AND THE WORKS OF RYAN C. THOMAS

"Fresh, bold and frightening. There are scarier things than a fast moving, flesh eating corpse. Open this book and see for yourself."

—J.L. Bourne, author of *Day by Day Armageddon*

"One of the best stories I've read this year... equal parts touching, compelling and gruesome."

—Nate Kenyon, award-winning author of *The Reach* and *Sparrow Rock*

"Ryan C. Thomas is not just a writer to watch, but one that has hit a stride that most others at their own game should envy."

—HorrorDrive-in.com

"Thomas has a free and easy storyteller's voice that lures readers in and leaves them helpless and naked when the shit gets real."

— Cody Goodfellow, author of *Jake's Wake* and *Spores*

HISSERS

RYAN C. THOMAS

Permuted Press
The formula has been changed...
Shifted... Altered... Twisted.
www.permutedpress.com

Special thanks to Dr. Isabelle Tancioni for her help with venomology.

A PERMUTED PRESS book
published by arrangement with the author
ISBN-13: 978-1-934861-60-8
ISBN-10: 1-934861-60-X

For Connor, Ethan, Cameron, Adam, Isabella, Abigail, Carly, and Leah...when you're old enough.

PROLOGUE

Lieutenant General Winston W. Davis, U.S. Marine Corps Special Projects Division, turned away from the video monitor with his mouth agape and his eyes wide. If he were alone he would have attempted a tap dance, but as he was not, he settled on a universal four letter expletive that conveyed his sudden excitement. What he'd just seen was going to revolutionize the world. It was going to revive long overdue fear in those damn bomb-loving camel-jockeys over there in the Middle Eastern sand pits of hell. Once again, America would raise its mighty democratic fist like it had in World War I and World War II. It would make the dictatorial lunatics in North Korea, China, Cuba, Somalia—you name it—think twice before even joking about America's demise. It was the scientific breakthrough of the century. Hell, it was so brilliant he was still having troubling believing it.

"Now that's goddamn amazing," he said.

Behind him the flatscreen monitor turned off. An after-image of a wounded soldier lying in a sterile hospital room some four floors below ground level faded to black. He flashed a smile at Dr. Haley.

She returned the smile, her hands behind her back. "It's not perfected," she said. "But we're getting close, real close. In fact even *I* was surprised at this latest progress. But I assume you know the adage about horseshoes and hand grenades." She raised her eyebrows and waited.

"Close doesn't count. Still, it's impressive."

"It's also unethical."

"How so?"

"We couldn't get the sequences to work at first, couldn't get the proteins to join until . . . well, we bound them in a virus."

"So?"

"So, we had to use an aggressive and modified strain of Lyssavirus, combined with a crotoxin to contain the protein."

"Cro . . . what?"

"Crotoxin. Drawn from the venom of a South American Pit viper. It inhibits immune and inflammatory reactions, which is necessary to block any transplant rejection. It was all that would work.

But, the downside—"

"There always is."

"The crotoxin is also neurotoxic. So if and when we perfect this drug, there will be a neural invasive side effect. You'll need a *second* drug administered to combat that effect."

Davis was lost. "Okay, wait. Back up. Explain the Lyssa thing?"

"Lyssavirus. Otherwise known as rabies. But it's been modified so—"

Now Davis laughed. "Wait. You gave that soldier rabies and snake venom?"

"No, not exactly. As I was saying, we've altered the virus considerably, added some of our own synthesized strands. This is the only way we can wrap up the proteins, get them into the body without instigating cellular death. You understand this is a very tricky bit of medicine you have us creating. Once the serum is injected, the virus breaks off. The proteins attack the wounded area of the subject and do their job. The new virus makes its way to the brain but—"

"Okay okay okay, I get it, we're back to needing a second drug. No big deal. What's the gist here?" He pointed to the black monitor. "Obviously it's working."

"It's starting to, yes. That boy you saw is our first brush with success. The proteins are like an incredible superglue. Tissue will accept tissue at an alarming rate. But the virus, the RNA strands—"

Just then Davis' phone rang. He waved her off, answered it, said yes and no a few times and hung up. "Sorry. My wife. Told her not to call now but she's planning a dinner party. Look, this is all making my head hurt, just tell me you're getting results and I'm happy."

"We're getting results."

"Perfect! Now, when I called you said you needed to talk business with me. What's that about?"

Dr. Haley nodded. "We need more money. The research has hit a couple of walls and—"

"Walls?" Davis' smile shrank back to a thin, determined line hidden under a graying mustache. "From what I just saw I'd say you leapt over a lot of walls. What kind of—"

"Unforeseen genetic anomalies. You have to understand we started on mice and cats, which is routine, so we allow for several negatives when we employ our tests on control subjects."

"And this subject . . . he's a negative? I thought you just said—"

"The secondary reaction was a negative, but an expected one."

6

"How expected?"

"Expected enough. We anticipated hitting some snags once we moved to human subjects. Such results are common in this type of research. We plan for them. It's how we perfect the process. We can iron them out in time."

"How much time?"

"Well, it depends on the funding. Which brings me back to the point of my original statement. Give us what we need and we'll get back to work immediately. Who knows? A year, two years tops."

It was Davis' turn to raise his eyebrows. "Two *years*? That long?"

"This is a delicate and untested procedure. You should be thrilled at how far we've already come. Two years more to deliver perfection is not much time in the long run."

"Says you. Black market chatter is rife with talk of the H-bomb. Not dirty bombs, you hear, full-on *nuclear devices*. We're gonna see more action in the deserts of hell before my next birthday. I'm telling you, you don't know how these psychos fight. Not like us. These idiots *want* to die. If they can blow us all to hell with an H-bomb strapped to their hairy-ass chests they sure as fuck will." Davis took off his hat and ran his hands through his hair. "If I put in for the money can you rush it?"

"Maybe. We'd still have to go through all the red tape before we can hand it over. Hell, the bid alone took us almost a year with the way you guys need everything signed in triplicate."

Davis laughed. "Don't hang that on me. I don't deal in signatures and photocopies. I deal in finding the right people to build me the shit I need built so I can make it safe for Mr. and Mrs. Smith to walk their dog in the park without fear of some Allah-humping towelhead blowing them into kibbles and bits."

"You do realize not all Muslims blow people up. I've worked with many Muslims in my time. They're good people."

"Tell me that after you spend a year in Afghanistan. Anyway, it's our money so we can expedite the process if we see fit. I can promise you if you can get this working properly—" he pointed to the blank monitor screen. "We'll take care of the red tape. Tell me, the soldier in the video . . . I couldn't help but notice the, um, arm.It moved."

"It surprised us all. There was a spontaneous grafting, an acceptance of foreign tissue without positive matching. About as uncommon as it gets. Which proves the serum is working. If this wasn't top secret, it'd be the top news story in every medical journal. He's being monitored."

"He looked beyond sick. Will he die?"

Dr. Haley took a moment to study her shoes. When she looked up there seemed to be new lines in her face. "We're not sure. For now all we can do it keep up the tests. We've altered the ratio of ingredients in the cocktail again and are planning to give him a new injection in two days."

"Altered?"

"Yes, I'm still working on it around the clock. The subject's brain chemistry was affected beyond our assumptions. Much like the arm."

Dr. Haley put her left arm forward. She was holding a disc. "As you requested. But please tell your superiors these are just hypothetical prognoses until we fix the current issues."

Davis took the disc, flipped it over. "I'll do that. Look, I'm gonna make a call. I want my bosses to get over here and see this stuff in action. I think they should see the video of the cat, too." He took out his cell phone again and spoke for a minute to someone on the other end. Dr. Haley waited patiently, occasionally tapping her foot. Finally Davis hung up and said, "Well, I told them what I saw. They're excited like pigs in shit, but there's been a change of plans. They want you to come to Washington."

"Washington?"

"You and your team. And the . . . " he pointed at the dark video monitor.

Dr. Haley shook her head emphatically. "No way, I can't move that boy."

"No, no. Don't bring the soldier. Just bring the equipment, the cocktail. They want you to show it to them in person."

"*What?* I don't have the right equipment to transport it. It's not safe. Tell them to come here."

"I already suggested that. You heard me with them. They said no. I don't question them and I *sure as hell* don't disobey them. They want to watch it work in person. I assume they'll supply a lab mouse or whatever it is you need. They're arranging a plane now."

"What?! General Davis, I appreciate—"

"Lieutenant General."

"I appreciate the honor of wanting to be seen by your superiors but I am not prepared to go to Washington nor can I just test this on anyone or anything. It takes days to set it all up. It's extremely fragile and needs a sterile environment with proper temperature control and—"

Davis waved her off. "Look, Doctor, I appreciate your dilemma but all you have to do is show them the video, maybe some tissue samples, a bit of the medicine under a microscope, and inject some in a damn rodent in front of them and you'll walk out of there with a blank check with your name on it. I guarantee it. If you want the additional funding—because they can still go to someone else—this is how you're gonna get it. A couple of days of your life to show them, in person, what you have. I'll even pay for the pizza and beer afterward. Just don't tell my wife, she gets suspicious." He chuckled but the joke was lost in the ensuing silence.

Dr. Haley looked at the black monitor behind the man in the dark green suit, thought of the young soldier they'd just been watching. He still hadn't recovered from the abnormalities, and sometimes at night she could hear his moans. It didn't matter that he'd signed up for the trial, was warned there were risks, he was *still* human and it *still* bothered her. There was, however, so much research yet to be completed before this project could be finalized.

And she needed the funding to do it so losing the account was not an option. Besides, if she was going to help cure the boy in the sub-basement below her, she needed to appease the investors ASAP. In the end it would help untold numbers of American soldiers recover from the horrors of war. Wasn't that why her team had bid on this account in the first place?

Sometimes the bottom line justified the anguish of experimentation and violation of human life. *Right?*

"Okay," she said. "But I need a *big* coffee first."

PART I:
SATURDAY NIGHT'S
ALRIGHT FOR FIGHTING

SATURDAY, 12:00pm

Connor heard the howling engine and sinister laughter and realized he was in danger. He pedaled his bike closer to the curb, his muscles going rope tight, bracing for the car to clip him and send him spiraling into the trees. He'd no doubt connect with a thick, jagged branch and explode in a pink mist of entrails and bone shards. By the time he looked back, adrenaline coursing through his chest, the dented and dirt-covered Camry's dark blue hood was already kissing the back tire of his bike.

The tire caught and skidded for a second, the handlebars jerking, threatening to dump Connor into the middle of the lane directly under the psychopath's car. He fought to maintain his balance, focusing on nothing except the stability of the bike frame beneath him.

The driver honked the horn and cackled, causing Connor to damn near shit his pants. The driver honked again and shouted a bully's battle cry: "Stay outta the road, pussyboy!" Then, with a screech of tires, the car swerved around him and sped away, launching gravel and dirt in Connor's face. A collection of teenagers, girls and boys, glared back at him through the rear window, everyone laughing and flipping him off.

Connor watched the car disappear, unaware he was still pedaling until the adrenaline dissipated and his thigh muscles began burning. Shaking, he pulled his bike off the road and onto the sidewalk. He sat still on the seat, staring down at dandelions growing up through the cracks, and did what he could to steady his breathing. Mostly that consisted of putting his face in his hands and whispering curse words to himself. He could feel his knees still wobbling. "Pieces of shit. Pieces of shit. Asshole pieces of shit."

He heard Seth pedal up next to him and skid to a stop. Connor looked up. His best friend was sweating and beet red, staring down the road after the car, looking terrified. Passersby would think it was him that just got run off the road and not the other way around. "You okay? Man, those guys were jerks. Lucky I was too far back or I'd have thrown my bike through their windshield or something. Like people have nothing better to do in this craphole town than run people off of bikes."

Connor appreciated his friend's concern, but knew the sudden bravado was a hollow gesture. Seth had never been in a fight his whole fourteen years. Sure, he was always *about* to do something to help people, but he never *did* anything. Nor was he in any physical condition to do so, the kid nearly had a heart attack just mowing his parents' lawn.

A moment of silence passed between them, then Seth picked his underwear out of his crack. "Did you see who it was?"

"I think I saw Jason Drake in the backseat. Can't be sure."

"That douche. I bet it was his brother driving. Maynard. You hear he pulled a gun on an undercover cop at the mall?"

Connor found that hard to believe. Maynard Drake was a jerk but he didn't carry a gun. "That didn't happen."

"Yeah it did."

"I highly doubt it."

"No, really, it did. But the cop didn't identify himself so they couldn't arrest him. It was almost a shoot out. I swear."

Seth was always full of dubious stories like this. Connor was getting tired of them. Most of Seth's stories were so outrageous they seemed culled from comics and movies. "So why did he pull the gun?"

"It was a drug deal, and the undercover cop was buying some blow off Maynard, but Maynard got real suspicious and thought the guy was gonna jack him for the Benjis and the blow and whipped his piece out. But they had to let him go because . . . um . . . something about a Trap Man."

Connor rolled his eyes. "First off, it's called *entrapment*, not a Trap Man. And secondly, are you officially retarded? None of that ever happened. Sounds like a bad TV show plot. You probably saw it on a *CSI* rerun or something."

"Whatever. Maynard's bad news and he almost just smeared you across the road so you'd better be careful. He's batshit psycho."

Connor kicked his pedal back into position near his knee and looked at his best friend. "Blow? Benjis?"

"You know! Benjamins. Dead presidents. Money. What? Don't gimme that look. If you're gonna survive in the streets these days, my friend, you gotta speak the lingo. It may save your life one day."

"You don't live on the streets. You live in Castor. The day we get hardened criminals here is the day I acknowledge Greedo shot first."

"Don't even go there."

"C'mon, I'm not gonna let those assholes ruin my day."

Connor and Seth pedaled up Draper Avenue, letting the summer breeze erase the past few minutes from their minds. Maple trees flanked the sides of the road, occasionally broken up by a house, business, or crumbling strip mall featuring the obligatory Radio Shack or GameStop. It was a fairly well-trafficked street so they rode on the sidewalk now to avoid any more run ins with homicidal drivers. The air still smelled of morning dew and freshly cut grass.

The warm September sun glinted off their tire spokes, casting white starbursts beneath them. Both boys stood on the pedals, mouths tight, knuckles white around their handlebars, pumping their feet to compensate for the road's slight incline. Connor, in the lead, glanced back once to make sure his friend was still close behind. Seth was portly for a fourteen year old, and it wasn't uncommon for Connor to have to stop and wait for the putz to catch up. He really didn't want to lose his momentum on this hill; starting up again would be a bitch.

When Connor crested the top of the hill he eased up on his speed. Seth fell in beside him, beads of sweat dotting his forehead, and they continued on. Neither boy spoke as they raced to their destination—-the only 7-Eleven in town. It was their summer ritual to come here, buy a couple of cans of Redbull and some hotdogs, nick some batteries by sticking them down their socks, and then go hang out in the fort in the woods looking at porno mags and playing with Seth's PSP until the batteries in the external charger ran out.

"You still alive?" Connor asked. The convenience store was close. "You look like you might pass out."

Seth was flushed and not amused. All summer riding up this hill and the boy was still overweight. Connor's ribbing did not lighten his mood. "Man, eat the skid marks in my shorts."

"Depends what's in them. What did you have for breakfast?"

"Your mom's crotch."

"Oh, yum. I'll have two helpings, please."

The 7-Eleven on Draper Avenue used to be a mom and pop convenience store called The Draper Deli and Soda Mart. It had been owned by an old married couple, the Frenches, who died before Connor was born, back in '92 or something. Connor's dad had told him you could get a fresh sandwich, can of Coke, the newspaper, bread and milk and maybe even a toy for about five bucks back then, which in those days was a steal.

Said Mr. French would always ask when he, Connor's dad, was gonna have kids and what he and the new wife were doing on Saturday because there was a community picnic at the park near the school, and they should come by. Connor's dad always followed up this tired tale with some lame nostalgic lament like, "You don't get that kind of neighbor these days. These days kids take guns to school and Starbucks runs the small business owner out of town."

All Connor ever replied was, "Why would you buy a newspaper when you can read it for free online?"

They cut across the parking lot and leaned their bikes up against the ice machine beside the front entrance. The interior of the store was air conditioned and had that 7-Eleven smell—floor cleaner, stale coffee, hot dogs, and sweat. Jared Higgins was behind the counter. He was a senior at the high school, one of the stars of the wrestling team and the kind of guy who was allegedly always getting girls pregnant but never actually dated anyone. He was muscular enough to bring down a rhino with one arm but dumb enough that multisyllabic words made him go cross-eyed.

His innate oblivion to anything that didn't have tits or an Anheuser-Busch logo on it was one of the reasons Connor and Seth could steal the batteries so easily. If he did happen to catch them it wasn't like a simple lie couldn't convince the idiot that the batteries *had* just fallen into their socks.

Neither Connor nor Seth were very friendly with Jared, but word traveled fast in their quaint town and even Connor's mom knew that Jared was being held back as a senior this year. That made him the only twenty-year-old in the high school.

And then it hit Connor, the knowledge that in just three days he and Seth would be walking the same halls as Jared. In just three days, come Monday morning, the summer would be officially over and they'd be starting on the path to adulthood. The thought filled him with absolute dread. It was worse than how he'd felt entering into the two-year junior high school. At least there you knew you only had to suffer as an underclassman for a year before you were king of the school, but this was different. This was a whole new game. Kids drove cars in high school, kids drank and fought and fucked. There were people like Jared in the school with you—big, muscled-headed idiots who could kill you with a finger.

And worse, there were people like Maynard Drake, who would run you over with his jalopy just to get a laugh.

There were girls there as well, girls like Reyna Heatherly and Paula Wheeler., legends in the boys' locker rooms. Sure, Connor and Seth had no chance of ever getting with them but they could at least look. And where there was one Reyna or Paula, there would be others coming up the ranks.

Yes, high school was where the golden treasure could be found. The elusive forbidden fruit. The power that made a boy's world go round: sex.

Connor tapped Seth on the shoulder. "Go get the Redbulls, I'll get the batteries."

Seth invoked Yoda. "Yes, master. Redbulls purchase, I will."

The batteries were down an aisle directly in front of Jared, but the goon was bent over a nudie magazine and playing with a Bic lighter. Connor grabbed a package of four double As, split the plastic cover off the top and slipped the loose batteries down his socks. A summer's worth of nicking batteries had made him a pro at this, and he was done in less than two seconds. He put the empty packaging behind a jug of motor oil.

"You get them?" Seth hefted the Redbulls to show he'd done his part.

"Yeah. Got 'em. Let's get the hot dogs."

They made their way over to the hotdog unit to make sure there were normal beef dogs rolling about. Sometimes the store had nothing but chicken taquitos and giant sausage dogs, which were good but cost twice as much as the regular dogs. Today they had an allotment of shriveled, sweaty links the EPA would probably confiscate in biohazard drums. They put their drinks on the counter and waited for Jared to notice them.

He did not. His eyes remained glued to the magazine.

"We're ready," Connor said.

Jared tapped the magazine. "Hold on, *Cochise*, I'm almost done."

Seth leaned over and whispered in Connor's ear. "Even if I believed he could string words together to form sentences, I don't think there are any on that page."

Both boys leaned slyly over the counter to get a look at the woman on the page. She was dressed as a baseball player if you counted the hat and bat. Beyond that she wore nothing but high heels. The pink wetness between her legs was entirely alien to Connor and Seth. Not that they hadn't seen pictures of naked women (they did have the Internet) but it still amazed them when they saw a vagina at such a close up angle.

Seth's jaw dropped open ever so slightly. Connor felt a bulge in his pants. Neither was concerned with the hotdogs anymore.

The bell over the front door rang. Jared didn't seem to care who'd come in, but he looked up nevertheless. For a second he just stared, then in what could only be described as a belated moment of decorum he closed the magazine just as two young girls walked to the counter.

Connor felt a tap on his shoulder. He spun around and found himself face to face with Nicole Fitzgerald. "Hi, Connor."

"Hey, Nicole."

She was dressed in tan pants and a white tank top, a bikini top visible underneath it. Her hair was tied back in a pony tail. Behind Nicole was her best friend Amanita Miller. As usual she was exposing as much of her skin as possible, walking around in shorts too small for her and just a bikini top. A pair of oversized sunglasses covered most of her face. What was visible was smeared in so much makeup she may as well have been in the magazine Jared was looking at. Connor could smell cigarette smoke on her.

Involuntarily Nicole glanced down at Connor's crotch and then looked away embarrassed.

Oh great! Connor stepped behind Seth and tried to hide his situation. "Um . . . what are you doing here?" he asked, as he pushed down on himself.

Nicole giggled. "Are you okay?"

"Yeah, fine, just—you startled me."

"Looks like you're startling yourself," Amanita added.

"No, it's . . . my fly, it's . . . stuck."

Both girls looked at each other and shared a laugh. Connor cursed. If only girls knew how hard it was for men to deal with this thing between their legs that had a mind of its own. It wasn't fair!

"We're getting hotdogs," Seth said. His eyes were locked tightly on Amanita's budding chest and tanned stomach. The girl noticed but didn't mind, such was Amanita's MO.

"Am wanted a Vitamin Water," Nicole replied. "We were walking to the park to lay out for a bit."

"Cool," said Seth, lacking anything actually cool to say.

With the help of some forceful bending, Connor's situation had returned to normal, so he stepped back out in front of Nicole. "So, um, how's it going? You psyched for Monday?"

"Kinda. It's gonna be weird, huh?"

All four were in the same grade. Connor and Nicole had shared a few classes last year but usually sat on opposite ends of the room. They were both in honors classes, as was Seth, but everyone knew Nicole was the smartest person in their grade and could stand to be in the honors classes a full grade ahead. You just knew she was going to go far in life.

"Is that a porno magazine?" Amanita pointed to the closed magazine on the counter.

Jared whisked it away and looked her up and down. He seemed enticed by the way she had her hands on her hips and Connor wouldn't put it past the guy to make a move. Hell, he wasn't sure Amanita would even mind. "I'm over eighteen, little girl. Don't judge me. You all gonna buy something or just stand around littering?"

"I think he means loitering," Nicole whispered.

Amanita put a twenty on the counter. "A pack of Parliament Lights. You can charge me ten dollars for them. You know, just in case." She winked at him.

"Ten? They're only six."

"But you can charge me ten. Like, to make sure there are no hard feelings, no feelings involving your job and all."

Jared scratched his head. "I don't know what you're talking about. They're six." He rang up a pack for her and gave her correct change.

Nicole and Connor both shook their heads and smiled.

"You fuckwads paying for these Redbulls or what?" Jared snapped his fingers on the cans, making a pinging noise.

Seth put some folded-up bills on the counter. "And two hotdogs," he said. Jared huffed and went to get the hotdog tongs.

"So hey," Nicole said, looking at Connor, "you going to Jason Drake's party tonight?"

Connor remembered the recent incident with the car. He and Jason were not friends by any means despite being in the same grade. Jason was not in the honors classes and spent most of his time in Home Ec classes or in detention. In fact he was in most of Amanita's classes. "Uh, no."

"Oh, c'mon. You should. It's gonna be fun. His brother does it every year the last weekend before school starts. Everybody goes. Jason said there's gonna be three kegs."

Amanita yanked the plastic off her cigarette box and began packing them against her palm. "Let it go, Nicole. I doubt they got invited." She glared venomously at Seth, who was still leering sideways at her body. When he caught her eyes he looked guiltily at his shoes.

"Oh please, that doesn't even matter," Nicole said. "Everyone's invited. It's like an all-inclusive school thing. That's what Jason said. So you guys could come."

If we show up we'll get thrown in the pool or pantsed or something, Connor thought. One brush a day with the Drake brothers was about all he could stomach. "Nah, we were gonna have our own little celebration tonight anyway so . . . I don't think we're gonna make it."

"Oh." Nicole nodded like she understood. "That's cool. Where?"

"Where what?"

"Where's your party."

"Our party?"

"You just said you're having your own celebration."

"Oh! You know, like, we were gonna hang out at the . . . fort and stuff."

"The fort? You mean that shitty wooden thing in the woods?" Amanita grimaced. "Sounds like a real blast. What do you do, reenact Star Trek Wars or something."

"*Star Wars* and *Star Trek* are two different things," Seth corrected. "And only *Star Wars* is cool."

"Neither is cool, actually."

"Well, maybe we could join you for a bit," Nicole said.

Connor could tell she was just being nice. He appreciated it but he knew no girl about to enter high school was gonna pass up a chance to meet four grades worth of high school boys at one of the most popular parties of the year.

"If you want," he replied.

"I'm going to the Drakes," Jared said, putting the hotdogs on the counter. "It's gonna be fucking awesome. You going?" He directed the question at Amanita. This time he made no effort to hide the way his eyes undressed her. "I could introduce you to people. I know lots of people. I could totally introduce you and stuff."

"I'll bet you could." Amanita took a pack of matches off the service tray on the counter. She was not amused. If her eyes could talk they'd say everyone around her was an idiot.

Seth took the hotdogs and Redbulls and handed Connor his share. "'Star Trek Wars'. What does that even mean? C'mon, we should get going."

Connor nodded. He felt weird enough as it was, if they stuck around any longer he'd surely do something embarrassing.

Nicole stepped in front of him before he could head to the door. "Well, look, I mean maybe we could just come by and hang for a little bit. Then when we go to the party—"

"I don't want to go to some stupid fort in the woods," Amanita chimed in.

Nicole glared at her, then looked back at Connor. "Then when we leave for the party if you want to come you can come with us. We could all go together. If you don't then no big deal."

"You're not listening, Nic, I don't wanna go into the fucking woods. I wanna go to the party and I need to do my hair and fix these tan lines."

Connor wanted to tell Amanita to shut the hell up but held back. She'd been Nicole's friend since preschool and he didn't want to insult their bond. It was similar to how the junior high school soccer team was all friendly with Connor for being a good scorer but made fun of Seth for being overweight. Why did people think you could insult someone's friend and they'd be okay with it?

"I dunno," he said.

"Look, Nic, They weren't invited. If they don't want to go they don't have to go."

"I could introduce you to a whole lot of people," Jared said. He winked at Amanita.

Nicole had finally had enough. "Am, we'll be there in plenty of time for you to shake your ass. You," she pointed at Jared, "we're fourteen, you know."

Jared shrugged. "Yeah, but not for long."

She turned to Connor. "And you, if you don't want to hang out with us just say so."

"Okay, look," Connor said, suddenly feeling like a real jerk. "You know where the fort is. We'll be there around eight or so. If you come, awesome. If not . . . "

"We'll be there," she replied, back to her giddy self.

"No we won't," Amanita added.

"I just want to eat my frigging hot dog and play some games. Can we go now?" Seth motioned to the door.

Connor pushed past his best friend. "Yeah, let's go."

SATURDAY, 1:30pm

The park wasn't a park in the normal sense. There were no lakes or streams, no hiking trails, no park rangers hassling people for leaving food where bears could get it. It was more of a community pasture. Two soccer fields and a baseball field served as the grounds for the local sports leagues, along side of which ran a football field's worth of green grass with occasional park benches and trash cans. The town called it the park though it was technically modeled after ancient Roman malls—meeting places where people came to mingle and barter goods.

Most of the people in the neighborhood only came to play Frisbee, cook burgers on hibachis, and in the case of underage hooligans, sneak beers in coolers when they could. Right now a pee wee soccer game was taking place on the far soccer field, and every now and then one could hear angry parents yelling at other angry parents. A Parks and Rec employee was cutting the grass on the baseball field, and the only other sign of life was two high school boys playing catch with a football way down at the other end.

Nicole and Amanita spread their beach blankets and stretched out on their backs. Amanita took off her shorts leaving nothing on but her bikini, but Nicole felt a little too exposed to go that bare and kept her pants on.

"Your legs will never get tan if you keep 'em covered up all summer," Amanita said.

"I'm Irish, I'll just burn."

"You used to be a shorts person. What happened, you outgrow them?"

"If that's a fat joke, then you're a bitch."

"D'oy."

"I like pants is all. They're comfy."

They both donned their sunglasses, stuck iPod earbuds in their ears, and closed their eyes. Everything was serene until the smell of Amanita's cigarette began to overpower the scent of the grass and summer wildflowers.

Nicole turned off her iPod. "Do you need to smoke that here?"

Amanita pulled her earbuds out. "Yes."

"You're gonna get cancer."

"So? You think anyone's gonna miss me?"

"I'll miss you."

"Well, you're the only one. You'll be in the White House or something by the time the cancer kills me so we won't even be friends anymore anyway."

"Just put it out, please."

Amanita huffed and pitched the cigarette into the grass. They both listened to the distant sound of a pigskin smacking into hands. "You weren't serious about going to that stupid fort were you?"

"Yeah."

"Why? I mean, Connor is okay, he's kinda cute and all, but they're pretty much dorks. We're about to go into high school, Nic. We should be looking for some older guys. Guys with cars at least."

"I like Connor. And I like Seth. There's nothing wrong with them."

"Gross."

Nicole propped herself up on her elbow. "What's so important that you have to be at Jason's right away, anyway? We'll have the next four years to go to this party. It's probably gonna be lame. For fuck's sake, Jared the Wonder Tard is gonna be there."

"Well, I sure as shit ain't going for him. What a pervert. He's like, as old as my dad."

"Well if you didn't dress like that in front of him . . . "

Amanita flipped her glasses up and stared at Nicole. "Okay, Mom, thanks for the advice."

"Well, I'm just saying. Guys are stupid and you never know what they're gonna do. So what's so important about this party tonight? I've never seen you like this."

"Nothing, I just really want to go. Like I said, it's time we start recognizing we're older. We're in high school. We need high school boyfriends."

"Seth and Connor are gonna be in high school too."

"You know what I mean. Not losers, real older guys. You don't want to be part of the lame crowd in this school."

Nicole gasped and hit Amanita on the shoulder. "Wait a minute! You like someone that's gonna be there. Who?"

"Why do you say that?"

Nicole hit her again. "Stop being coy. Who is it? Holy shit is it Jason? It is, isn't it?"

Amanita hit Nicole back. "Jesus, will you be quiet. So what? So I happen to think he's hot. You act like it's a tragedy."

"I'm just shocked is all. I mean, you were in his classes last year. Did you even talk to him?"

"Sometimes. I dunno. He isn't that smart, y'know. But there's something about him. At the end of the year he just started to look really good. He's starting to look like Maynard with the chest muscles and all. Besides, I don't need to talk to him. I just sort of want to mess around and stuff."

"Ew, gross. I don't think he's hot, he looks greasy. And you shouldn't put yourself out there so easily. You don't know where he's been."

"God, you sound like my Mom again. It's just sex. We're gonna do it sometime anyway. You really think it's gonna be all special like in some movie? Do you even know how boys feel about a girl who makes them wait? It pisses them off."

Nicole lay back down and was quiet for a minute before replying. "Well then, I guess I'll be pissing a lot of guys off."

"Well, I don't care. I mean, you lose your virginity once and it's gone and then it's all meaningless anyway. Might as well just get it over with."

"You talk like you know."

"I know more than you."

"Oh really, how far have you gotten?"

"I told you, I got naked with my cousin's friend. We almost did it, but he didn't have a condom. I'm not a slut, you know."

Nicole laughed. "I told you before I don't believe you. Stop making up stories."

"It's not a story. What about you? All you ever did was kiss that ugly boy you met at the mall."

"So, he was a good kisser. You know, I don't want to talk about this anymore."

"Why? Afraid Connor will be bad kisser? I doubt he even knows how to handle a woman."

"We're not women, we're fourteen."

"Speak for yourself. Like I said, there will be real men at the party tonight. If you want a good kisser, find one there. Not at some stupid fort in the woods."

"You're really not going to come to the fort?"

"I sure as hell don't want to."

"What if I promise we'll be at the party by nine o'clock? Just come so I can convince Connor to come with us. For me, okay?"

"If I come then you owe me."

"Put it on my tab."

Amanita's cell phone began to play a Fallout Boy song. She checked the number and grunted. "It's Alicia. She's texting me."

"What's she saying?" Nicole asked.

"She wants to know what I'm wearing to the party? God, she's so ridiculous."

"Why can't she decide for herself?"

Amanita began texting to Alicia yet, true to teenage girl form, started talking about her at the same time. "Oh my frigging God, did you hear what she said about Mandy the other day? She's such a bitch sometimes. But, that's why I love her."

Nicole was all ears. "Mandy Robinson? No, what?"

"So get this. She was IMing Danielle Riccard last week and Danielle said Mandy said that Alicia should go to the sale at Forever 21 because they had these tattoo shirts that are way better than the ones Alicia bought at Hot Topic, which she said look like they were found in a trash can, and Alicia got all pissed and called Mandy a fat, nappy-haired cow and—hang on, she's texting back—ok, so it turns out fucking Mandy was sitting right next to Danielle! So Mandy post-ed a comment on Alicia's Myspace about how Alicia shops at the Salvation Army, which she actually used to do when she was young because her mom was poor because her dad left for some crack-whore—no offense to your mom, who you know I love, and I meant that for the dad-leaving part not the crackwhore part—and took all their money and Alicia had lice in her hair—I think I remember that happening in like second grade—and anyway where am I—oh yeah she put up a picture of Alicia in this totally ghetto outfit from when she was young but photoshopped her head on it now. It's actually pret-ty funny but I think David Moore did the photoshopping because he's like in love with her and would do it for her, which is sad because Alicia kind of likes David, too. So Mandy said she was gonna kick Alicia's ass next time she saw her and I think she's going to be at the party tonight. I'm telling her I'm wearing jeans and a tank top. Should I wear those black stilettos I got, you think?"

Only teenage girls can follow so many thoughts without getting lost and Nicole was true to form.

"Well, Mandy did gain some weight," Nicole replied. "She eats those pretzels at the mall like it's the end of the word. She has a bad carb addiction. And Alicia's shirts really are kinda skanky. And I'm just wearing my Nikes so if you wear heels then I have to and I don't want to. Plus we're gonna be meeting with Connor first so I'd just wear sneakers."

"Crap, I forgot about that. Way to ruin my mood again."

A football suddenly landed in between them. One of the boys from the other end of the grass field came over to retrieve it. He was wearing running shorts and a gray t-shirt. Sweat ringed his armpits and neckline. "Hi, girls," he said. Like most boys, his eyes seemed to linger on Amanita. "Sorry about that." He hefted the football. "It got away from me."

"Doubt it," Nicole said.

The boy looked confused. "Excuse me?"

"We saw you playing earlier. The trajectory of your throw would've had to change a full ninety degrees in our direction with increased velocity to get the ball over here. Even with a strong gust of wind blowing in our direction, with the weight of that ball, the angle of difference would at most be ten degrees. Ergo, you did it on purpose." She could see his friend walking over now behind him and knew she was right.

"My friend is all smart and stuff," Amanita added. She saw the boy staring at her but made no attempt to cover up. Instead she lit another cigarette and blew the smoke at him. It dissipated before it got anywhere near him, but the gesture had been made.

"Just wanted to come say hi. Jeez, forget it." He turned and intercepted his friend's approach, said something under his voice, and they both went back to where they'd been playing earlier.

"He was kind of cute," Amanita said. "Think he'll be there tonight?"

"I hope not."

The two girls laid in silence for the next couple of hours, letting the summer sun bronze their bodies. Nicole thought of what she'd say to Connor later. She really hoped he would come with them to the party. She'd had a crush on him for so long now, and she swore tonight she would finally muster the courage to tell him. Hopefully Amanita wouldn't screw it all up.

Saturday, 3:40pm

The fort had been a town institution for generations. Built to the blueprints of a bad dream and haphazardly nailed together by what was no doubt a team of blind imps, the contraption made the House of Usher look like Buckingham Palace. A series of twelve palettes formed the main chamber, while broken pickets, bundled tree branches, a few squares of plywood and some torn-up rug created additional crawlspaces. Two leather bucket car seats that looked like they'd lost a fight with a panther were the prime accommodations. A wooden spool served as a table between them.

Over the years it had gone through some changes. Posters were stapled up and torn down, holes had been cut in the roof for smoking and then mended with strips of rubber tile, an additional chamber built of broken up bookcases had housed a couple of mattresses before someone realized they were infested with bugs and trucked them away before the CDC could get involved. That chamber had then been torn down in an attempt to create a fire pit, which was later lined with a tarp, filled with water and covered with twigs as a makeshift booby trap. The hole had long since been filled in, but bits of the tarp still poked out of the ground.

The surrounding trees were scarred with initials, marking the passage of the fort's ownership over time. Many had plus signs and jagged hearts between them, but to this day no one knew who had first built the fort. Some believed hippies had erected it during the Vietnam War as a place to hide against the authorities after protests and sit-ins. Others claimed it was the hideout for satanic cult members in the 80s, who stole neighborhood cats and sacrificed them during occult rituals.

Connor's dad said that it was just a place some kids he went to school with built so they could have a place to make out with girls, and that he should stay away from it because it was dirty and probably infested with diseases. Connor seemed to think this was the best explanation, and of course neither he nor Seth stayed away. In fact, they were the only ones in town who seemed to come up here anymore. It was the perfect place to chill and hide away from idiots like Jason Drake, who was always out looking to start trouble with other kids.

Besides, there was a collection of porno mags from the '90s still lying around so it was easier to view this porn than trying to bypass the parental controls on the computers in their homes. They knew the magazines were from the '90s because the women had a lot of hair down there, and they never had any hair on the Internet nowadays.

Seth sat in one of the car seats and took the batteries from Connor. He put them in the back of the PSP's external charger (the internal one usually died right in the middle of a game) and started playing a World War 2 shooter. "I've got it saved on the battle of Bastogne," he said. "I can't get past the effing Panzer tanks."

Connor made a half-hearted attempt to suggest a strategy but the truth was he didn't really care. He'd been thinking about Nicole since they'd left the 7-Eleven. He felt weird around her. She was not bad looking but he'd never really thought about her in that way before, like a girlfriend. But today he'd sort of felt . . . different. He suddenly wanted to know what kind of stuff she liked. Did she like video games, too, and if so which ones. Did she know how to play first person shooters or online role playing games? Did she even have an Xbox or a gaming PC? He'd have to ask her later if she showed up.

That thought made his palms sweat. What if she really *did* show up? What were they supposed to talk about if she didn't play video games or watch baseball? More importantly, what if she *didn't* show up. Would that mean he pissed her off?

Man, girls are so frigging weird!

"Fuckballs!" Seth slammed his fist on his knee. "That stupid tank! Every time. Hey, are you listening to me?"

"Yeah. Panzer tanks. Can't you find a bazooka or something?"

"No. All they give you is a BAR. They don't even give you a sticky grenade. If I had something to take the tank's treads out . . . but I don't think the developers animated the treads to break. What if I use a claymore?"

Connor looked through the hole in the pallet that formed the south wall. He could see the woods around them, could see the edge of the hill that ran down toward the town park. It sounded like a game was happening on one of the fields.

"I wonder if Nicole and Amanita are down there. Think we could see them?"

Seth hit pause on the game and shot an angry look at his friend. "Who cares? They're stupid."

"No they're not. Nicole is cool, at least."

"Amanita is a bitch and I hate how she looks down on me. She looks down on everyone like her shit don't stink or something. Tucker said she blew on his dick in the bathroom."

"Blew on his dick?"

"Yeah, something like that. Who knows. Tucker also said she said that video games are for nerds. I mean, she's an idiot. Does she even know what kind of dexterity it takes to play this game? I'd like to get her in an online death match and see how smart she in then. Why is Nicole even friends with her?"

Connor shrugged. "They used to live next door to each other. I guess they just get along. You can always ignore her."

"So then you're gonna go with Nicole tonight?"

Connor resumed looking through the hole in the pallet. All he could see were branches. He wanted to go out and make his way over to the edge of the trees and look down on the fields, see if he could see the girls down there. But he knew Seth would be upset. "No, I'm not going. We don't need to go to some lame party to be cool."

Seth returned to playing his game. "Actually, we do. But they wouldn't let us be cool even if we went. I mean, I'll understand if you wanna go. I know I'm the reason you weren't invited in the first place. They don't like you because of me."

Connor turned back to him. "Don't say that."

"Well, it's true. Seth the Donut Boy, Slim Seth, Waddle Butt, Spherical Seth . . . Fat Ass. I hear it all."

"Nobody says that."

"Yeah, I'm an idiot. I make it up. They all call me that, I don't even care. I was born fat and it's in my family genes, I can't help it. But you know what, I kick ass at video games and when I'm a million dollar developer they'll all be regretting it. When they're working at Burger King and I have my own private jet, we'll see who laughs."

"If you get a private jet you better let me fly it."

"Of course." Seth kept his eyes on the game as he talked. "We'll fly to Vegas for the world championship Halo tournament, we'll fly to Los Angeles for E3,and we'll have a hideout like this in a cave in Hawaii."

Connor looked around the dirty fort, glanced at the torn and crumpled porno mags, black strips of rug that were once red, discarded batteries from a summer's worth of handheld gaming, and yellowed bits of paper and God knew what else that had found a home here years ago. "Like this?"

"Well, not like this place, but a fort with defense systems and eye scanners and an emergency helicopter escape pad."

"Sounds sweet. Sign me up."

A silence passed between them for a minute and then Seth swore as his character was killed. He put the PSP down. "I'm serious, though, if you want to go tonight you can. I won't be mad. I have this clan on Halo 3 I want to try out for anyway."

It was hard to tell in the dim light of the fort's interior, but it almost looked like Seth might cry. Connor sometimes thought about what it must feel like to be the butt of fat jokes all the time. It didn't help that even he made cracks now and then. Hearing Seth now, seeing his downcast eyes, it started to really sink in.

"I said I'm not going. Maynard tried to run me over. I don't care if Nicole is going, nothing could make me go to that party."

"I'm sorry I make you unpopular. It's not like I planned this when I met you."

"Seth, you don't make me—"

"*Yes, I do!*"

Connor could see Seth really was on the verge of tears now.

"All the girls talk about you, Connor. They like you. You score goals all the time in soccer, you get put on the front line, you're a fast runner and thin and you're in the honors classes. You'd be way more popular than you are if you didn't hang around with me. I'm just a fat fuck who people like to throw food at. Everyone hates me."

"No, they don't."

"Just stop. I know they do. I'm a joke. Even God hates me. Look what He did to me when He took my sister! He hates me!"

And there it was, the real catalyst for this sudden spiral into depression and self loathing. Like always, Connor didn't know what to say when Seth started talking about his sister. What *could* he say? What did you tell a boy who's sister had been kidnapped right in front of him. They didn't teach this stuff in school, and it was not a topic generally covered by cartoons or MTV reality shows.

"Wasn't your fault," he mumbled. The words felt so hollow and meaningless.

Seth waved him off, picked up the PSP again. "Yeah yeah, I know. Eight years of therapy and all I know is it wasn't my fault. It doesn't make Mom and Dad look at me any differently."

"You were frigging six years old, Seth."

"I didn't scream. That's what they don't get. That's what they can't accept. *I didn't scream.* I don't know why either. I didn't scream and now I'm doomed to a life of guilt and humiliation. A fat fuck of a joke. Just go to the party without me."

Connor watched his friend wipe away his tears as he blasted more German troops. He knew the story well enough, at least as much as Seth had told it to him two summers ago when his family had moved to town. They'd been living in a small 'burb in Ohio, in a two bedroom house on a quiet residential street. Seth's father, Frank, was a network engineer and his mom, Debbie, worked as a CPA in a local tax firm. They both put in long hours, they both came home tired and went to bed after a quick meal and cup of tea. Seth and his little sister Joana didn't know how hard their parents worked, didn't know how much overtime was required to support the two children they adored.

Not seeing them for most of the day was just their daily routine. This meant Seth staying after school for the in-house daycare program and Joana being dropped off at a different daycare for toddlers until they both could be picked up.

The day their lives changed was like any other. A light drizzle fell like a film grain effect from the clouds overhead that October Thursday. The trees were starting to go bare, the last few dried-up orange and brown leaves dancing to the ground to decay before the obligatory onslaught of winter snow. Seth was six and Joana four. Debbie had picked them up around six and brought them home, made them dinner, and surprised them with hot chocolate and a Disney movie from Netflix. Frank came home around eight and played with his children for half an hour before putting them to bed. Then he and his wife shared a few quick stories from their day, discussed a bill or two, and did the same. Hours passed while everyone slept.

When the sky was at its darkest, and the moon was lost behind deep purple rain clouds, one of the bedroom windows in Seth and Joana's room slid open. A lanky figure in jeans and a hooded sweat-shirt crawled in the way a spider might enter a crack in the wall—long legs first, arms and cephalothorax second, abdomen last. The stench of garbage and dirt swirled in with him and seemed to settle on the floors and walls. The strange figure's bones creaked as he moved.

Seth woke up, watching in the glow of a bumble bee nightlight as the figure moved closer on the stick-like legs and leaned over him. A gaunt, scruffy face looked back at him from the depths of the hood; sunken eyes black and slick like olives, a gray beard peppered with mud, and a gin blossom nose. The man slowly lifted a finger to his thin, cracked lips. "*Shhh.*"

Stricken with enough fear to immobilize every muscle and bone in his body, Seth felt a shroud of helplessness engulf him. He was old enough to know what a burglar was, knew he must scream for his mother and father, yet he couldn't find his voice, as if the man's shushing had cast a spell over him. He felt his crotch go warm and wet but the sensation did nothing to spur him into action. A subtle shaking, like a deep winter shiver, overtook his legs and chest. His teeth chattered. His heart pounded. Yet he could only lie there and watch and pray to God for help.

The man in the sweatshirt took a long step across the room on his spindly legs, more dirt wafting in his wake, bent down over Joana and kissed her forehead. The twiggy fingers on the ends of his mantis-like arms cracked as he slid them under her small frame and scooped her up. Still asleep, she rolled her face into the man's chest and gripped his sweatshirt. Seth knew she thought it was Dad, but he couldn't find his voice or his feet to tell her it was not.

The insectile man looked back at Seth for what seemed an eternity. His eyes reflected pinpricks of light from the bumble bee, his mouth twitched and made faint smacking sounds as if he were chewing meat. He measured Seth's features, imprinting the young boy's face in his mind, perhaps for later use. Again, he put one bony finger to his mouth. "*Shhh.*" Then he turned, carried Joana out the window into the night, and was gone.

It was the last time Seth or anyone else ever saw his sister.

The next four years were spent dealing with the police, missing persons experts, the FBI. Seth met with more councilors and therapists than he could count. He was the only one who had seen the man enter the house, which made his description gospel for a long while, but as the years went by the experts began to insinuate he'd seen things differently. "All this talk of bug legs and arms is a dissociative mechanism, a way to make sense of the nightmare," one therapist had told his parents. "By turning the kidnapper into some kind of magical demon, it helps him rationalize his shock. It's common in small children who suffer the intrusion of a stranger, and pretty prevalent in sexual abuse cases. Unfortunately he has become so accustomed to seeing this demon in his head that he may not actually be describing the man accurately for police. We need him to remember what the man really looked like if we're going to ever catch him."

In the end the police and FBI had never found a credible suspect. All Seth's parents could do was ask him why. Why didn't he scream? Why didn't he run or make a noise? Why had it taken him a whole hour to get out of bed and come crying into their room? Why why *why!*

"Still not going to the party," Connor said. He slipped out through the opening between the pallets and pushed through the trees until he got to the edge of the hill that looked down across Farmers Road and into the park. As he'd suspected, a soccer game was taking place in the closest field. From the way the players were all running in various directions, completely missing the ball, and even standing still trying to catch butterflies, it was clearly the pee wee league. Beyond the far field he could see the grassy area people picnicked on, but it was too far away to really see anyone's face. He scanned it nevertheless, looking for a sign of—

There! He was sure he could see Nicole and Amanita laying out on big, white towels. Of course it could be anyone, but he wanted to think it was them. He sure did hope Nicole showed up tonight. Especially now that he told Seth he wasn't going to the party it would be the only way to see her.

He sat on the hill and looked out over the town, followed the line of small mountains that ran around it on three sides. From this height he could see the Jefferson Bridge into Victorville, could see the rock walls of the Jefferson River ravine—now nothing but a dried up creek bed full of empty beer cans and old tires. He could see most of the town as well; the high school he'd be attending in two days, the public library, the 7-Eleven at the top of Draper Road, the pizza place his folks ordered from every Wednesday night, the garage Dad said ripped everybody off, the Dennys where the high school kids hung out and ordered coffee, the used bookstore where he'd discovered George R.R. Martin just last summer and, in the distance, the shopping mall.

If he squinted just right he could make out his street, but the trees that ran down it pretty much blocked out the view of the houses. Still, he knew whereabouts his house should be. He could look two streets over and see Nicole's street. She'd lived so close to him for so long but they still didn't know much about each other outside of school. He knew she was a brain, she knew he played sports, end of story.

Heavy footsteps alerted him to Seth's approach. The boy sat down, crossed his legs Indian style, and looked out over the town as well. "Sorry about that back there."

"About getting your pansy ass kicked by Germans? Forget it. You suck at games, what can you do?"

"You know what I mean." Seth held up the PSP. "Here, wanna play? You did steal the batteries after all. Your game is still saved on the memory card."

"Nah, it's okay. I played so much yesterday I dreamed I was hiding in hedgerows in the South of France all night."

"Suit yourself. What are you thinking about?"

Connor smiled. "About tonight."

"What about it?"

"I don't know . . . " Connor pitched a rock out toward the road. "Something just feels weird."

Seth pitched a rock out as well. It didn't go as far. "Yeah, girls are weird."

SATURDAY, 8:11pm

The sky was striated with bands of amber and violet as night settled in. Connor took in the view, finding Rorschach patterns in the clouds as he and his friend once again returned to their sanctuary. It was, after all, the last weekend night they would share together here that wouldn't involve worries about homework for many months.

"How was your dinner?" Seth asked.

"Okay. Dad made hamburgers on the grill. You?"

"Leftovers again. Mom said she didn't want to cook. I think the docs upped her anti-depressants. C'mon, let's go."

Trudging up the hill to the fort at night was a real pain. The summer foliage was thick and seemed to absorb any trace of light that got in its way. The streetlights on Farmers Road bounced some glare back up through the trees, but mostly Connor and Seth had to navigate the path by moonlight and two small flashlights.

Thankfully the path was wide and traveled frequently enough that even in the dark you had a sense of where it was before you. Besides, Seth and Connor had been there enough times at night to be experts at finding their way even if there wasn't a path. The only real danger, aside from getting too close to the hill over the road and falling a good hundred and fifty feet straight down, was walking through a spider web.

"Mosquitoes are hungry," Seth said.

"I've got Off in my backpack. Wait 'til we get there."

Through the trees they could see the lights on at the baseball field in the park. *Must be another little league game letting out*, Connor thought. They usually ended at eight o'clock.

Seth entered the fort first and lit the dozen citronella candles inside. In the enclosed space they lit things up like a sun.

"Here, let's go outside to spray this on so we don't light the place on fire." Connor handed the can of Off to Seth.

"Well, d'uh."

Both boys ducked back out into the woods for a moment and sprayed themselves with the insect repellent. As they were finishing up, they heard twigs snapping back on the path.

Connor's chest grew tight. "You think that's them?"

"It's either them or the trees are walking. That part always scared me in *The Wizard of Oz.*"

"That's because you're a pussy."

"And you're a douchebag."

"You're a level 18." Connor burst out laughing.

Seth gasped. "Oh my God, you dick. Not cool. Besides, everybody on that game cheats. They all have modded controllers!"

Seth was referring to the Halo 3 videogame, which they often played on his Xbox console. The game allowed you to rank up depending on how skillful you played. Connor was at 30, but Seth had been stuck on 18 for months. It was a sore spot with the boy. Seth didn't fare well with real sports, Connor assumed he only signed up for them so they could still hang out together during soccer season. Videogames, however, were another story. Seth was a master at gaming, and could usually beat a game in under a week. Connor was pretty terrible at gaming, he just couldn't move the characters the way he wanted to. For some reason he excelled at Halo 3's online gaming system, where he had a knack for anticipating other player's moves before they made them.

The snapping twigs grew into footsteps that got closer and closer. Someone in the dark swore and made a comment about how they could be at a party. Amanita. The cherry tip of her cigarette appeared in the blackness like a rogue firefly.

A second later the two girls stepped out of the gloom and into the spotlight glow of Seth and Connor's flashlights. "Hi, Connor," Nicole said. She was smiling. She had changed into jeans and a t-shirt with a sparkly star on the front. Her hair had been straightened as well. Even in the low light Connor could see the purple eyeshadow dusting her lids and the reflection of her lipgloss. She looked . . . adult. More adult than he'd ever seen her in school.

Next to her, Amanita, also in jeans and a t-shirt was huffing and picking a leaf out of her hair. "Yeah, hi, Connor. Nice hangout. I walked into a goddamn tree," she said, bending down and rubbing her knee. She took another puff of her cigarette.

Nicole laughed. "It was pretty funny. Just all of a sudden she fell backwards."

"I've got frigging heels on. It's not funny."

"I've got some Band Aids in my backpack," Connor said. "Did you get cut?"

"No. I'm fine. Just leave it alone." She pushed past them and leaned on the fort. The rickety construction allowed some candlelight from inside to leak out and create a yellow aura around the whole structure. "So this is where you two cuddle up together."

"We didn't build it," Seth offered. "It was here—"

"I know. The whole town knows about the hippies that built it. Looks like it should still have their corpses inside."

"My Dad says the hippy stuff is just a myth," Connor added.

"Whatever. I'm gonna go out on a limb and say there's no fridge in there?"

Connor shook his head. "No. Why would there be?"

Nicole opened her Dooney & Bourke tote—Connor knew the brand name because he'd overheard the girls talking about it at school when Nicole got it for Christmas—and pulled out a pint of Jack Daniels. "We brought something to drink." She shook the contents in the bottle.

"It's better if you drink it cold," Amanita added. "But we'll have to make do. Come on, let's go inside so the bugs don't bite."

"We have Off," Seth said.

"As if. I've got expensive perfume on and I'm not ruining it with bug spray." Amanita pushed her way inside the fort, made a dozen comments about the cleanliness of the space, and finally plopped in one of the car seats. The others followed her in. Seth, who knew nothing of chivalry as it was not a common aspect of video games, took the other chair, leaving Connor and Nicole to find spots on the floor.

When they were seated, Nicole unscrewed the cap of the Jack Daniels and held it up. "Who's first?"

"Where did you get it?" Connor asked.

Amanita, still sucking on her cigarette, held out her hand for it. "I stole it from my parents' liquor cabinet."

"Won't they be pissed when they find out?" Seth asked.

"They won't care."

"What? They don't care if you drink?"

"You got the first part right." She put the bottle to her lips. They all waited with baited breath to see if she'd take a swig.

The interior of the fort began to stink like bourbon and smoke. It reminded Connor of the few times he'd visited his father's friend's bar up state. All they needed was a toothless man talking to himself in the corner, a digital dartboard that didn't work, and a jukebox that played nothing recorded after 1978 and the facsimile would be complete.

Connor looked at Nicole. "You drink this a lot?"

"Me? No. I've only had a beer or two before. Am talked me into trying this." She moved a little closer to Connor until her knee accidentally touched his. "Oh, sorry." She looked away.

Connor blushed and scootched away from her.

Amanita rolled her eyes. "Nic is all goody two-shoes when it comes to drinking. She's afraid—"

"Am! Shut up—"

"—but we're going to a drinking party later and I'm gonna help her change all that. It's fine, Nic, they don't drink either, right?"

Neither boy nodded.

"See. Okay," she continued, "let me show you how it's done." She closed her eyes, tilted her head back, and took a bug gulp. The liquor came out so fast it spilled down her neck. Instantly she coughed and spit bourbon all over the wall. Seth yelped as her cigarette, tossed aside as she choked, landed on his lap. He quickly stomped it out. Nicole rushed over and slapped Amanita on the back like she was a baby in need of burping. Connor sat wide eyed, unsure what the hell to do.

Finally Amanita finished coughing, wiped her mouth with her hand and handed the bottle to Connor. "See, nothing to it. Your turn."

Connor took the bottle and smelled the lip of it. The caustic fumes burned his eyes.

"You don't have to if you don't want to," Nicole said. "We just thought, you know, since everyone was going to be drinking tonight—"

"No, it's okay. I mean I've had some beer before. It can't be much worse, right?"

Seth pointed at Amanita. "I think she almost just died, dude."

"I didn't almost just die. It's hard stuff is all. You have to acquire a taste for it. Least that's what *Cosmo* said."

Connor didn't really like the smell of the liquor, but he could sense some kind of eagerness in Nicole. Maybe she just wanted to go the party and drink, or maybe she just wanted to see if he was a pussy or not. Tentatively, he took a small sip. The liquid burned as it slid down his throat and lit his stomach on fire. He let out a small cough. "Not bad," he lied.

Nicole went next. Like Connor, she took a baby sip and winced as she swallowed it. "Jesus, Am, this tastes like crap."

"Yeah but it'll get you drunk fast."

"I don't want to get drunk."

"No, but remember what we talked about?" The two girls shared a look that made Connor uneasy.

"What'd you talk about?" Seth asked.

"More *Cosmo* stuff," Amanita said and laughed. Nicole laughed with her, but for some reason it felt forced.

Nicole, still fighting the burning sensation in her stomach, handed the bottle to Seth.

"I don't want any," he said.

"Oh, come on," Amanita teased, "you can't stay a geek your whole life. Just take a sip."

"I'm not a geek."

"Don't be a bitch, Am." Nicole looked at Amanita as though she might shoot fire out of her pupils and burn her friend to ashes.

"Oh please, I'm just kidding around. C'mon, Seth. Take a sip. It won't kill you. I read that bourbon drinkers are refined. You could use some refining."

Seth gave the bottle back to Amanita. "Look, just because your parents let you smoke and drink doesn't mean it makes you cool."

Amanita took another sip and this time didn't cough. "What is that, some kind of peer pressure speech? What are we in junior high still? If you don't want any then don't drink it. I was just trying to be nice. It's not like I even want to be here with you . . . " She was clearly going to add some kind of epithet but cut herself off.

"Then why did you come?" Seth pressed. "It's not like you're exactly wanted here."

"You're a fat piece of shit."

"Am, just drop it," Nicole said. She turned to Connor. "Look, maybe we should just go to the party. Are you sure you guys don't want to come?"

The truth was he did kind of want to go. He wanted to be where the in crowd was, and he wanted to talk to Nicole, which he'd hardly had a chance to do so far, but he'd pretty much promised Seth they'd hang out here for a while, play some more PSP. *All this confusion sucks*, he thought. "No, it's okay. Maybe we'll go to the next one. You go and have fun. I'll see you in school on Monday. Who knows, maybe we'll be in the same classes."

The look in Nicole's eye made it clear she was let down. "Yeah, I hope so. Well, it was cool seeing you. I like your fort."

With that, she turned and followed Amanita out into the woods. "Well, thanks a lot," she whispered.

Connor poked Seth in the shoulder and motioned for him to get up. "C'mon, we should walk them down the path to the street."

"Why?"

"Because girls like that. And it's dark out there and we have flash-lights."

"I don't care. Amanita is a bitch with a capital B."

"Then do it for Nicole."

"Don't see why I should."

Connor thought for a moment. "Because I'll rank your Halo stats up to 20 for you so you get the lieutenant badge."

Normally Seth would never accept help on a video game, but he really hated being called a *noob* by the other players and wanted a better badge. "Fine. But only to the street. I'm still not going to that dumb party."

"Thanks."

Together, they snatched up their flashlights and caught up to the girls, who were only a few feet away from the fort, moving slowly in the darkness. "Here, let us guide you back," Connor said. Once they played their flashlight beams over the path everyone was able to walk normal.

Amanita lit another cigarette. "Can't believe I wore my good heels into the woods."

"You'll be fine," Nicole said.

"The party probably already started."

"So?"

"Everyone is already there. We're gonna get there late and look like losers."

"I don't think everyone's there," Connor said. "See, you can see Jason Drake's house from up here. Next to the pizza place. Doesn't look like a lot of activity."

"What do you mean? There's like a hundred people there already."

Nicole added, "Wow, that's a cool view."

They all followed her, moving through the trees to the edge of the hill looking out over the town.

Amanita pulled her cellphone out and took a picture. "Have to admit, it is a cool view." They all looked at the picture but it was pretty blurry. "Well, what do you want," she said, "it's a cheap phone."

"I don't even have one," Connor said. "My parents said I have to wait until I'm sixteen."

"My parents took mine away," Seth added. "I didn't know they charged you to download the video games."

Nicole took her iPhone out of her purse and took a photo of the view. The quality was much better than Amanita's. "I'll put it on

Myspace tomorrow so we can all see it."

"I'm not your friend on Myspace," Connor said.

She smiled playfully. "Well, send me a friend request, dummy."

They all looked back out over the town again, lost in the view. "Which one is your house, Connor?"

He knew she knew where he lived but he pointed it out anyway. "Over there. The trees are blocking it but you get an idea. Your house is over there."

"Over there?" she asked, pointing too far to the right.

"No, um, over . . . " he took her hand and moved it to the left. Her skin was warm and soft and standing this close to her he could smell her shampoo and perfume. It was weird to smell the scents of a girl so close up. He could feel the tiny soft hairs on her arm and, somewhat embarrassed, withdrew his touch.

She turned back and smiled, so close that he could almost taste the Jack Daniels on her breath. "Thanks."

"You guys hear that?" Amanita asked.

Connor was frozen still, looking at Nicole's eyes. He was afraid that if he moved at all he might throw up. "Um, no," he said.

"No really. Listen."

"I hear it too," Seth said. "Sounds like a motor."

Now that Connor listened, he could hear a strange noise, like a combination of distant screaming and a truck rumbling by at high speed. No, it was more than that. It sounded like a freight train. And it was getting louder. Damn loud.

"What the hell is that?" Seth asked.

All four of them looked out over the town, trying to find the source of the noise. There was something dangerous about it, something that felt entirely out of place.

"Oh my God." Nicole pointed up into the sky.

Connor looked up. Every hair on his body stood on end.

SATURDAY, 8:24pm

At first it was just in the clouds. A light, blue and glowing, turning the clouds into pulsating purple blobs. Then tiny red flashing pinpricks joined in, and everyone knew what it was—the familiar strobing lights of an aircraft. The jet engines sounded too low to the earth. As the lights grew brighter, the sounds got louder. Nicole, Connor, Seth and Amanita stood fixed on the top of the hill, eyes watching as if in a trance.

Then . . .

It swam down through the lowest layer of clouds, a massive steel beast angled at some sixty degrees. If the angle was any steeper it would be in a complete nosedive, its speed in excess of five hundred miles per hour. The wings tipped too far to port, showing the four teens the metallic underbelly of the craft and the collection of desperately winking safety lights. It threatened to roll over but whoever was flying it was fighting to roll it back and it pitched like a canoe on heavy waves. The tail swung, as if the plane were skidding in the air.

Connor heard the screams from next to him, knew it was his friends, but could not register it as more than background noise. The thunderous sound of the plane almost drowned out all sound and threatened to burst his eardrums. He knew nothing of the plane's make, just that it was giant and fast and flying the wrong direction. *Down!*

He felt his pulse race and his body go cold with sweat as his brain finally made sense of what he was seeing.

Nicole grabbed his arm and screamed in his ear. Her grip threatened to rip his skin off. He couldn't understand what she was screaming, couldn't turn his head away. She was in hysterics but he didn't care. He was frozen.

The plane slammed nose first into the ground with a force that shook the entire town.

Connor, Seth, Nicole and Amanita fell backwards as the concussive wave of heat from the explosion screamed up the hill and slammed into them. All four threw their arms up over their faces and yelled but there was little coherence in anything they cried before they were hurled backwards into the dirt.

"Jesus Christ!"

"Oh my God!"

"I'm on fire!"

The last was not true, but their close proximity to the crash, and the severe temperature of the fireball, made it feel like they were.

The blast wave passed over them with a howling *whoosh*. Connor sat up and rolled to his knees. He crawled on all fours back to the edge of the hill and looked out over the town. The fireball was turning black with carbon smoke, debris flew in every direction, almost like a fireworks show. He could see something soaring through the air at them, something large and on fire and coming at a speed too fast to outrun.

The thing in the air was on a trajectory for them.

He turned back to his friends, trying to issue a warning from his quivering lips. He saw Nicole standing up, brushing dirt from her eyes, trying to get her bearings. Suddenly he felt like he was on the soccer field again—the ball in front of his feet, the goal a few yards away and closing, adrenaline pumping, a massive defensemen chasing him, threatening to sweep his legs out. He sprinted at Nicole and hit her full force in the stomach, hugging her, driving her to the ground, spinning as they fell so she'd land on him instead of the other way around.

The force of the impact knocked the wind out of him. He looked up and saw her looking down at him, total surprise and fear written in her eyes. He watched as the massive, flaming wing of the airplane sliced through the air above them, missing them by mere feet.

It severed the trees around them like a scythe through wheat, crashing through the woods with the squealing protest of twisting metal. Tree tops and bifurcated trunks toppled to the ground, rumbling against the forest floor. Branches exploded outward and struck the dirt with enough force to crack a skull. The flora rained down on top of them, cutting their bare arms, breaking their skin like BBs shot from an air rifle at close range. For a fleeting moment Connor thought his actions would be for naught, that they'd be shredded by the trees, but the wing lodged itself in a towering pine with an ear-splitting crunch, gave one last creak, and finally came to rest.

"You okay?" Connor asked, his breath coming back to him. He could feel Nicole's lips just about touching his.

She pushed off of him and brushed her hair out of her face. She was shaking, and had a superficial cut above her eye, but otherwise looked in one piece. "Yeah. Thanks."

"No problem." Connor stood up and took note of his own injuries. Twigs had lacerated his shin pretty badly, cutting through his jeans. Blood was running into his sock from a deep gouge. The entire area felt numb, but it didn't hurt to stand on. He could feel a bruise forming on his shoulder. "Seth? Amanita?"

"Over here." Seth's hand stuck up from a mound of broken branches.

Connor and Nicole rushed over and pulled the larger ones off of him. He emerged covered in dirt and bleeding from his nose. "What the hell was that?"

"I think it was the wing of the plane."

"I felt the air from it."

"Yeah, it was close."

Nicole stepped over a fallen tree and picked up the broken bottle of Jack Daniels. "Where's Am?"

Both boys spun in a circle, kicking aside the piles of branches now littering the ground. Amanita was nowhere to be found. They found Nicole's purse and handed it back to her. She accepted it with a thanks, too concerned about Amanita to bother checking inside.

"She's got to be around here somewhere," Seth said.

Nicole put her hand to her mouth. "Oh my God, she wasn't standing when that thing . . . when it . . . "

Nobody dared finish the sentence for her, the thought was too horrible. If Amanita had been standing when the wing flew over them it would have crushed her instantly and sent her flying through the air like a ragdoll. She would be nothing but a lump of broken bones deep in the woods.

Nicole began to cry, which prompted Seth and Connor to start overturning branches at a frantic rate. They called out for Amanita but got no response. Connor started to think Nicole might be right. Amanita must have gotten hit by the—

"She's here!" Seth exclaimed.

Nicole and Connor rushed over and found Seth lifting up one of the pallets from the fort. It must have ricocheted away from the fort when the wing did its damage. Amanita was lying under it, her eyes closed. She looked dead.

"Oh no, Am. No, please be okay." Nicole bent down and lifted Amanita's head, put two fingers against the girl's throat. "I . . . I don't know how to check for a pulse. I mean I do, but I've never done it. Not for real. I don't feel anything. Oh my God, she's dead!"

Connor knelt down beside her. "Is she breathing? Feel her chest."

Nicole put her head on Amanita's chest. She actually cried harder.

"Yeah, she's breathing. She's alive." She wiped her tears away and sniffled.

Connor shook the unconscious girl and gave her a little slap in the face—the same kind of medical treatment he'd seen in so many bad movies—hoping to jar her awake.

Amanita's eyelids began to flutter. *Shit, it actually worked.*

"She's coming to!" Nicole yelled.

"I'm to already," Amanita said. "For fuck's sake stop yelling in my ear."

"Sounds like her," Seth said.

"Can you walk?" Connor asked.

Amanita rolled herself onto her knees and then steadily got to her feet. She moved all her joints and didn't scream out in pain. Like the others, she had cuts on her bare skin, and her shirt was torn near her right hip, but she was fine to travel. "Something hit the back of my head," she said, rubbing the spot in question. She pulled her hand away but there was no blood.

"You might have a concussion," Nicole said. "Do you feel dizzy or is your vision wobbly?"

"I'm fine, McDreamy. Really. Except my fucking shoes are gone. I just bought those shoes. Damn!"

"So we're all okay, then?" Connor asked.

"McDreamy is a guy," Seth added. This generated looks of disbelief. "What, it's a good show."

For the next few seconds everyone checked themselves over once more and concluded they were all just the worse for wear. The worst of the injuries seemed to be Connor's shin, which needed stitches and a bandage.

"What do we do about that?" Nicole asked, pointing into the woods where the wing had gone. A pool of fire was casting orange light up into the surrounding treetops.

"More importantly," Amanita added, "What the hell do we do about *that?*" They followed her finger as she pointed out over the town.

A trail of fire cut through the center of Castor. Flaming debris was spread out in what had to be a mile-wide radius. Nearby houses had been torn to pieces, businesses reduced to kindling, trees and cars smashed to bits. The smell of burning wood and metal was everywhere. The plane itself, throwing walls of fire into the sky, was situated just beyond the pizza place.

As the four of them stood on the hill, looking down in awe, rubbing bruises and wiping blood off their skin, they heard the cries of the entire town float up the thermals from the crash site and wash over them like a nightmare.

Their friends and families were injured, dead or dying.

Saturday, 8:29pm

As a tight group, the four teens hobbled through the dark woods, careful to find footing over the newly fallen trees. Their flashlights were gone, and even though the severed wing was still burning and lighting nearby vegetation on fire, dense shadows still made it dangerous to walk.

The path led down to the south end of Farmers Road, which was flanked on both sides by woods. Farmers Road cut like a river through the center of town, passing by the park and angling up toward the Jefferson Bridge on the north end, winding through many miles of wooded nothingness on the south end until it met State Road 134 to Wallington. It was just the one road into and out of town unless you counted a few dozen dirt "roads" that cut through the wooded hills encircling the majority of Castor. There had once been second bridge over the Jefferson River's deep but empty riverbed, but it had been deemed unsafe after a wild storm had loosened its struts in 1987. The town had voted and eventually torn in down.

Connor, Nicole, Seth and Amanita reached the bottom of the dirt trail and began jogging down Farmers Road. The blaze from the crashed plane seemed brighter, hotter.

Connor stopped at the edge of the park and pointed across the giant green lawn. "We can cut across the soccer fields to Union Avenue and hop over the chain-link fence around the supermarket. That'll put us on top of the hill near Pizza King."

Nobody protested, but Nicole pointed to his leg. "Can you climb like that?"

"I'll be alright."

"I have a feeling you're not going to be high on the ER's list of priorities," Amanita added.

The park lights were off, the games having ended for the day. In the near distance they could see the orange glow of the blazing fire reflecting off the low clouds. It looked like a gigantic pit from hell had opened under their town and was trying to crawl up to the sky.

"I can't get service." Nicole held her cell phone up, trying to find reception. "One hundred and twenty bucks a month and it doesn't work."

"There's a cell tower on top of the high school," Seth said. "That's not too far from the crash. Maybe some debris hit it? Knocked it out?"

Connor shook his head. "We have to have more than one tower."

"I can't get Internet on it either," Nicole added.

Amanita took out her own cellphone. Its face was cracked and dirt fell out of the battery housing. "Mine's busted. Shit, I don't even have insurance on it."

Connor said, "The plane must have messed up the town's system. But we can hear sirens so somebody already called."

Not that the whole town wouldn't have felt that, he thought.

Nicole put a hand on Connor's shoulder and stopped him for a second. "I need to make sure my Mom's okay."

"Yeah sure, but—"

"But what?"

"I feel like we should get to the crash and see what's what. I'm sure we're not going to be able to do anything anyway, but we witnessed the whole thing so you never know. We'll head home right after."

Nobody spoke as they crossed the remaining fields and emerged onto Union Avenue. The backside of the local supermarket was before them, the fence to the truck loading docks already locked for the night to keep riff raff out.

Amanita climbed up first, cursing as she went, but her body was toned and she had no problem lifting her weight. Nicole went next and Connor stayed back to help her in case she fell. But like Amanita she proved athletic enough to hold her own.

She landed on the other side and waved for Connor and Seth. "Come on, let's hurry."

Seth went next and got halfway up before he stopped. He was having difficulty getting his weight up to the top. On the other side of the fence Amanita rolled her eyes. "Oh for fuck's sake just put your foot there—"

"I can do it," Seth yelled back. With a grunt he rolled himself over the top and almost fell all the way down to the ground on the other side but both Amanita and Nicole put their hands up to stop him, allowing him to get a grip.

Connor went last, and while he had no problem getting over, he felt his shin burning as he used his calf muscles. At one point the open wound grazed a link and sent shockwaves of pain up his back. He winced when he landed next to Nicole.

They walked around the side of the supermarket, across the small parking lot, and onto the road. They followed it up a steep grade until it was level with the rooftops of the surroundings homes and businesses. Here they stopped and stared at the scene before them.

The Pizza King was gone. The gas station across the street was just a pile of flaming tinder. Up and down the street debris burned and keened as it melted. The fuselage of the plane lay in the middle of what had once been a house, now torn in half, passenger chairs piled up around it, everything alight. The cockpit had driven further into the surrounding homes, leaving a trail of destruction and fire in its wake. The other wing was nowhere to be seen, neither were the jet engines. The tail of the plane had been sheared off as well and was also missing. It was hard to tell what had gone where, but judging by the number of burning houses surrounding the crash it was obvious the rest of the plane, like the wing that almost crushed Connor and his friends, had been flung off on impact.

Sprawled on the street at varying intervals were dead bodies, some of them in one piece, others missing essential parts. One of them was headless. Limbs poked out from under burning bits of metal. Some limbs were not attached to a body.

A fire truck sped to the scene, joining two others that were already on site. Long arcs of water shot into the towering flames but did little to extinguish the blaze. The entire town's collection of police cruisers was on site, red and blue lights all but lost in the intense orange blaze of the fire. An ambulance appeared out of the black smoke and pulled to the stop near one of the fire trucks. More sirens could be heard approaching. All of the emergency personnel were so overwhelmed they looked like baseball players caught in a pickle, frantically running back and forth but not sure what to do.

But worse than this, worse than the sight of the giant mangled and burning plane sitting in the middle of a residential street in Castor, worse than the dead bodies with broken bones splayed at unnatural angles, were the people on fire, running around in the street. Even from the top of the hill Connor could hear their wails of agony and wanted to cry; they were burning alive.

Firemen and police officers emerged with fire blankets and portable extinguishers and tried to spray down the victims, but there were too many to attend to at once. The lucky ones were hosed down, their skin blackened beyond recognition, the unlucky ones writhed on the hot street while their flesh melted off.

None of the four friends made an attempt to move any closer. This was disaster on a scale they had never seen. This was more than the town of Castor was ever meant to handle. Seth finally stepped forward and said what they were all just realizing. "The plane hit Jason Drake's house. It's completely gone. I mean, look, it's just gone."

Nicole turned to Connor but was unable to speak. There was something she needed to say, something profound, but the realization that they could have been at the party was too fresh for her. Tears welled up in her eyes and fell down her cheeks.

Connor wanted to say something to let her know everything would be alright, but he stopped short, because as he turned back to the scene, the final puzzle piece fell in place. The people rolling on the ground on fire were their schoolmates. The plane had barreled right into them, a massive bullet burning at a thousand degrees. The flaming bodies on the street would turn out to be people he knew. The motionless ones had been lucky. What was it they always said in the movies about disasters? The lucky ones die quick.

Amanita bent over and threw up on the street, almost falling to her knees in the process. She was crying, and somewhere in the back of Connor's mind he realized it was the only time he'd ever seen her cry. Next to him Nicole started to shake and began tugging on his sleeve. "We have to help! We have to do something!"

At the crash site, firemen were doing their best to shoot suppression foam on anything with flames, including the burning people. It wasn't doing much good. The fire was so intense and so hot that it incinerated anything that got close to it. The terrified screams of pain grew louder.

Connor felt his knees go weak but knew Nicole was right; they had to help their fellow students. "Okay, follow me."

He led the way down, eyeing a teenage girl rolling on the grass of a well-manicured lawn, her hair burned off, her legs still on fire. Connor broke into a run, desperately trying to ignore the blinding pain in his shin, and tore his shirt off. He slid on the grass beside her and beat the flames with his shirt. His back began to burn from the hot air surrounding the nearby burning fuselage, like standing too close to a bonfire. It was all he could do to ignore the heat and focus on the girl. As he whipped at the flames on her legs she howled in pain and flailed like a wild animal. "Stay still! I'm trying to—"

"Get off her!" Two large arms reached around him and threw him several feet to the side. He rolled over and saw two firemen spraying the girl's legs with foam. Their faces were streaked with soot, their eyes beet red. Even working together the two large firefighters could not control the poor girl's kicking. He realized then it was Danny Williams' older sister Carrie.

He could tell from her necklace, a Sailor Jerry Sparrow tattoo. Never took it off. She worked at the pretzel stand in the mall and would be a junior this year. Boys found her attractive and stood around ordering pretzels all day just to sneak a peek at her. Right now, her lips were dangling down beneath her chin, her bald head was slick with bubbling hot blood, her cheeks were singed into strips of meat, and her left eye was nothing but a black olive. Half of her head was burned beyond repair.

Nicole, Amanita and Seth reached down and helped Connor up.

A police officer ran over and began shoving them off the lawn. "Get the fuck out of here now! I mean it!"

So much for helping, thought Connor.

"They're still burning," Nicole said. "Somebody needs to put them out. They're going to die!"

The cop started to yell at her but stopped when another burning teenager came running past them and fell, rolling to the ground.

For a fleeting second Connor considered chasing after the cop, lending his help whether the bastard liked it or not. But something stopped him cold. It wasn't fear of pissing off the authorities or the possibility of causing more harm than good to the victims, but rather the sight of a large man with the bloody face running full tilt at them, running so fast he looked like a blur. The *slap slap slap* of the man's shoes on the pavement rattled like gunfire.

Something about the way he ran, hunched forward like a baseball player about to slide into base—arms thrust out, fingers splayed, his mouth opened as wide as it would go—it didn't feel right.

He's not screaming, Connor noted. *He's not even flailing. He's just running at full speed, straight for us, reaching for us.* He glanced quickly at Seth and saw the same kind of confusion in his friend's eyes. Amanita and Nicole saw it, too. Everyone watched, wondering what the hell was happening, nobody could put their finger on why it was strange.

Then it hit Connor. The man was one of the flight attendants, the dark blue dress uniform melted into his skin, and he was hissing.

Hissing.

"Everybody run!" He grabbed Nicole and yanked her up the lawn to the burning pile of rubble that was once a house and ducked down behind a car that was now crushed and covered with broken two-by-fours. Seth and Amanita didn't need a second warning and hauled ass to hide beside them. They peeked out to watch.

When the flight attendant hit the edge of the lawn he changed course, veering toward the cop and plowed into him with everything he had. The cop flew over the teenager he'd been trying to put out, rolled into a ball and came up dazed. The flight attendant, still hissing and never losing his momentum, hit the cop again and took him down like a sack of laundry.

As they hit the ground the flight attendant tore at the cop's eyes, sending gouts of blood into the air, and bit down on the cop's face, frantically shaking back and forth like a shark. The blood-curdling scream that let loose from the officer as the mangled flight attendant yanked his nose off and went for his throat was all but lost in the din of the surrounding scene.

But Connor and his friends heard it. They heard it loud and clear, they just couldn't believe what they were seeing.

The flight attendant leapt off the cop and sat on his haunches, quickly scanned his surroundings, caught site of the firemen working on Carrie Williams, and bolted after them, now on all fours like a rabid dog.

"Look out!" Connor yelled. But it was too late; the flight attendant tackled the two firemen and went for their faces with his teeth. All Connor and his friends saw were bursts of blood and pieces of flesh spitting into the air. It was over in seconds, both firemen lying still, and the flight attendant was off chasing another police officer.

Amanita spoke through chattering teeth. "What the flying fuck was that shit! He ate that guy's face! Did you see it? What the fucking hell was that! I wanna go I wanna fucking go I wanna—"

Nicole grabbed Amanita and hugged her, the curse words still spewing into her shoulder. Seth and Connor exchanged worried glances. This was not right, not right at all.

"Okay," Connor said, huddling them together, "I don't know what that was. I don't even care right now. None of this is good to be around and I'm thinking everyone has their hands full so let's leave this whole thing—" he pointed toward the burning plane "—to the cops and stuff. We need to get home to our parents. *Then* we can deal with what that crap we just saw was all about."

"You need to fix your leg." Nicole put in. "We should run through the . . . " she stammered for a second but found her resolve. "Run through the back of the Drake's house and get on the next street."

"Can't."

"Why?"

"Because if the plane slid into the Drake's house that means the cockpit probably broke off and went further. The houses on the next street will be burning too. Maybe even the houses on the street after that. And we can't get down the road here, which would be easiest, but we *can* head back up Union and go around the gas station—"

"It's gone," Seth said. "Look."

"Right. I forgot. But we'll just go that way anyway and stick together and—"

He never finished his sentence. Over the shoulders of his friends he could see the street, the plane, distraught and curious people from the neighborhood being ushered away by angry and confused policemen, firemen maneuvering their fire hoses, and the cop who'd just been attacked at the edge of the neighboring lawn.

The cop was standing. Just a few feet beyond the car they were hiding behind.

Not just standing, but swiveling his head back and forth so fast it looked like he might snap his own neck, arms flexing like a television wrestler acting tough. His face had a gaping hole in the middle of it where his nose and lips had once been. His cheeks and forehead were split wide with deep gouges. What really concerned Connor was the way the cop was hissing.

Just like the flight attendant.

Before Connor could mention what he was seeing, the cop looked right at him, locked his bile-colored eyes with him, and burst into a sprint.

Connor felt ice shoot through his chest. "Run run run!"

Everybody's eyes went wide and Seth screamed but they were all up and running in a flash, nobody looking back. Connor knocked one of the two-by-fours off the top of the car and it hit the faceless cop in the knees, taking him down.

"This way," Connor yelled, aiming for Union Avenue. The other three ran toward him but suddenly jumped apart as the cop tore into the middle of the group. Seth and Amanita ran back to the car, got it between them and the frenzied cop. Nicole reached Connor and yelled, "He's gonna kill them!"

If the cop doesn't get them, Connor thought, *those two firemen certainly will.* They were standing now as well, and even at this distance he could see the way their heads swiveled and their chewed-up lips snarled in a hiss.

What the hell is going on?

"Seth, behind you!"

Seth and Amanita turned, saw the two firemen running at them, screamed, and broke out toward the burning plane and firetrucks. The cop went around the back of the car and joined in the chase as well.

Connor's stomach lurched, knowing his friends were done for, knowing Seth was not fast enough and Amanita was handicapped by bare feet, knowing there was nothing he could do to save them, hating himself for being so worthless. Oh dear God he was about to watch them die in the most heinous way he could have ever imagined. One human being biting the flesh off of another until death.

Seth and Amanita reached the nearest fire truck, gunning for the handful of firemen working the hose on its back, just as two more yellow-eyed, animalistic cops came out of the black smoke and swarmed the unsuspecting men.

The pursuers—the faceless cop and two mangled firemen—saw the new attack and decided on the easier prey. Seth and Amanita leapt behind the truck as the entire pack of ravenous hissing authorities fought the firemen to the ground and bit off their faces. An eyeball flitted through the air and was quickly scrounged up and eaten. Other bits, noses and lips and chunks of gooey flesh, met the same end.

"C'mon!" Connor shouted, waving them back over.

Seth saw him, started to run, but stopped. He pointed at Connor. "Get out!"

Connor turned, saw a neighborhood resident, a woman in a Disney Land sweatshirt, her neck ripped to shreds, running at them in the now familiar FUBAR sprint of the insane. She was a substitute teacher around the schools; he'd had her a few times. Running almost hand over foot next to her was Melissa Hodges, a quiet girl a grade ahead of him, her mouth agape and coated in crimson blood, face burned to a waxy slick. She must have been at the Drake's party too. Something was spreading and it was happening damn fast.

He grabbed Nicole and ran toward the demolished gas station, praying she could keep up. Luckily she'd worn sneakers, unlike her friend, and was lithe enough to move almost as fast as he. Were it not for her purse she might even be faster, but he didn't think to tell her to leave it. Besides, it had a phone in it, and even though it wasn't getting service, it was a link to reality.

They hit the street beside the station and he glanced back, saw Melissa Hodges and the substitute teacher being halted by an EMT. The freakish teacher jumped on him, Melissa wrapping her legs and arms around him like they were lovers reuniting after years apart. They all went down to the ground and the bloodshed began.

"Where's Am?"

Connor took a second to scan the insanity. "There. With Seth. Running to the backyard of that house. See them?"

"We have to go get them."

The scene spread out before them and Connor finally saw the new element that had been thrust into the night's events. Everywhere around the plane people were savagely attacking one another. Someone would bite a chunk out of someone else's face or neck or chest or arm, and within seconds that victim would be running around hissing as well, their eyes now glassy yolks. As he stood and watched, he estimated about twenty trauma victims tearing through the streets, hissing and sinking teeth into anyone they saw.

Residents who'd rushed out of nearby homes to gape at the crashed plane were now screaming in terror and running away from bloodthirsty police officers and firemen and even their own friends. They took off down side streets, into homes, through yards, all of them hunted and chased. It was pandemonium. Homicidal pandemonium.

"No," Connor said, finally answering her question. "Seth knows the neighborhood as well as anyone. He'll get them to another street. He'll get them home."

"Are you sure? This is madness!"

Hell no, he wasn't sure. If this were all a video game then yes, Seth would get home safely no problem, but this was something else. He had no idea if he'd ever see his best friend again. The only thing he did know was that they couldn't go back. People were turning into these lunatic monsters so exponentially fast it would only be hours before the whole town was seized.

He spotted the flight attendant scrabbling over a police car, completely covered in blood, his clothes torn like a caveman, jumping off the hood and sprinting down the street into the heart of the surrounding neighborhood.

The edge of the same neighborhood where he and Nicole lived.

"Shit. We need to go. *Now.*" He looked back once and prayed for his friends' safety, then turned and ran back up the hill toward the supermarket, Nicole by his side.

Saturday, 8:58pm

The streetlights were off and the power was out in every house along the street. Inside some windows people could be seen lighting candles and checking flashlight batteries but they were few and far between; everyone had rushed down to the crash. Only two cars passed as Amanita and Seth emerged from the backyard of an unknown house. They had pushed through tall hedges, scrambled over one four-foot fence and were now three streets beyond the crash. The clouds over-head were still orange with the reflection of the fire, the towering flames still bright. The chorus of screams from the crash site contin-ued to ride the night air.

Amanita pressed herself against the side of the house's garage, looking out at the dark, lifeless road running perpendicular before them. "What street is this?"

"No idea. Maybe Madison? Recognize any of the houses?"

"No. But it's either Madison or Monroe. My house isn't far away, maybe six more blocks. We can go left two blocks and catch Maple. That runs all the way down to my street." Another scream echoed from behind them, on the street they'd just crossed. She turned and looked at him, her unspoken request plain as day on her face.

"What, you want me to go with you?"

"It's called chivalry."

"It's called I-don't-care. I live that way." He pointed to the right.

"So you're gonna let me run home alone in bare feet while every-one is eating each other?"

"Yeah, that's pretty much the plan."

"You know, you're not just a geek, you're a dick."

"Oh, as if you've ever been nice to me. Like I owe you anything."

"Nice to you? I don't even talk to you! How can I be mean when I don't talk to you?"

"You don't talk to me because you think I'm a geek."

"Well, you are a geek. And a jerky one at that. Try putting down your stupid video games for a minute and joining the rest of us who have social lives. You're really not gonna come with me?"

Seth patted his cargo jean pockets, fished his hands around in each one and then swore. "My PSP is gone."

Amanita threw her hands in the air. "Oh my God, are you serious? What the hell are we gonna do now? We have no PSP. We're totally fucked." She paused. "What the hell is a PSP?"

"My video game console."

"Seth, forget the fucking video games. I'm running down to Maple in two seconds. If you're not with me then I hope you die."

Tentatively, Amanita stuck her head out and scanned the street, saw it was still empty and eased down the driveway, past the car, and began to jog into the adjacent house's lawn. Seth banged his head lightly against the side of the garage, listening to the incessant screams coming from everywhere, whispered, "Screw it," and followed her.

He caught up with her and ignored her middle-finger welcome. "Whatever, I'm a jerk. I'm here aren't I? Stick to the fronts of the houses. If we have to, we can duck in bushes."

Her slight nod was the only confirmation she wasn't going to slug him.

They moved quietly across the lawn and onto the lawn of the next house, and then the next one after that. They made it all the way to the house at the intersection of Maple without incident, stopped behind a weeping willow tree on the property. Sirens and screams were still audible here. "Okay," Seth said, "we jet across the street to that parked car, then up the lawn and stay close to these houses until we get to yours."

"Way ahead of you."

"Wait. Before we go, take back what you said."

"What? About you being a geek?"

"No, about hoping I die."

Amanita put her head in her hands. "It was a joke."

"Wasn't funny. I want an apolo—"

"Oh for fuck's sake, I'm sorry. Will you shut up before some face-eating asshole jumps out and kicks your ass?"

"Apology accepted."

"Jesus fucking Christ."

"You know, you swear a lot."

"Yeah, well I'm sorry but a plane just crashed on my friend's house and now people are biting each other to death and I'm a little messed up. I'm gonna swear a little bit, okay? You know for all the insults you claim I sling at you, you sure as shit have a lot to say about me."

Seth thought about that for a second. "Alright. Sorry."

"Good. Now let's just do this, I want to get home."

"Okay then, Lara Croft, on three. One . . . two . . . "

Someone hissed.

Seth felt a shiver race through him. The hiss came again, close by. Directly to their left.

Standing on the adjacent lawn, the one they'd just run across, was a man in his pajamas. He was covered in dark stains, his hair wild, his eyes yellow orbs, sniffing the air like a wolf. The front of his pajama top was torn open and a wound like a red saucer was oozing fluids over his right pectoral. He stepped toward the willow tree.

Seth and Amanita huddled together, rotating around the tree trunk as the hissing man drew closer. He stopped short, turned and ambled onto the street, moving jerkily as if he'd been given new legs, chuffing with his mouth open the whole time.

Both Seth and Amanita fought back the urge to scream as the clouds parted and illuminated the man with moonlight.

The man had three arms.

The one sticking out of his back was wearing the black and yellow fire retardant sleeve of a firefighter. As the man moved off down the road, stopping to sniff the air every few feet, the arm swung back and forth, grasping.

Saturday 9:01pm

The gouge on Connor's leg was starting to swell so badly he thought he might have to take his shoe off. Dried blood was caked up along the edges of the torn skin, but fresh blood still continued to dribble out. He did his best to ignore the pain that shot up his leg as he and Nicole rounded a parked car and emerged onto his own street. He paused for a second, then pointed down the road. "Okay, we're here. So far no one's noticed us. I think I should get you home first and then—"

"No way. Look at you, you're leg is about to fall off. We'll get to your place and I'll call my Mom to come get me."

The mention of the phone got Connor thinking about how he was going to tell his parents about what they saw at the crash site—people biting and killing one another. Mutilated people who *should* be dead racing around like cannibalistic savages. They needed to call the cops and report it but it sounded so outlandish he was afraid they'd laugh at him.

As if challenging him, a scream erupted into the air from somewhere nearby. It was cut off with a choke.

"Seriously, we have to go." Nicole began jogging toward Connor's house. "I don't want to be out here any longer. Please, Connor. Please!"

She was right. It was dangerous out in the streets. There was no telling where those crazy people were. Together they ran down the middle of the street, keeping an eye out for anyone or anything strange. They made it to the end of the street without incident and started up Connor's driveway.

He lived in a gray two-story house with brown trim. A collection of Green Mountain Boxwood bushes grew up against the front of the house. A Toyota Camry and Mazda 323 were parked side by side in the driveway. Typical family fare. He never noticed how bland it all looked until now, standing next to Nicole. He almost felt embarrassed.

Something else caught his eye. "The lights are off."

"They're off everywhere. The plane must have really done a job on everything, knocked down more than a few telephone poles. No power."

"Then wait, if you're cell isn't working either, how will you call your mom?"

Nicole stared back at him, at a loss for words. Immediately he felt bad for ruining her hopes of calling her parents.

"No problem, I'll have my Dad give you a ride. C'mon."

Nice save, he thought.

He opened the front door, knocking as he swung it in. "Hello. Mom? Dad?"

No answer.

"Maybe they're upstairs?"

"Maybe." Connor closed the door behind them and headed to the kitchen. Behind him he heard Nicole bump into the rocking chair near the bookshelf.

"Sorry," she said. "Can't see anything."

"No, my bad. Should have warned you. I stub my toe on that damn thing all the time, even when the lights are on." *Strike two*, he thought. Jeez, he kept messing up with her.

He tried the light switch in the kitchen just to be sure. It was dead. From the dining room he saw an orange glow. "Mom?"

"In here," came his mother's voice. "Lighting a candle. The power is out."

Connor rushed into the room and hugged her, fighting back the urge to cry.

"Connor, sweetie, you're gonna break my ribs."

"Sorry." He let go of her just and turned to find Nicole standing against the wall. "This is Nicole."

His mother placed the lit candle next to the other six already lit on the dining room table and blew out the match. "Hi, Nicole."

"Hi, Mrs. Prudhome. I think you should look at Connor's le—"

"You're Nicole Fitzgerald, right? I met your mother at a PTA meeting a few years ago. Very sweet."

"Thanks. She's okay. Connor needs—"

"Hang on a sec. Let me throw this out." Mrs. Prudhome made her way back into the kitchen and disposed of the match. "So, what is going on out there? We heard a huge explosion of some kind and then a lot of sirens. All the power went out and I can't get anyone on the phone. I'm telling you the whole house shook! Your dad is looking for a flashlight and a radio, as if he can find anything in that disaster zone he calls a garage. I've got food in the fridge that's gonna go bad if it doesn't come back on soon."

Connor followed her into the kitchen with Nicole in tow. "Mom, a plane crashed near the Sunoco station. People are—"

Mrs. Prudhome spun around so fast it looked like she was dancing. "*What?* A plane crash! Oh my God, is anybody hurt?"

"You could say that. Mom, something weird is going on. We saw people—"

His mother struck another match and gasped. "Connor! Jesus Christ what happened to you? Mark! Mark!"

Connor's father came racing into the kitchen. He was screwing the top onto an old flashlight. "What? What?" He pressed in the flashlight's rubber button and shot a weak beam of light across the dark kitchen. When he saw Nicole and Connor covered in soot and dirt and blood, his jaw dropped. "Connor! What they hell did you do to your leg?"

Mrs. Prudhome went to Connor and bent down in front of him, delicately examined her son's shin. "What in the name of God were you two doing?"

Connor shook his head. The sudden barrage of meaningless questions was driving him nuts. "Mom, you're not listening. A plane crashed and—"

"That was a plane crash?" his father asked. "That loud bang we heard that knocked the power out?"

"Yes, a plane crashed and a lot of people are dead—"

His mother was on the verge of hysterics. "Did you get hit? Were you near it when it happened? Jesus, Mark he needs to go to the emergency room. This is really bad. I think I can almost see bone. Oh my God, where's the gauze?"

"Mom, chill out, there's no way they're seeing me at the emergency room. You have no idea how many people are hurt right now. The bodies alone . . . "

"It's a lot of people dead, Mrs. Prudhome." Nicole was crying now. Connor's dad put his arm on her shoulder to comfort her. Nicole looked a little awkward so Connor got up and stood next to her. She didn't look any more comfortable.

Mrs. Prudhome checked the cordless phone again. "It's still dead. Mark, we need to get him to a doctor."

Connor's father took out his cell phone and dialed a number. "Okay, get your coat. We'll drive over and see what kind of resistance they give us. And we'll drop . . . um . . . "

"Nicole," Connor said.

" . . . Nicole off at home. Where do you live, Nicole?"

"I'm a couple of streets over. On Poplar."

"This is Jenny Fitzgerald's daughter," Mrs. Prudhome explained, taking her purse off the kitchen counter, "from the PTA fundraiser?"

Mark Prudhome said he remembered but it was obvious he didn't. Lucky for him this was no time to for his wife to argue about white lies. He finally closed his phone and clipped it back on his belt. "I can't even get an operator. It just makes a beeping noise."

"I have no service either." Nicole took her cell phone from her purse and tapped the screen to light it up.

Connor said, "I'd try, but I'm not allowed to have a phone."

"Not now, Connor." Mrs. Prudhome ushered him into the living room. "Let's get going before you get an infection."

Mark Prudhome led Nicole to the door and swung his flashlight around. "Where are my keys? They were in my jacket. Where's my jacket?"

"Jesus, Mark, can't you keep track of anything?"

"Well next time I know our son is going to be wounded in a plane crash—"

"It was a tree, actually, Dad."

"—I'll be sure to file them in the appropriate disaster drawer."

"Well, the wing hit the trees so I guess—"

"Found 'em! They were in my pocket."

"Can we please go now," Mrs. Prudhome said.

Mark opened the front door and all four walked out. Nicole and Connor hung back, Connor's parents taking the first step.

The *slap slap slap* of someone running down the street drew their attention. Nicole squinted, and let out a shriek. Connor saw what she saw: two men in tattered rags, their mouths agape, running full tilt toward them. They were only three houses away.

"Inside!" Connor yelled. "*Inside now!*"

Mr. Prudhome jingled his keys but didn't move. "What the hell do they want?"

"Dad, get the fuck inside now!"

Mrs. Prudhome turned on Connor as if she might throttle him. "Connor!"

"No, he's serious," Nicole said, "They'll get us!" She was already opening the door back to the house and retreating inside.

The running men were one house away now. Their hissing carried straight to Connor's ears. Their mustard eyes caught the moonlight for a second and then winked out of existence. "C'mon, go go go!"

Now Mr. Prudhome recognized there was danger, and whirled and ushered everyone back inside. He slammed the door and spun the deadbolt just as it rocked with the impact of something crashing into it with incredible force.

"Who are they?" Mrs. Prudhome yelled.

"From the crash," Connor said. "I was trying to tell you. Something happened at the crash."

The door pounded again in its frame, shaking the entire front wall of the house. Again and again. The muffled and rage-filled hissing was incessant.

"Leave us alone! I've called the cops!" Mr. Prudhome shouted through the door.

Nicole was having trouble catching her breath but nobody seemed to notice. Connor ran to the window next to the door and made sure the latch was locked.

The front door took a mighty blow, and even in the dark of the house everyone heard the audible crack.

"What do they want?" Mrs. Prudhome yelled. She was steadily backing toward the kitchen, her purse in front of her like a shield.

Mr. Prudhome yanked his phone off his belt and tried to dial 911 with shaking fingers. "Get away from this home right now or I'll . . . *Shit!*" He tossed the phone aside and grabbed a desk lamp off the small end table where they kept a basket for the mail. The cord broke as he pulled it from the wall and held it up as a weapon. The door thundered again, the glass in the small window at the top splintering and falling out onto the front step. Bone-chilling hisses swam into the room.

"Dad, forget it. We need to get out of here. They're gonna get through."

"Back door?" Nicole asked.

Connor shook his head. "We'd have to go out the gate near the driveway. They'd see us."

"Okay, everybody upstairs." Mr. Prudhome wrapped the lamp's broken cord around his wrist and pointed up to the bedrooms. "Now!"

Connor, Nicole and his mother raced up the stairs. Mr. Prudhome stayed near the door as it took another blow from the two crazed men on the other side.

"Dad?"

"Connor, get up the stairs and lock the bedroom door. Find a weapon. Anything. If anyone comes up that's not me I want you to hit to kill. Look at me. You hit to kill. Go go go!"

"But, Dad—"

"*GO!*"

Connor turned and raced back up the stairs, threw himself into his parents' room where Nicole and his mother were taking golf clubs out of Mr. Prudhome's golf bag. He locked the door just as his mother looked up. "Where's Mark?"

It was weird hearing his mother call his father by his real name. It made him realize they had a life outside of being his parents. "He's . . . he's . . . "

The sounds of shattering glass blared up the stairs. The hissing was suddenly coming from inside the house, like demonic canned laughter in a bad sitcom. Now the sounds of fists on flesh and people being slammed into tables and walls. Furniture screeched across the hardwood floor. More glass shattered, something slammed hard into the stairs, strong enough to shake the entire upstairs. Mr. Prudhome's gurgled yell—"*Run!*"—was cut off with the wet noise of teeth tearing into his flesh.

Mrs. Prudhome shook her head. "No! What's he doing?" She ran for the bedroom door. Connor blocked her.

"Mom, you can't." He was on the verge of tears and trying to keep from fainting. He pushed past his mother, grabbed the nightstand from beside the bed and threw it toward the closet. It landed on its side, spilling the content of its drawer all over the floor of the nearly pitch black bedroom. Without losing momentum he started pushing the king size bed in front of the door. "Help me!"

Nicole saw why he'd moved the nightstand—to make room to slide the bed—and got beside him and pushed as hard as she could. Together they got the bed in front of the door just as the two men on the other side reached the top of the stairs and slammed into it. The lock on the door held but it wouldn't for much longer. They shoved the bed closer, butted it against the door. Mrs. Prudhome was shaking her head back and forth, fighting her fear and disbelief. The door took another impact, hissing spilling into the bedroom. The bed moved backwards.

"Mom!"

Mrs. Prudhome suddenly snapped out of her shock. Perhaps it was the sight of watching her only son try to save her, or acceptance that her husband was dead, but she was running to help hold the bed against the door.

The two men on the other side were fueled by rage, an advantage that let them push the door open despite the weight against it.

Connor let go of the bed and yanked open the window overlooking the front yard. It opened onto the overhang covering the front steps. "Quick, out here."

The door slid open further, pushing the bed backwards, and consequently Nicole and Mrs. Prudhome with it. Four arms hooked their way in and grasped for anything within reach.

Nicole climbed out the window and sat on the overhang. She waved for Connor to hurry and follow.

The door slid open further. Two heads burst in, dead eyes visible even in the dark, mouths hissing at nothing. Arms frantically reaching. A leg working its way in.

"Connor, take these." Mrs. Prudhome drew her keys from her purse.

"Mom?"

"Just go. It's not hard. Make sure the emergency break is off."

"Mom, I can't—"

"Connor get out that fucking window and get out of here! Now!"

Tears finally spilled down Connor's cheeks. He could not believe what he was seeing or hearing. *This was not happening.* He was not losing his parents right in front of his eyes. "Mom, please don't."

His mother grabbed him and hugged him harder than she had ever done in his life. "I love you. You're my angel. Now go. Go!"

The two men were inside the room now, scrabbling madly over the bed. Mrs. Prudhome swung the golf club and connected hard with the nearest man's face. He stumbled and fell to the ground.

Connor felt himself being yanked backward. Nicole was reaching through the window, grabbing his shirt with one hand and holding the window open with the other. "Please, Connor. We have to go!"

He looked back once, saw his mother swing the club at the second assailant, saw the club bend in an L around the man's face and knock him off the bed, saw the first attacker up again and tackling her to the floor, the sounds of face cartilage and bone cracking under human teeth filling the room.

He spun and dove out the window, letting it shut behind him just as his mother's screams of terror and pain reached a crescendo.

Saturday, 9:21pm

Seth and Amanita rushed up the front lawn of her house, constantly looking over their shoulder at the empty street.

Seth was panting. "Hurry. Open it."

Amanita's hand shook as she tried to insert her key in the lock. "Stop rushing me. You're freaking me out."

"I'm not rushing you, I just don't want to die."

"You're rushing me." The key turned and she pushed the door open. They raced inside and shut the door behind them, locking it again. Seth drew the curtains on the front picture window and then peeked out through the slit. "I don't see him. He must be on another street."

"Well get your head out of the window so he doesn't see you, idiot."

"I'm making sure he's not coming. And stop calling me names."

Amanita tried the lamp near the door but the bulb gave no light. "Still out." She moved further into the house, ignoring Seth, who was still peeking out the window. "Mom! Mom!"

Seth rushed after her, found her in a small family room. An entertainment center sat in one corner housing a television and DVD player. A loveseat and recliner were pushed up against the opposite wall. A bookshelf containing more chotchkies than books finished off the décor. "Shhh! You're screaming too loud."

Amanita continued to ignore him and moved into the kitchen. Stacks of dirty dishes filled the sink. A collection of cereal boxes were arranged in a row on the small table against the wall. What looked like a pile of newspapers was on the kitchen counter.

"Mom! Dad!"

Seth peeked out the window over the sink but saw nothing in the small backyard except a couple of plastic chairs and a crabapple tree.

Amanita ran down a hallway and opened the door to her parent's room. She hit the light switch out of habit but again there was no juice. "Mom!"

"Please stop yelling."

"They're not here."

"Check upstairs."

"I don't have an upstairs, Captain Observant, unless you built one in the last four seconds."

"Basement?"

She began to retort but cut herself off and went back to the kitchen. She opened the door to the basement and looked down the pitch black steps. Seth stood next to her, feeling the wet, coldness of the cellar creep up the stairs.

"Mom! Dad!" she yelled down into the darkness. "It's me. I'm home."

There was no reply.

"What's down there?" he asked.

"Just a washing machine and dryer. The boiler. I dunno what else. Boxes of shit my dad refuses to throw away." She shut the door. "I'm not going down there. There's no reason they'd be down there anyway."

Seth shifted uncomfortably and looked at his feet. "Maybe they had to run an errand?"

Amanita pulled out a chair and sat at the kitchen table. "What errand? The car is in the driveway."

"Maybe they just, um, went for a walk?"

Amanita leaned forward and put her head on her knees. "They don't walk. They watch the same damn TV shows every night. Why aren't they here? They hate me. They just left."

"We don't know that. Maybe they're at a neighbor's trying to use the phone or something? Maybe . . . " Seth moved closer to her and started to put a hand on her shoulder but stopped, feeling a little awkward. He'd never had to comfort anyone before, let alone a girl. Especially a fiery girl like Amanita.

"They don't talk to the neighbors."

Seth gulped. He didn't want to suggest that Amanita's parents might have given in to curiosity when they heard the explosion but what other possibilities were left. "Do you think they would have gone down to the crash? Maybe walked down . . . ?"

Amanita looked up. She was stone faced. "If they did, they're dead. Those . . . things . . . probably killed them." There was a moment of silence before Amanita repeated, "They hate me. They just left."

Saturday, 9:22pm

Nicole grabbed the edge of the overhang and swung herself down to the steps below, landing with a grunt. "C'mon, Connor. Hurry."

Connor's legs would not stop shaking, the wound on his shin now beginning to itch maddeningly. Behind him in the bedroom his mother's screams turned to gasping breaths, accompanied by the constant banging and thumping of voracious cannibals fighting each other for fresh strips of flesh.

"Connor! Jump!"

Nicole's voice came from below. He glanced down and saw her standing on the lawn near the driveway, staring up at him with palpable terror. Her soot-covered face was streaked clean where she'd been crying.

Connor took hold of the overhang and lowered himself down, landing awkwardly on his torn leg but managing to stay upright. He hobbled down the three front steps, raced around the front of his mother's Camry and hit the lock button on the keychain. The doors unlocked and he climbed in the driver's seat as Nicole got in the passenger seat, drawing the seatbelt across herself.

"Do you know what you're doing?"

"No. I mean, maybe. If it's like a video game I think I can get it."

He put the key in the ignition and turned it. The car roared to life, sending goosebumps up his arms. He felt so small behind the wheel, staring down the car's hood to the garage. All the times he'd sat in the passenger seat he'd never been able to register the sheer power of what it felt like to drive. "Lights," he whispered, searching frantically for the knob.

"It's usually on the stick near the wheel," Nicole said.

He grasped the stick to the left of the wheel and pushed it. The high beams flashed on and then off. He pulled it and the same thing happened.

Above them, the bedroom window exploded outward, raining shards of glass onto the car's windshield.

"Turn it!" Nicole screamed.

Connor spun the stick and the lights came on and stayed on. "Got it."

One of the rabid men was crawling out onto the overhang, mouth dripping fresh blood.

Connor grabbed the shift and tried to look at the letters written beside it. "One back is reverse. Right?"

"Just go!"

He stepped on the brake and yanked the gear stick back one notch, felt the car buck. Nicole threw her hands against the dashboard as the savage man leapt off the overhang and landed on the hood of the car.

"Connor!"

"Hang on!"

He stepped hard on the gas pedal, throwing the car backward into the street at such a rate he and Nicole nearly banged their heads on the steering wheel and dashboard respectively. The man rolled off the hood and landed on his back in the driveway.

The front door of the house opened and Mr. Prudhome came racing out on all fours, the skin on his face completely missing, his clothing now in rags. He started hissing at the car and charged for it.

From the bedroom window the second savage man jumped out, followed closely by Connor's mother, each one landing on the grass of the front lawn. Mrs. Prudhome was up in a flash, her lips and nose bitten off, her yellow eyes feral and mad.

"Don't look, Connor. Just drive. Just drive!"

Connor shook his head no. He could not believe what he was seeing. His mother and father, their faces nothing but scraps of sinewy flesh coated in ichor, running for him, intent on killing him. The two people he needed most in the world.

"The pedal. Step on the pedal."

"I can't."

"Do it! Please!"

Connor stepped on the gas pedal, backing the car into an out of control turn that moved them twenty feet further down the road. Knowing he could not control the car in reverse, he shifted to drive and hit the gas.

The car picked up speed and raced by his own driveway just as his mother and one of the savage men sprinted into the street. The car hit them both, throwing the hissing man into the bushes of his neighbor's house and dragging his mother under the hood. The car lurched up and down as it rolled over her body.

Connor screamed, an incoherent wail that locked every muscle in his body, a sickening cry of sadness and rage.

In the rearview mirror he watched as his mother's body flipped and tumbled out from the back tires and rolled to the side of the road.

He put his hand over his mouth, tears streaking down his cheeks. "Oh my God oh my God oh my God—"

The car slowed. Mr. Prudhome smashed his face against passenger side glass, leaving a face print of thick blood. Nicole screamed and tried to crawl across the seat into Connor's lap but the belt restrained her. With her head in Connor's lap she screamed as Mr. Prudhome hit the glass again, his amber eyes staring at her through the smears of gore. The second madman ran on top of the car, beating the roof with his hands.

"Go go go!" Nicole urged.

"My mother . . . " Connor looked at this father, met his yellow eyes. "Please, Dad, it's me."

The roof of the car dented inward under the force of a pounding fist. Mr. Prudhome swung his arm back to punch the window.

Connor hit the gas, spinning the tires, watching his father's bloody fist cocked and loaded. The tires caught and the car bucked forward, the velocity pinning Connor to the seat. His father's punch landed on the trunk. The man on top fell to the street but got up and started running after them at an amazing speed. Mr. Prudhome came after them as well, both men running as fast as humanly possible. For a split second Connor thought the car might not even outrun them, but the engine shifted and the car hit 30 miles per hour and began to widen the gap.

He took a right turn onto Asheford without braking and the car skidded sideways, hit a telephone pole on the driver's side. Connor smashed his head against the side window hard enough to see stars. Thankfully, the seatbelts pulled tight across himself and Nicole, holding them in place. The car straightened out, decreasing speed.

Nicole shook her head and looked behind them. The two men were still running, still intent on catching them and tearing their flesh off.

"Just go," she said. "They're getting closer."

Connor hit the gas again, this time easing the pedal down to avoid a spin out, and did his best to steer the car down the residential street until Mr. Prudhome and the other savage man were lost by distance and darkness.

Saturday, 9:31pm

The streets were filled with the susurrations of treetops blowing in the summer night breeze. At least Seth hoped to God it was just the leaves making that sound. The alternative was too scary to think about. He and Amanita had left her house almost ten minutes ago, sticking to the front lawns of the neighborhood houses, staying in the shadows. Each house they passed was as dark and ominous as a tomb. Seth imagined himself shrunk down to action figure size and placed in the scenery of the train sets they displayed at the mall each Christmas, only the power had been turned off in this satanic Dickens' Village.

"What was that?" Amanita ducked down behind a freestanding trellis supporting a rose bush.

Seth cocked an ear and felt a shiver run through him. From the end of the street he heard running footsteps and labored hissing. In the darkness they could not see who it was.

"Don't even breathe," he whispered.

"No shit."

The footsteps continued on to another block and were gone.

"Sounds like there are more and more of them."

"You think the people in these houses are home?" Amanita asked.

"Don't know, and I'm not knocking to find out. We were in your house long enough for this shit to get over here, obviously."

"How much farther is your house? I need to piss."

"Why didn't you do it at your house?"

"Because I just wanted to leave, okay. Don't mention my house again."

Seth dropped the subject. Ever since leaving Amanita's house she'd been growing angrier. They'd stuck around for a few minutes and still could find no trace of her parents. The only logical explanation was that they'd run down to the plane crash to be lookie-loos. It had been Amanita who finally suggested they go to Seth's house.

"It's not much farther. Can you hold it?"

"No, I'm gonna piss my pants right here in front of you. Of course I'm gonna hold it. Why do you think I asked, Einstein?"

"I dunno, because my mom always goes to the bathroom like every twenty minutes. She says girls can't hold it like boys."

"Well I can. Can we go now?"

They detached themselves from the trellis, waited behind a parked car for a few seconds, then ran to the next house. They kept up that pattern for a couple more blocks.

"That's my house. Right there."

"Wait!" Amanita grabbed Seth and yanked him down flat to the ground. "Look."

In the yard across the street from Seth's house, two twitchy adults were huddled over what looked like a pair of legs wearing black and white Chuck Taylor sneakers. The top half of the body was missing. The two men tore at their prize with slashing, bloodied nails. When they flipped their head's back and grunted into the air, their teeth were stained with darkness, strips of fresh, *human* meat dangling like spaghetti down their chins.

"I'm gonna puke," Amanita said.

"I think that's Mr. Farrell. He always wears those sneakers. He thinks he's still living in the sixties."

Amanita put her head down and spoke into the grass. "Who's that? Who's Mr. Farrell?"

"Just my neighbor. Oh jeez, he's . . . he's dead."

"Ya think! Where the hell are his head and arms?"

"They're really eating him. I mean look, their swallowing the . . . Oh, man, this is bad. Oh, man, I need to get home. I can't do this. I need my Mom and Dad. This isn't happening. This doesn't happen in real life. I have to go."

Without looking up, Amanita gripped a fistful of his hair and pulled him so close to her he could feel the heat of her breath. "No. We're going back to my place."

"Like hell. My mom and dad are right there. My dad has a gun."

"What kind of gun?"

"Um . . . well it's a B.B. gun but—"

"Seth, we can't make it to your house without being seen."

"We're like, one hundred feet away! I'm not leaving my Mom and Dad. They just got me that PSP. They just bought it this summer."

"I don't care about the frigging PSP!"

"But I have to get them."

"Seth, what if these things see you? What if they're inside your house?"

From behind them came the sounds of stampeding feet on hot summer cement. More than two, more than three, maybe even more than five. Seth peeked over his shoulder just in time to see a loping group of bloodied men and women charging up the lawn for him.

Where he found the strength or speed to get up and run was beyond him. But he was up and screaming bloody murder before he knew what he was doing, racing for the front door of his parent's house.

"Fucker!" Amanita was up and racing beside him, the footfalls of their attackers gaining behind them, almost on her heels.

Seth hit the front door and pushed it open. Amanita flung herself in under his arm, knowing instinctively that in his terrified state he had forgotten she was even there. Seth slammed the door and threw his body against it as the group of hissers slammed into it like a battering ram. The door snapped open and three different arms reached in and waved like snakes, looking for anything to drag outside. As much as Seth was overweight he wasn't big enough to fight off this group of mad men and the door began to slide open.

"Push!" Amanita threw herself against the door as well. It opened even further, shoving the two teens toward the wall. Both were screaming, both were trying to dig their feet into the rug to get enough traction to force their weight backwards.

"Get away from there!" The voice came from the street. Old and gruff like someone who'd been swallowing gravel for the last decade. "That's right! I said get the hell away from that house!"

BANG! Something small ripped through the door right between Seth and Amanita, spitting splinters into their cheeks. Whatever it was hit the ceramic lamp across the room and made it explode into fine dust.

"What the hell are you freaks? What the hell is your problem? Help!"

Bang! Bang! Bang! A second small hole punched through the door next to Seth's head, close enough that he felt it move the hair above his ear. This time the mirror above the recliner spider-webbed and fell in daggers to the ground.

The door finally fell back into its jamb and closed. Seth flipped the deadbolt.

"Who's that yelling?" Amanita knuckled the tears from her eyes, fighting to catch her breath.

Seth stood on his tip toes and looked through the peep hole in the door. "No idea. Some guy with a gun. They're pulling him down. They're—Oh geez."

He spun around and put his hand over his mouth. Before Amanita could ask what was wrong the sounds of one human being torn to shreds by a group of others sang out into the night. There were no more shots from the gun.

"I need to find my dad. I need to find my mom and dad. Mom!"

"Shh! They'll hear."

"Anybody!"

"I don't think they're home either. They would have heard all that. They definitely would have heard the gun. That frigging guy almost shot us. He almost killed us. Hey, are you listening to me?"

Seth took a couple of steps forward and sat on the couch. He stared through Amanita, as if trying to see out the door. "They're really not here. The door was unlocked."

"Get up! We can't rest!"

"But the door was unlocked."

"So what. Who cares. We have to get out of here. Those . . . things . . . are right out there." She pointed through the door. "They're gonna come back any second."

"That door is never unlocked. None of them are. If I leave one unlocked my Dad . . . well I just can't leave it unlocked. Can't happen here."

"Well thank fucking Christ it was."

"My mom and dad don't leave it unlocked. You don't understand. Not since Joana."

"Who's—"

Someone screamed an unholy wail of pain from down the street. The hissers on the front lawn took off running, the thudding of their feet growing distant. For a moment Amanita thought all their unwanted company might leave them in peace, but a second later the sounds of teeth tearing into the gunman's flesh resumed. There was still a pack of wild man-eating humans on the front lawn. How long before they finished their meal and came back to the house?

She finally moved from the door and brushed past Seth. "I can't see shit. Where's the kitchen?"

"To your left."

"C'mon. We need weapons. Anything. Knives, a frying pan, something. And be quiet."

Seth suddenly rose from the couch. "Hang on. Be right back." He took off running up the stairs.

Amanita found herself alone in the dark living room, listening to the smacking sounds of wet mastication outside. Curiosity drew her to the door again where she put an eye to the fresh bullet hole. In her limited line of sight she could see about ten or twelve flesh-eaters tearing the skin off of the man with the gun, whom she only recognized because the weapon was still in his hand.

She drew away from the hole and started to make her way to the stairs but stopped short. Something on the floor caught her eye. She bent down and lifted it up, waited a second for her eyes to adjust to the gloom. It was a picture of Seth with his parents. With a gasp she moved back to the door and peeked through the bullet hole again.

Oh my God, how am I going to tell him this? Seth's parents were on the front lawn chewing apart the gunman's cheek.

She heard him return, looked back slowly.

"I have this." Seth held up a katana sword. "Dad wanted me to take karate. I think he thought this would help. I don't know how to use it but it's sharp as shit."

"Seth . . . your parents . . . "

"What?"

She needed to be sure before she told him. She turned and looked back through the bullet hole. Yes, it was most definitely his parents eating the man on the lawn.

They'd been turned.

Suddenly a yellow eye appeared on the other side of the hole, so close it filled her entire view. The door shook as the hisser beat on it with all of its weight.

Seth and Amanita screamed.

Saturday, 9:45pm

Driving a car should have been an exhilarating experience for Connor, but he felt nothing. A numbness had overtaken him. He focused on staying on the road, not hitting any parked cars, and not going too fast.

In the passenger seat Nicole took out her cell phone again and tapped the touch screen. "Still won't connect." She held it up to the windshield as if that might make a difference.

Connor took a right turn onto Willmington Road and remained silent. What did phones matter now anyway? His parents were dead. He'd killed his mother. Left her to die. Run her over. Who could he call now that would take it all back, turn back time? No one. That's who. No one. So what did phone service matter?

It didn't. Not to him.

"Connor! Look out!"

He hit the brakes, jarred from his silent stare. Ahead of them in the middle of the road, bathed in the headlights' beams, stood a pack of crazed, half-mutated people. Every one was drenched in blood and wrapped in torn clothing. Many were missing body parts, fatally wounded in several areas: an elderly man with his trachea exposed, a short fat woman with a hole in her belly big enough to dunk a basketball in. They should be dead. Just like the people at the plane crash. But they weren't dead, they were in the middle of the damned road, twitching and snarling and pissed off at something.

Some of them sported more body parts than biology should have allowed: a woman with three legs, a man with a hand growing out of his neck, a small boy with fingers jutting from his forehead.

"Turn around! Turn around quickly!" Nicole reached over and pulled the manual shift into reverse. "Hurry!"

The pack of maniacs let out a collective cry and raced for the car. They ran so wild they nearly knocked each other over. Yet their determination was so intense they merely jumped over any fallen cohorts to get to the car first.

"I can't," Connor said. "I can't. I don't want to do this anymore. Why's this happening?"

"You can do this, Connor. Just hit the gas. Please, hit the gas." She put her hand on his thigh and squeezed it.

Something about her hand registered in his mind even as the first cadaverous lunatic leapt onto the hood, sliding up and smushing his mangled face against the windshield. Her hand was warm. It felt good, reassuring, it sent a message. He realized his inaction was going to get them both killed, and he'd seen enough people killed in the last hour. He didn't want Nicole to die too.

The entire pack swarmed the car. In every window snarled a face full of gore, mad as hell, trying to get in at them.

Finally Connor put the pedal to the floor and the car rocketed backwards, breaking through the pack. The force of the acceleration caused the car to weave from side to side. Connor fought to keep it under control but the wheel was fighting back. It was all he could do to keep it steady. He'd seen the way his dad always looked back over the headrest when reversing and knew he should be doing that, but he was too afraid to take his eyes off the charging pack ahead of him.

"Stop! Go forward! Hurry!"

Connor hit the brake, shifted into drive, and stepped down hard on the gas. The car shot forward and rammed into the crowd, sending bodies flying to the curb.

He took a series of lefts and rights without paying attention to street names. As long as he could get them somewhere free from these people, it didn't matter.

Five minutes later he stopped the car. He was sweating. The street was deserted. The power was off in all the houses, same as everywhere else. "I think we're okay here," he said.

"Where are we? Is this near Pioneer?"

Pioneer High School, where they were bound on Monday. Maybe not anymore. Who knew if they'd even make it to Monday.

"I don't know. I think we're near the park again, actually. Like, it should be a little ways that way."

"Then we're back near the crash. We have to leave. I need to get home still."

"Yeah. I know. Hang on." Connor opened the door and stepped outside. The now familiar sounds of distant screams and screeching car tires played their macabre melody all around. The picture window of the house in front of him had been smashed. The bushes were trampled. A bloody handprint punctuated the center of the front door. He glanced toward the horizon and could still see the faint orange glow of the plane crash. It was dimmer, but still there. The world was still going insane.

He bent over and threw up on the street. What came up was not just his last meal, but the realization that he was suddenly alone in life.

He had no family anymore, no mother or father, no home, and he had no idea why. More vomit crawled up his throat, threatening to choke him into unconsciousness. When it passed and spattered on the asphalt near his feet he sucked in a great breath and wiped the tears and snot from his face.

"Connor," Nicole said. She was next to him now, her arm over his shoulders. "I'm sorry."

He had not even heard her approach, but was very happy she was there. He barely knew her, yet he knew he needed her somehow. Needed to protect her, needed her to keep him focused.

"I'm sorry about what happened back there. I can't even imagine what you're thinking right now. It makes me want to crawl up in a ball and die but I can't. We just can't."

"I felt her under the car," Connor said. "I think I heard her bones breaking. I . . . "

"It wasn't her. I know that sounds ridiculous but it wasn't her. It was something else. Whatever these . . . things . . . are, they're not human. These people shouldn't even be alive. I don't know how they are but they shouldn't be. So you didn't kill her, you hear me. She did what any mom would do to save you. She protected you."

"I should have stayed. I should have at least tried to help her. I could have thrown a punch or a kick. Something."

"You'd be dead too, and I'd be dead. Hell, even worse, we could be one of them."

"I don't even understand what they are. It's like, they just change. They're dead, then they're up."

"Something viral. I don't know. It's not our problem. We just need to get out of here."

"The walking dead. They're the walking dead, like in the *Bible*." Connor finally stood up and scanned the street. "I'm not religious. Are you?"

"Not anymore, no. There was a time—"

"I know it says something in there about plagues and stuff. You think this is one?"

"No. I think that plane crashed and everyone started going batshit insane, that's what I think. It's something about that plane, but I'm not going back there to peek around and find out why. I don't care. Not right now." Nicole walked back to the passenger side of the car and got in, waited for Connor to sit behind the wheel again. "You saved us, Connor. Don't forget that. Which means we have to use this time to get out of here and find someone to help. The police station is not far from here."

"I know where it is. I'll get us there but if we see more of those things we're gonna have to take some back roads. They seem to be in packs now."

"But we have to go to my house first. I have to know if my mom is okay. If she's not, and I'm beginning to brace myself for this, then we'll go to the police. But I have to go there first or I'm just going to wonder."

Connor put the car into drive but kept his foot on the brake. The thought of someone else still having parents almost made him cry, but he swallowed his misery and waited for the feeling to pass. "Seth has this video game, Grand Theft Auto 4, and you can run people over in it. We used to just drive the cars around and smash into the humans. They go flying in the air and bounce off of things and even bleed . . . it was so much fun. We would sit there and laugh hysterically. But this . . . I've hit at least a dozen people in the last ten minutes, and I don't know if I'll ever laugh again."

As soon as they started driving Nicole suggested they put the car radio on and search for news. Several of the stations were playing music or commercials or the latest pop tunes, what her Mother called screaming-idiot-music. Finally she found a news channel but they were talking about economic hardship and a governor in Maine who siphoned public funds to pay for a golf membership to some club. She kept flipping through stations, sighing when the topic did not involve plane crashes. Finally something caught her ear.

" . . . large plane crashed in Castor just a short time ago. No details yet but our reporter is on the way. We repeat we have news that a plane has crashed in the town of Castor. No word on any survivors at this time but we are trying to get all the details as fast as we can. Hang tight and hopefully we'll have a better idea of the situation there, after this." It cut to another commercial.

"What station is that?" Connor asked.

"I dunno. It's 105.7 but I don't know where that's from?"

"I don't know either. Try the AM stations."

The AM stations proved to be pretty useless, full of religious talks, sports commentaries, and light music from the '40s and '50s. "Nothing. It must be too soon. They usually wait for it to hit the AP wire. That's what my aunt says, she's a journalist. Maybe in a few minutes we can—"

The car skidded to a stop and Connor pointed past Nicole, out the window to the street. "That's Seth's house down there. I know where we are."

"Oh crap, there's an army of those things all around it."

Saturday, 9:52pm

They were barricaded in the living room, the couch pushed up against the door, the double-paned glass, installed on every house Seth had lived in after the disappearance of Joana, doing what it could to withstand the beating fists of the angry, bloodied mob. The entire house shook as the pack of crazies outside tried to punch and kick their way in.

Near the fireplace was a bin holding tools for tending a fire. Amanita yanked a poker out and held it like a bat. "What the hell do they want?!"

Seth hefted his sword. It was shaking, along with his entire body. "How the hell do I know? Obviously to eat us!"

"Go away!" Amanita shouted. The command did not deter the yellow-eyed monsters outside from trying to tear their way in. "Leave us alone. We didn't do anything to you! Just go away!"

"They can't hear you, and even if they could I don't think they'd care."

"We have to hide. If they get in they'll rip us up in a second. Where can we hide?"

"Under my parents' bed?"

"What? No, not there! Like a basement or an attic. Is there a crawl space in a closet or something?"

"No. And the attic is in the family room but you need a ladder."

"What! Why—"

"It's an old house and the family room used to be a garage and that's where the fucking attic was. I didn't build the damn place."

"Fine, does the basement have a lock?"

"Don't know. Never checked."

The front window cracked, a jagged stitch running down the very center. The faces outside didn't even seem to notice, just went on hissing and beating the pane. A few more direct blows and it would break.

Amanita pointed with her poker. "Look, it's the guy with the gun."

Indeed the man who'd come to their rescue just minutes ago was up and baring his teeth at them through the glass. His neck had been bitten into crimson threads.

"He's still got the gun," Seth said.

"If he shoots the window we're dead."

As if on cue, the window broke, falling in three deadly sheets of glass to the living room floor. Amanita backed up, trying to keep her bare feet from the razor sharp shards.

The first hissing man threw his arms over the sill and flailed as he hauled himself up. Tiny daggers of glass still set in the sill sliced into his arm, spilling blood down to the living room's baseboards.

"No!" Amanita shouted. "Do something!"

Seth stepped forward and swung the sword, but in his fear did not put enough power behind it. The blade hit the man's hands but only left a thin dark line of blood across them.

"Again. Hit him again!"

This time Seth put his shoulders into it. The sword came down and lopped off the man's hands. He did not seem to mind, other than he lost his grip and fell back into the attacking mob of creatures.

Seth shrieked and leapt backwards toward the couch, exposing Amanita to the next wave of hissers pulling themselves into the house. With a string of expletives, Amanita jabbed her poker at the first one inside, a teenage girl she recognized from the high school, someone she would have seen in the halls on Monday, maybe even at Jason's party earlier. The poker pierced the girl's eye, caught it on the poker's barb and pushed it backwards into the brain.

The girl fell down on her back, twitching and grasping at her face, the poker jutting up from her eye like a victory flag.

Three more creatures scaled their way inside. Their hands grasped wildly for their prey, mouths open and tongues flicking like snakes.

Headlights came out of nowhere, backlighting the mob at the window. The car screeched up the lawn, tossing bodies to the side, sped up and slammed into the house, rocking it on its foundation, pinning the hissers to the vinyl siding and bursting their bodies like bugs squashed under a shoe.

Seth, who had flung himself into the hallway, peered around the corner. "Where are you, Amanita? What's going on? What the hell was that?"

"Over here." Amanita lay half in the fireplace, curled in a ball, only her legs sticking out. "Who's in the car?"

Seth leaned out, saw a handful of the monsters still pinned to the front of the house, waving their arms in a struggle to free themselves. They spit at the car that had them wedged tight.

The car horn sounded. Twice. Three times. Voices yelled from inside the vehicle.

Covered in soot, her pantlegs soaked in blood, Amanita rolled out of the fireplace and studied the car. "You gotta be kidding me. It's

Connor."

"And Nicole," Seth added. "That's Connor's mom's car."

From the street a dozen more creatures ran full speed at the Camry. They tried to tackle the vehicle but bounced off of it, then tried a new tactic and started climbing on it, pounding on its surface.

"He's saying something," Amanita said. "Sounds like . . . back door! *Back door!*"

"This way. C'mon!"

Saturday, 9:54pm

So many creatures were on the car Connor and Nicole could see nothing out the windows except arms, legs and torsos with gaping wounds and copious amounts of viscera; they had almost no way of knowing whether or not Seth and Amanita even saw them waving.

Connor reversed, releasing the monsters who were pinned between the car's hood and the front of the house. They fell forward with crushed bones and burst stomachs, their entrails dangling like ropes, still reaching for the fresh meat inside.

The monsters on top of the vehicle rolled off and landed on the ground near the tires. The car bounced up, rolled over them, and spit them out the front again where when they went flipping across the lawn like ragdolls. Connor shuddered and thought of his mother, the way he'd heard her bones breaking under the tires, but suppressed the images. It was more important to get around to the garage, which was to his right. He hoped Seth and Amanita had understood his direction to exit out the side of the house.

Grass and soil kicked up into the air, the wheels barely finding traction. Yet it seemed to glide slowly and gracefully to the driveway.

"Where are they!" Nicole screamed.

"I can't see anything out the windows."

Behind them on the front lawn, any creatures whose legs hadn't been broken under the car were righting themselves again. The rest were pulling themselves forward on hands and elbows, their mangled useless legs sliding behind them. The first and only one to hit the car placed two hands on Nicole's window and head-butted the glass. He wore a Boston Red Sox shirt and had a crew cut. A shard of jagged sternum stuck straight out from his chest.

He's really dead, Connor thought. *This confirms it. How is it happening?*

"Open the door! Open the door!" Amanita came running down the walkway on the side of the house. Seth was close behind. *Thank God they got the message,* Connor thought.

Nicole leaned back over her seat, grabbed the handle of the back door and opened it to show them it was unlocked. Amanita yanked it open further and threw herself into the car. Seth leapt in next, his sword stabbing across the car's interior just inches from Amanita's face.

The creature in the Red Sox hat saw them through the window and head-butted it again.

"Lock it lock it lock it!" Nicole yelled.

Connor hit the power locks just as three more undead body-checked the car and hissed at them through the windows. They raged and threw fists and kicked but the vehicle held together. He backed the car up onto the road, where it shot backwards as the tires finally caught on the asphalt.

He turned and looked out the back window just in time to see a red Hyundai speeding by them on the street. A thunderous boom filled the interior and all four passengers were slammed back into their seats as the Camry plowed into the side of the Hyundai. Metal wailed in protest. Tires squealed. The sword flipped up and struck Amanita in the forehead, opening up a gash that flicked blood onto the seats. "Fuck!"

The engine died.

"The hell was that!" Seth screamed, unaware he'd cut Amanita.

As one, they turned and looked out the back window. The red Hyundai sedan was pushed into the yard of the house across from Seth's, its car horn now blaring incessantly. The driver's side door was crumpled in and the window was blown out. Steam was billowing out from under the hood.

"We hit that car," Connor said, stating the obvious. "I didn't see it coming until—"

"*Goddamit!* You almost cut my head off!" Amanita put a hand to her forehead and then held it up. It was coated in blood. "My head. Oh my God, is it bad?"

"You'll live," Nicole said, grimacing. "But that woman looks bad."

Through the blood-smeared back window they watched a young woman with bleached blonde hair sit up in the Hyundai. Her face was lacerated and she was crying. She gave them a cursory glance then frantically tried to restart her car, unconcerned with the accident, but the engine wouldn't turn over. The more she turned the key and got no response the more her obvious anxiety grew. Her faint, *"No no no,"* transferred the panic to the four teens watching her.

"Oh my God," Nicole said. "She's real. She's not one of them. She's speaking."

"We have to get her," Connor said. "Seth, tell her to get in. Tell her to—"

The sound and force of the undead running over the top of the car cut him off. In an instant the pack of hissers jumped off the battered Camry and zeroed in on the crying woman.

"No!" Nicole cried. "Leave her alone!"

The pack of raging undead yanked the blonde woman through the broken window, pulling her arms and legs in different directions at once as if she were a wishbone, her body now the focus of a blood-thirsty tug-o-war. Her screams of terror were so shrill Connor thought they would shatter all the glass in the neighborhood. She finally went down under a storm of slashing fingernails and buzz saw teeth, her legs still kicking.

"Start the car," Nicole said. "She's gone. We can't help her. Just get us out of here while they're busy. Please, hurry."

The words were almost sinister in their disregard for human life but Connor could not disagree with them. The innate need to survive overrode all thoughts of heroism. He turned the key and the engine rolled over and caught. As he put it in drive, he heard the sounds of a baby crying. They all did.

Nicole grabbed the steering wheel. "Wait. That's a baby. We can't just . . . "

They all turned and watched through the back window, wondering where it was and how to save it, but what unfolded next nearly sent them into shock.

The blonde woman rose up, her eyes dark yellow, her face a mess of ragged flesh. She wore only a bra now, and large divots of flesh had been gouged out of her torso. Striated muscle and gray ropes of intestine hung loose from her abdomen. The other undead backed off her and were momentarily confused by the baby's cries. With a snarl the blonde woman pushed her way through the ravenous monsters and lunged inside the broken Hyundai car window. She slid over the front seat into the back. The entire car began to shake. The baby's cries cut out right before a gout of blood splashed up against the inside of the back window.

The rest of the hissers tried to pile in through the broken window as well but only managed to bunch themselves up. Then, the blonde woman must have accidentally opened the back door because she fell out onto the street with her baby in her mouth, the car seat still wrapped around its tiny feet. It wasn't moving as she tore her head away from the infant's neck, chewing up a mouthful of meat. The baby's head fell over its back, dangling on a strip of gristle.

Seeing the fresh kill, the pack of undead converged on the blonde woman, fighting for scraps.

Except one. The man who'd had the gun on Seth's lawn. He was staring in at Amanita, his bloodied mouth showing ruined gums where teeth had been torn out. He still held the gun. It was over his head now, coming down.

The window smashed and Amanita screamed.

Saturday, 10:03

They drove in a daze. Red, sticky goo coated the car.

"I never realized how dark the streets get without power. The houses look creepy." Nicole was looking out of the passenger side window as the car turned onto Spring Lane.

"Anyone could be hiding in any of these yards and we wouldn't even see them," Amanita added. She was wedged between Connor and Nicole in the front seat, doing her best to keep her knees from bumping into the steering wheel. The tiny car was not made to sit three across and they were scrunched shoulder to shoulder.

"I don't think they hide in shadows," Connor said. "They don't seem to care a whole hell of a lot about staying hidden. We'll see 'em if they make a run for us."

"And then what?" Amanita asked.

"I don't know. I don't want to think about it."

Nicole spun around and gave a quick look at Seth in the backseat. He was huddled up behind the driver's seat, doing his best to stay away from the broken window across from him. The side he'd been sitting on was tacky with drying blood. "How you doing?" she asked.

Seth gave her a slight nod but remained quiet.

Nicole exchanged glances with Connor, let the implied thoughts about Seth remain unspoken. The boy was retreating into himself. "Haven't seen anyone in the last few streets," she said, doing her best to stay positive. "Maybe that's a good thing. Maybe they didn't make it down this far."

"They're everywhere," Connor replied. "They may have come here and moved on already." He regretted saying it but he knew the reality of the situation better than any of them so far. His mother and father were dead, torn apart by people he'd once called neighbors. There was no hope for a happy ending to any of this. All they could hope for now was to get to safety, find someone who could come in and wipe out every one of the savage monsters that had taken his family. But even *that* hope felt hollow when one considered the nature of the curse that had befallen Castor. Whatever was making these . . . things . . . behave in such a violent manner was spreading too fast to outrun.

"Well I haven't seen any signs of struggle anywhere," Nicole responded. "It may be okay. Turn here."

Connor took a right onto Jasmine Road, slowed the car while he scanned the street. Ahead of them, the quaint residential road was illuminated only by moonlight. Cars sat parked on both sides all the way down, obscuring the majority of lawns, creating numerous hiding spaces. *Anybody could be behind them,* Connor thought, *living or dead or . . . changed.*

But they don't hide, he reminded himself. That was one attribute they could rely on. Whether or not it would help them was anyone's guess.

"Park here."

Connor pulled to a stop outside of Nicole's house. It looked so forgotten without any lights on inside.

"The car is in the driveway," Amanita said.

Nicole put her hand on the door handle. "Yeah. That's good. I mean, at least she didn't drive off. And the house looks okay. Everything seems, you know, together."

Nobody spoke for a good five seconds. Then Seth sat up. "Let's go already, I'm exposed back here."

Connor turned off the car but left the keys in the ignition. Everyone exited and waited while Nicole fumbled in her purse for her house keys. The now-familiar sounds of screams still managed to make the hairs on their arms stand up, even from a distance.

Nicole opened the front door and stepping inside, caught the smell of something cooking, a sweet mix of onions and grease. She waited to see if Missy, her Mom's Pomeranian, would come running up as usual, but she didn't. Nicole's heart sank and her pulse began to race. *Please dear God no,* she pleaded silently, *don't let it happen to me, too.* The other three teens followed her inside the dark house. Amanita shut the door and locked it behind them.

"I smell food," Seth said.

"She said she was going to make tacos tonight."

"Mom? Mom? Missy?" Nicole called out for her mother and the dog but got no reply beyond the echoes of her own voice off the walls. The kitchen was empty, a frying pan on the stove with browned ground beef still waiting for a cook to stir it. It was an electric stove but she turned the burner's dial to the off position just in case the power came back on. She continued on into the dining room, which was empty, and the bedrooms, which were also empty. She came back to the living room and found her three friends waiting for her.

"Sorry," Amanita said.

"But the door was locked. There's no indication anyone broke in," Nicole said. "Wouldn't there be broken windows and overturned furniture? I don't get it."

"My house was fine," Amanita said. "I think most people stepped outside to see what happened."

"But we're far enough away . . . "

"It's spreading fast," Connor added. "Who knows how quickly it got to this street. People go outside to talk, stand around, some undead thing comes charging out of the shadows a few minutes later. Who knows."

Connor's thesis made sense, and in fact was almost surely what had happened. Her mother must have heard the explosion, grabbed Missy like she always did—the dog had separation anxiety if she wasn't picked up every ten minutes—and stood around gossiping with Mrs. Henry from next door. Maybe they saw the orange sky over the plane crash, stayed outside a while waiting for news. It would only take two minutes, maybe three, for one of those undead creatures to run over here or at least start a domino effect that backed up this way.

"But why? Why do they want to kill everyone? *Why!?*"

Nobody answered or offered much in the way of consolation and Nicole didn't really expect it. Connor's parents were dead, Seth's and Amanita's were missing as far as she knew, and now her house was empty. It was par for the course.

She sat down in the middle of the floor and began to cry. "Why? I don't understand any of this. I don't want to be here any more. I don't want my mom to be—" she pointed through the front door. "—one of those things." The tears came so fast they stung her eyes.

She felt an arm around her and let her head fall into the chest of her comforter. She'd expected it to be Amanita but it smelled like a boy. *Connor.* She'd been hoping to get close to him tonight, but not like this. There was nothing exciting or romantic about this and *Cosmopolitan's* "How To Get Your Man" advice column sure as hell didn't cover this scenario. She'd wanted to steal a kiss from Connor after a beer or two, after she'd worked up the courage, just a little lip-to-lip action to dwell on for the next few days, but instead she was sobbing in his arms because their parents were dead and they were probably going to die themselves if they didn't find help soon and the world was going to hell.

Amanita sat down beside them, put her hand on Nicole's head and stroked her hair. "Nicole, I really am sorry. You know how much I love your mom. But I need to ask you something."

Nicole ran a finger across her eyes to clear her tear-streaked vision. "What?"

"I need to borrow shoes. My toes are cut to shit. What size are you again?"

"Um . . . six."

"Damn. You have big feet. I need a five."

"My mom is a five. Well, five and a half."

"Close enough. Where does she keep her sneakers?"

For a split second Nicole almost said she didn't want Amanita wearing her mother's sneakers. Every one of her mother's possessions suddenly felt very sacred to her. She didn't want to ruin the memories associated with them by covering them in blood.

Oh, what does it really matter now, she asked herself. *We need to get help and Am needs to be able to run. Self preservation first, grieving second. Get a grip on yourself or you'll be dead in no time. And don't you think for one second Mom wouldn't want you to get out of here and get help.* "In the hall closet. Just dig around and you'll find a pair. There should be a couple of different ones in there."

While Amanita rooted around for the sneakers, Connor got up and checked the phones which, he reported, were still dead. Seth randomly flicked on lights and then gave up and said he'd look around for a flashlight. Nicole remained on the floor, letting the reality of her new life sink in. She was alone now, just like Connor. Her mother was just a passing moment in time that had ended without warning. The last thing she'd ever said to her mother was that she was staying over at Am's house and would be home by noon tomorrow. A lie. Her last words to her mom were a lie!

Now she couldn't apologize, couldn't tell her how much she loved her. All that was left was stuff, mementos that could not ask her how her day was or hug her when she needed it. Just stuff. The family pictures on the table near the couch, the folded up jacket draped over the easy chair, the chotchkies on the shelf near the far wall—most of them bought by Nicole as birthday and Christmas gifts when she was little, two cheesy paperback romance novels on top of the entertainment center—dog-eared as Mom was wont to do to keep her place. Just stuff you couldn't apologize to now, no matter how badly you wanted to.

"The sneakers fit," Amanita said, sitting back down beside Nicole.

"Can you do me one more favor? As my best friend?"

"What?"

"Be real. Tell me what my forehead really looks like? Because it's throbbing like a motherfucker and I don't for one second think it's a scrape. Be honest."

"Honestly . . . you're gonna have a scar if we survive."

"Fucking Seth."

"There are bandages and ointments in the bathroom. C'mon, I'll fix you up."

Nicole used the light from her cell phone to find gauze and hydrogen peroxide under the bathroom sink. The sink itself was still working, which she took as a good sign, a sign that civilization was still intact. Unfortunately she still could not get cell phone service but decided to tackle that after she cleaned up the sword wound on her friend's head. For now, it felt good to be occupied with something, anything, that would get her mind off of her mother's disappearance. "Here, hold the phone up like this so I can see what I'm doing."

Amanita took the phone and held it above her head, bathing most of the bathroom in a light blue hue.

"Now hold still, this might sting." Nicole poured the hydrogen peroxide onto a wad of toilet paper and dabbed it at Amanita's cut.

"*Motherfucker* that burns!"

"I told you. Geez, it's deeper than I thought. This might need a stitch or two."

"I'm gonna kill Seth, I swear to God."

"Well, don't kill him yet," Connor said, sticking his head into the bathroom. "He just found us a flashlight. And when you guys are done, we need to figure out where to go next. We're gonna need all four brains working here."

"Why can't we just stay here?" Nicole asked. "We can hole up in the basement or something. The phones and power are bound to come on soon, right? And there's food and water and . . . and . . . " She trailed off, afraid to say what she really wanted.

Connor said it for her. "And maybe your mom will come back? Nicole, I know how you feel, we all do, but we can't wait around hoping that—"

"Don't make me feel bad for wanting that. I'm sorry about your parents but my mother could still be—"

"I'm not trying to make you feel bad. Honestly. I just think . . . if this situation keeps progressing like it is, we're going to have company soon enough and I think we should get out of the neighborhood. Sure there's food and water here but there's no way to call for help, and you saw what just two of those things can do to break into a house. If they see us in here they won't stop until they get in and get us. That's why we need to talk about this."

Nicole felt bad for jumping down Connor's throat. His parents had just been feasted upon and morphed into raving lunatics right in front of his eyes after all, and even though she had no idea where her own mother was, it didn't mean she should assume nobody else felt for her. *God, I'm losing my mind on an emotional rollercoaster.*

"Okay, two seconds and we'll be right there."

"No sweat, we're gonna eat some of this taco meat if that's cool. We're starving and it'd be better to be fueled up in case we have to hide for a while."

"Go ahead. I know you have to heat the taco shells up in the oven, but that's not working, so there's probably bread or something on the counter near the fridge. Forks and spoons are in the drawer near the dishwasher. Plates are in one of the cabinets. Just open them all 'til you find 'em."

After Connor left, Nicole used her phone again to find some Band Aids in the medicine cabinet. She put one across Amanita's new battle wound and washed her hands.

"He's nice," Amanita said. "He's no hottie like Jason but if this night had turned out differently maybe it would have worked for you two. I mean, if he liked you back. Not that he wouldn't because you're a hot piece of ass, but, well, you know what I mean."

Nicole dried her hands on the towel near the shower. "Yeah. But this night has ruined my life. All our lives." She sat on the toilet and began to cry again.

The sentiment was contagious, and within seconds Amanita was crying too.

"I want my mom," Nicole whispered.

"I want your mom to be here, too."

Saturday, 10:32pm

They all sat around the kitchen table with a bowl of taco meat and a slice of bread in front of them. Amanita used her lighter to light some of the candles they'd collected from various shelves in the house and it felt very much like they were going to tell ghost stories around a campfire, which wasn't half wrong, except this particular ghost story was true.

"The guy from the plane had to be dead," Connor said.

"You mean the steward?" Seth asked.

"Yeah, the steward or whatever you call him—"

"Pretty sure they're flight attendants these days," Amanita corrected.

"My point is the steward/attendant had to be dead. I mean, could you survive that crash?"

"It's possible," Nicole said. "Lots of people survive crashes. It just doesn't always get reported. I saw a late night news show once about plane crash survivors. One guy flew out of the plane and smashed through the wall of a house and lived. He had like a million broken bones, but he survived."

"Well the steward didn't appear to have broken bones. He was running. And it took all of what? Ten seconds for the cop he mauled to stand up and come after us. Whatever is changing them acts super fast, within seconds. It was the same with . . . with my mom."

Nobody said anything. The topic of dead parents was becoming too tough to discuss. It was easier to let these moments float in the air collecting sadness. At least it was a way to acknowledge their parents' passing, however brief and insufficient for the grieving process. Still, Connor knew they had to get their heads around what was happening so he forged on.

"With my mom, it took about ten seconds. I suck at math but I know that with all the people in this town, this thing could spread like wildfire in minutes. It feels like it already has."

"Do you think they're really dead?" Seth asked. "Like zombies. Doesn't seem possible. I love cheesy bad horror movies and all, but zombies aren't real. I mean, we know about zombies, everybody does. Shoot 'em in the head, kill the brain and—*boom*—they die."

"Like that one who broke the car window. You stabbed him in the head—"

"He does that a lot," Amanita interrupted.

"—and he fell over. The sword went in almost to the hilt, out the back of his skull. It had to have hit the brain. Did anybody see if he stopped moving?"

Everyone shook their head no.

"I also did it to some chick at Seth's house," Amanita added, "with the fireplace thingy. She dropped like a rock but she was still moving when we left."

"Maybe you didn't push it in far enough," Seth said. "Either way they're not human. And they *do* want to eat people. And they *are* dead. Shit. I don't get it."

"I thought you had to *shoot* zombies," Nicole asked. "Maybe a bullet does something different?"

"I don't know, a brain's a brain," Connor said. "If the sword didn't kill it, I don't know a bullet would."

"But we don't know for sure."

"Well no, but I don't have a gun to try it. Unless your mom had one." He caught his use of the past tense and saw that Nicole did as well but let it pass. Normally he'd apologize, but he was too angry and too scared to worry about it right now. He could see Nicole was a strong girl and would get over it. She was taking this all pretty well, and she'd been calm under pressure in the car. Hell, they'd all been able to hold themselves together so far. Fairly well anyway, considering the circumstances.

Only her brief breakdown in the living room had shown any weakness, and that was more than acceptable. She hadn't seen it, no one did, but when he'd put his arms around her and held her, letting her sob in his chest, he'd cried as well. For her. For himself. For everyone.

"She doesn't have a gun, no. I don't know who in the neighborhood does. We have no cops as neighbors as far as I know. Hell, I don't even know where to buy a gun."

"Which means we have no real weapons," Connor said. "All we had was the sword, but that's gone."

"Thank Christ," Amanita said, "or we'd all have our heads cut off by now."

Seth put down his piece of bread. "My dad got me that sword, you know. I'm sorry I hit you with it, but it meant something to me. Stop putting me down for using it and remember I managed to save your fucking life with it."

"You almost slashed my throat when you did! You thrust it out right in front of my damned neck."

"And stuck it in that shithead zombie's face!"

"I repeat, you came an inch from my jugular."

"I'm surprised you even know what a jugular vein is."

"Oh, what it that? A joke about me being stupid. What, because I'm not in the honors classes with you three you think I'm an idiot? Because I don't read a nerdy science fiction novel every week like you bookworms I can't possibly know anything about biology and anatomy? Well guess what, I know just as much as you and maybe more."

"You only know stuff because Nicole is smart and you hang out with her, so I don't doubt it. Doesn't mean *you're* smart."

"You'd be surprised what I know, you video game nerd. Not everything is learned from reading books about spaceships and dragons."

"Watching the Discovery Channel doesn't mean you're smart either, it means you're filled with useless knowledge."

Amanita took out a cigarette and lit it up at the kitchen table. "Sorry, Nicole, it's either this or I punch him. I'll go out back if you want me to."

"No, it's fine. Doesn't matter anymore, anyway," Nicole said.

Seth picked up his bread and dipped it in the meat sauce. "Yeah, go ahead and smoke, because the first thing we need is for the smoke alarm to go off and tell every undead thing in the streets where we are."

Amanita leaned in close to Seth's face. "One—smoke alarms are triggered by thick smoke breaking up the electric current inside them. Unless I blow the smoke directly into the alarm, the cigarette smoke dissipates before it even reaches it. But I didn't learn that on the Discovery Channel so I guess it's not true and I'm just a dumb idiot. And two—there are a million noises going on outside right now. Screaming, fires, cars, I'm sure we'll be fine."

"God, I *should* have slashed your throat. Then I could've killed two birds with one stone—that zombie bastard and you."

"Enough, guys." Connor picked up his plate and set it in the sink next to some dirty dishes. He sat back down and took a sip from his glass of water. "Back to the plan. We have no real weapons so we'll need to find some. Anything that we can swing or stab with."

"What about fire," Amanita said, punctuating her question by holding up her cigarette. "Didn't we see one go down on fire near the plane?"

"I don't know. A lot of them were running around on fire. Maybe it eventually burned one enough to kill it but I can't say for sure. It's worth keeping in mind."

"My mom has some scented oil for the oil lamps in her bedroom," Nicole said. "She never lights them because she's afraid she'll fall asleep and the house will go up, even though I tell her they're built to stay lit without supervision. It's in a bottle under the kitchen sink."

"Okay," Connor said, "We'll take that too. Now, once we load up, our first stop needs to be the police station. It's not that far from here. I assume if there's one safe place to be right now that's it."

"It wasn't safe in *Resident Evil II*," Seth said. "And as far as we can tell the power is out everywhere so who knows. We could get there and those things could be waiting for us inside."

"The front door is glass and looks into the receptionist area. So we'll be able to tell. There's always someone sitting at the desk."

"Arrested a lot?" Amanita took a drag and blew the smoke down toward her feet.

"No. There was a comic book store across the street from it for a while. Mom would take me when I got good grades. Sometimes we'd just park in front of the station and walk across the street. Anyway, it's still the safest plan for now."

"I wish there was a comic book store there now," Seth said. "I have to order them online. Still haven't gotten my latest copy of *Gambit*."

"And if we get there and it *is* overrun by these things?" Amanita stood to flick her ash into the kitchen sink.

Connor nodded. "Then we leave town. The two quickest routes are . . . um . . . Jefferson Road—"

"Jefferson Bridge over the river gorge and into Victorville," Nicole said. "We can be out of town in fifteen minutes."

"Right, or we can go the other way. Take 134 into Wallington."

Amanita took another drag and the cherry glowed bright orange. "But that's back near the park, and near the crash. And I just realized this shirt is sticking to me with blood. Can I borrow a shirt, Nicole?"

Nicole sighed. "Yeah, sure. Go in my room and get one."

Amanita stubbed her cigarette out in the sink and left the kitchen.

"So it's settled?" Connor asked.

"Honestly," Seth said, "I don't really care. I don't know where my parents are, neither does Nicole or the She Beast in there changing her shirt. All I really know is I want to find them. I've lost my PSP and my sword, I don't want to be here in Castor right now, but leaving scares me even more because what if my parents *are* here? What if we leave and they're out there hiding? I can't lose anymore . . . " Seth left his final thought unspoken.

"I agree," Nicole said. "I can't make a decision on anything right now. I want to get out but I need to know where my mother is first. So right now if you think this is best, then I say we do it. I trust you."

Connor knew they were saying this because he was the only one whose parents were dead, or at least changed. There was nothing impeding his decision-making ability. He had nothing to live for here anymore. *They* still had hope.

And that annoyed him. Hope was going to continue affecting their ability to think rationally. What would he do if they got to the police station, saw it was under attack, and decided to come back here and look for their parents? Would he just let them?

Yeah, you will, he thought. *It's what they need to do. You may be with friends but you're more alone now than you've ever been.*

"Okay, then we're doing it," he said. "Start gathering weapons."

Amanita returned wearing a long-sleeved, maroon V-neck thermal top. "I know it looks bad but it's comfy and warm. Deal with it."

"Nobody said anything about you," Seth said, taking some steak knives out of the utensil drawer.

"Well, d'uh. It was just a joke. And I heard what you called me. I thought we had made a truce."

"We did, but you kept bitching about the cut on your forehead. I said I was sorry like a million times."

Amanita let out a long, deep breath. "Alright, fine, I'm sorry too. It's just, you know, I kind of like my face scar-free. But since you saved me from having it eaten off, I'll let it go. But you gotta stop whining about losing your PSP thing. That's gonna drive me nuts. You sound like you lost a child or something."

Seth put the knives on the table, looked at Amanita without so much as a smile, and walked out to the living room. The moment of silence that followed seemed to slow down time for everyone.

"Geez, I was apologizing. What's up his ass?"

Connor set the bottle of lamp oil next to the knives, careful to keep it away from the burning candles. "The missing child comment. You shouldn't have said that."

"Why? It's just a damn video game machine. You guys act like it's the world. Trust me, girls don't dig that strongly on video games. We'd rather the attention be on us."

"It's not that. Seth had a . . . Forget it. We're leaving in a few minutes. Get something long and sharp. Hurry."

Saturday, 11:04pm

They all piled into Nicole's mom's SUV, the interior of which was now so full of knives, garden tools, broom handles, and even screw-off table legs that if the vehicle took a funny turn they might all end up diced and concussed before they knew what was happening.

But at least all the windows were intact.

Nicole begrudgingly left her pocket book in the house, and only took her cell phone. Better to not be carrying something bulky if they had to run.

Amanita once again sat in the back next to Seth. He had not spoken to her since she'd made the dumb joke about the PSP and still had no idea why it had upset him. For some reason just seeing his dumb frown made the gash on her head pulse. He was too sensitive about material possessions. Or maybe she wasn't being sensitive enough to his position—the boy valued gifts from his parents, they must have loved him very much and he them.

And what about you, she asked herself. *You should really cry over them, Am. Your parents are probably dead. Don't you want to cry? That's what a normal person would do in this situation. Jesus, you're so fucked up. You don't even care, do you? No wonder nobody loves you.*

She pressed her face hard against the window until pain ran up her nose. It made the voice in her head go away.

She looked back at Seth, studied the distant look in his eye. *I should tell him about his parents,* she thought. *He deserves to know. I'd want to know. But how do you tell someone you saw their mother and father eating someone?*

She decided not to bring it up right then. Maybe when they got to the police station and were safely inside, then she'd mention it.

Connor turned around from the driver's seat. "I feel high up in this thing, like I'm too far above the ground to see the road."

"Do you even know how to drive this?" Amanita asked.

"Not really. Do you?"

"No. But I don't want you to kill us either. Maybe we should find a smaller car. If you don't feel comfort—"

"Nah, I drove the Camry okay and this is an automatic too. It's actually not that hard. I don't see why we need to be sixteen before we get our permits. It just feels so frigging big."

A moment of silence passed, enough time for Amanita to wonder where her parents were and whether or not they were okay. If they were, were they looking for her? Did they even care? She'd always wished her parents were more like Nicole's mom, interested in her day and encouraging her no matter the endeavor. But her parents were not like that, they didn't care what she did so long as she didn't cost them more money than was required by the state to raise her.

It didn't even matter if she left a pack of smokes out on the table or not, they were just goddamned automatons—-paying bills, going to work, microwaving Lean Cuisines for dinner, watching shitty television shows from the 70s on *Nick at Nite*, buying her shitty birthday gifts from cheap stores, ignoring her grades.

"Hurry up, Nicole," Connor whispered. "She's been in there for five minutes already. We need to go."

"She said she had to go find her mom's spare keys," Amanita replied. "Give her a sec."

"I am. I don't mean to be so frantic, I just . . . I'm scared and I'm not afraid to say it."

"Join the club," Seth said.

Amanita pulled her seatbelt over her and locked it in place. "By the way, that was sweet how you hugged Nicole. She kinda likes you, you know."

"I like her too. I mean, you know, she's nice. But I'm a dork and she's probably gonna see lots of boys . . . " He let the thought die out.

Amanita knew why he stopped. Because there may not be any more boys in the high school after this.

"Found 'em!" Nicole said, running out of the front door, holding the keys aloft. She got in the passenger seat and handed them to Connor. "Okay but wait. Before we go—when I was leaving I noticed Missy's leash is gone. I didn't think to look for it before because it was dark."

"So," Seth said.

"So, sometimes Mom likes to walk Missy, especially in the summer when it's warm. I think they just went for a walk and aren't back yet. We should wait a little while and see if she comes back."

The other three teens traded glances in the dim interior. No one wanted to say what needed to be said. Finally Connor came up with a compromise. "How about if we drive up a couple of these side streets. If she went for a walk she wouldn't be far. And if we see her and you want to go home with her then fine. If not, we stick to the plan."

"But—"

"No buts, Nicole," Amanita finally said. As much as this whole night was driving her mad it was killing her to see her best friend suffering from profound false hope in the face of impending defeat. She had to start facing the fact her mother was probably dead or undead. "We need to get to help. I love you and I love your mom but we were here for over a half hour and she didn't come back. There was food cooking and everything. She probably *did* go out to see what the noise was, put the dog on the leash, and then . . . Let's just let Connor drive."

Nicole spun around in her seat. "I just want to know if she's okay."

"We'll help you find out," Connor said, "I promise. But after we get somewhere safe. Okay?"

He turned the key and started the SUV, backed out of the drive. They went up two streets before they saw the first mob of hissers. At least a hundred of them, speed walking all over the place, their noses in the air, their mouths agape. When they saw the headlights the entire pack charged.

"Hang on!" Connor yelled, and attempted a three-point turn which became more of a nine-point turn before he got them facing back the way they'd come. It was too little too late. The hissers engulfed the car, pounding on it, spitting blood onto the windows, pressing their mangled faces against the windshield.

Amanita screamed, Seth yelled something unintelligible, Nicole began crying. Connor fought the wheel of the car and tried to accelerate through the dense mob of flesh-eaters but their collective bodies created a wall.

Amanita didn't know what was more infuriating, the thought that the hissers might flip the car over and yank them out of broken windows like they'd done to the blonde woman, or the way Seth was repeatedly yelling something in her ear. By the fifteenth time, she was able to make out the words: "Second Gear! Second Gear!"

Amanita had no idea what it meant but Seth was adamant as shit that Connor shift the SUV to second, so she espoused the cry. "Second gear, Connor! Second fucking gear!"

Finally, Connor grabbed the gear shift and yanked it down one notch, slammed on the gas. The SUV jerked forward with a burst of energy, appeared to suck bodies under the front grill as it rolled over everything in its path, bounced violently up and down over the creatures as if it were off-roading over moguls. All four passengers were flung about, stabilized only by their seat belts. A kitchen knife whipped by Amanita's face and pinged off the window beside her before flying off in another direction. The SUV then sideswiped two parked cars, tearing the side mirrors off, and made it five hundred yards down the road before the engine suddenly sputtered out and died.

"What the fuck!" Amanita yelled. "Keep going. They're coming!"

Connor jiggled the key. "It's not me. It's dead. Something happened to the engine."

"What do we do?" Nicole asked. She was visibly shaking. The meat cleaver in her hand vibrated so badly Amanita thought the girl might accidentally fling it across the interior.

"We've got to check the engine. Anyone know anything about engines? Seth?"

"Don't look at me," Seth said. "I only knew about second gear from that racing game. You can upgrade the engine if you win races but you don't ever have to fix it."

Amanita turned and looked out the back window. The hissers were sprinting down the road toward them. They had maybe a thirty second lead. "Well whatever you do do it fast because they're coming!"

Before anyone could respond Connor reached under the dash and popped the hood. Then he was out the door and running around to the front of the SUV.

"Where's he going?" Seth yelled. "He doesn't know anything about engines."

"Fuck it," Amanita said, grabbing a carving knife and leaping out as well. She met Connor around the front as he was lifting up the hood. He cursed himself for not grabbing the flashlight. The sound of hundreds of stomping feet and rasping breaths grew louder and louder.

Thankfully the small light underneath the hood lit up the smoking engine. Strips of flesh, like stringy cheese, were bubbling on the hot engine block. The cables were spattered with red ooze. A collection of human hair was wound tightly around the fan blades. The hair was still attached to half of a woman's face.

Connor gagged but managed to keep his food down. "I know shit about cars but that looks like a problem."

Amanita turned away. "I'm gonna be sick."

Shoes running on asphalt began to rebound off the houses on either side of them. The pack was almost at the SUV.

Connor reached in and grabbed the head, tried to yank it out. "The hair. I need a—"

"Here." Amanita thrust the knife in his hand. "Hurry."

He reached his hand down to the fan and started hacking at the tangled hair. It cut away in long clumps, wrapping itself around the knife. "I need to use both hands. Yank on the head as I do this," he said.

"Are you crazy?"

"Do you want to die? Do it."

She reached her hands into the engine and let her fingers touch the warm half-moon face. She didn't know if it was warm from the engine or because the undead body had still been circulating blood. Either way the skin felt waxy and tough, the texture of someone who spent too long in a tanning bed.

There was something so incredibly *wrong* with what she was doing. *This was a human head. It was a living person just hours ago.* Now, its one eye stared back at her malevolently, as if blaming her for this.

Connor hacked away another strip of hair. The head jerked but was still tangled.

"More. Get that big clump there."

Connor sawed with the knife, eagerly, sweating, his arm moving as fast as he could make it go. Up and down, up and down, up and down. Amanita thought of a porn video she saw online recently. *A stupid thing to be thinking at a time like this. I really am going nuts, aren't I? Get your head straight, Am. Yank this face out.*

Connor zipped through one last ribbon of hair. The mangled half-face pulled free, sat in Amanita's hands running blood all over her feet. The exposed white skull felt like coral against her hand. A chunk of gray brain fell to the road in a wet slop. She shrieked and dropped the head, kicked it away. It rolled a few feet and came to rest still giving her the stink eye.

"Connor!" It was Nicole, her voice muffled from inside the SUV.

"Let's get outta here." Connor slammed the hood down. Through the windshield Nicole and Seth were waving frantically for them to get back in the car. Connor sprinted to the driver's door. A step behind, Amanita ran to the SUV's back door but stopped short, as she felt her bladder let loose. A lunging wall of wild, spitting undead maniacs were passing the back bumper. A pair of bloody arms swung for her head as if to hug her. She only briefly saw the yellow-eyed man whose tongue dangled through a hole under his chin before she dropped straight to the ground, rolled under the vehicle.

Stampeding feet raced around the SUV, flashing by her eyes, cutting out almost every last bit of moonlight. She could hear her three friends screaming bloody murder inside the SUV, see the car start rocking above her. Heard the engine knock, fail to turn over. She anticipated arms to come probing underneath, reaching for her, but the hissers had forgotten her and were now preoccupied with the meals visible through the windows.

"Don't leave don't leave don't leave," she whispered, staring up through the SUV's undercarriage, her lips trembling. "Pleasepleaseplease."

She heard the engine turn over and catch, and suddenly felt like the butt of a cruel joke. *Oh man,* she almost wanted to laugh. *This is some funny shit, Am, the way you finally bite the dust. You're friends are gonna drive off and leave you in the middle of the road! Do they even realize you're not in the backseat?*

Above her, the exhaust pipes and muddy undercarriage shimmied in time with the engine. There were a couple of handholds above her that she might be able to grab onto if she were a stuntwoman, but this wasn't the movies, she couldn't ride under here like she was Indiana Jones or something. She'd fall and end up as a road pancake.

This was like that "Hobson's Choice" column she always read in *Cosmo*: marry the starving artist or the asshole jock? Scream for help and expose yourself to the gum-smacking lunatics around the car, or try to run out between all those stomping feet, bolt for the nearest house and hope the doors are unlocked.

She chose the former. It just felt quicker. *"Heeeeeelp!"*

Immediately two faces snapped down to her right, upside down, arms reaching in for her. A mottled, graying claw gripped her jeans at the thigh and yanked her an inch toward the edge of the SUV. She gripped a small rod above her, tried to hold on, screamed until she felt her throat go dry. With barely enough room to move she pried at the fingers. The hand kept dragging her.

Saturday, 11:12pm

"Connor, where's Am?" Nicole looked in the backseat. "She's out there!"

Connor locked the doors just as the faces slammed into the windows. The pack seemed even larger now than it had before. Maybe it was just the close proximity. They all seemed to move as one entity, like an ocean of yellow and gray tentacles and teeth and popped eyeballs and striated muscle and blood. His heart was threatening to rip out of his chest. He put the keys in the ignition and turned it. It sputtered once, died.

"Am! Am!" Nicole was turned around in the seat now, looking out the back window at the friendly faces plastered there. "Where is she?"

"I don't know! She didn't get in," Seth said. "She's still out there."

Connor turned the key again. He realized Amanita wasn't in the car, too, but what could he do about it? If she didn't make it in she was definitely dead by now. And if she hadn't been torn to ribbons she'd be changed in another few seconds. "C'mon, do it. Start." This time the engine turned over. "Thank you."

"What about Am?" Nicole had her hand on the wheel, keeping him from turning it. "Are you just gonna leave? Oh my God what do we—"

There came a plea for help from somewhere around them. Distant but somehow close. The voice was unmistakable, it was Amanita. *But where the hell . . . ?* Then Connor had it. *Smart girl. Smarter than she wanted people to think anyway. Now be even smarter,* he prayed, *and stop screaming before they hear you.*

"She's alive. I hear her."

"Me too," Seth said.

"Here, Nicole, take the wheel and drive when I when get out."

"Get out?! Are you crazy?"

"Just do it."

"I can't drive!"

"Neither could I until two hours ago. It's not hard, step on this, turn with this, put this in the D position. Just don't go anywhere until I'm gone and you're alone. Got me? *Got me?*"

"Yes. Shit, Connor what are you doing?" She scooted over into the driver's seat as Connor climbed into the back. A hisser lay across the hood and tried to bite her through the windshield, his teeth scraping down the glass.

"Where are you going?" Seth asked. His whole body was shaking in fear.

"She's under the car. I'm gonna run for—"

"What?" Seth was shaking his head no. "What do you mean under the car? What do you mean run?"

"No time. Seriously. Just meet me at the police station. Now beep the horn and hold it. Now!"

Nicole beeped the horn, the hissers backed up for a fraction of a second, confused, and then continued beating on the side of the vehicle. Connor hit the power button on the sunroof, the whirring noise masked by the horn. As soon as he could squeeze through he climbed up onto the roof. All around the car a crowd of angry yellow-eyed monsters looked up at him. The ring of creatures was four and five deep. *I can't make it*, he thought. *It's too far.*

Then die trying. What do you care anymore, anyway?

He took a step and launched off the roof, leapt over the heads of the hissers, landed and rolled on the grass of the nearest house. The wound on his shin screamed in protest. He rolled up onto his feet and took off running down the street.

I can beat these guys. I can beat these guys.

Her leg was exposed, she saw blood-stained teeth leaning in for a bite. She kicked and yanked and kicked and yanked. Whacked her shin into the monster's nose, and then got her leg back under the SUV. Her screams were so loud she could not tell the difference between the vehicle's incessant horn and her own shrill voice.

Amanita slashed her nails at the faces creeping in after her and convulsed at the sight of an eyeball opening with a razor thin slice.

Then the faces whipped out of sight. The crazed flesh-eaters stood up, remained bow-legged for a half a second, and then took off running down the street. It made no sense but she didn't care. She rolled her head and looked out from under the SUV. All the feet were charging away as well.

Tears cascaded down her cheeks, ran into the corners of her mouth. Her chest continued to rise and fall in panic and she had to fight to catch her breath.

Finally, the horn stopped. Only the sound of her wheezing remained audible over the gentle purr of the SUV's engine.

"Am! Hurry up! Get out!"

It was Nicole, her voice clear as if she were leaning out of the window.

"Nicole? Are they gone?"

"Yes. Hurry up and get in the car."

She squirmed out from under the car and stood up. Nicole was indeed leaning out of the driver's side window. "You okay?"

Hell no I'm not okay, she wanted to yell. Instead she glanced down at her legs and ran her hands around her jeans. They were torn and the shin of her right leg was exposed but the bastards had not broken her skin at all. "I'm fine."

The back door opened and Seth was there, moving across to his seat. "Then get in. We have to get to the police station."

Amanita climbed in and shut the door. Something felt wrong about the empty space in the front seat, about Nicole being in the driver's seat. Hadn't she seen Connor get inside? Was he hurt? Did he die?

"Where's Connor?"

"Somewhere out there," Seth said, looking out the window.

"Okay, this might be rough." Nicole stepped on the gas. The car jumped forward and everyone flew off their seats. "First time, guys. Sorry." This time she applied gentle pressure and the SUV moved forward gracefully.

"You smell like piss," Seth said.

Amanita looked down at the wet spot on her lap and began to cry.

Saturday, 11:15pm

This was worse than doing sprints at soccer practice. There was no reprieve at the end of the field. This was constant exertion for one's life, legs pumping so fast they burned. Stitches ran up Connor's sides as he cut right at the end of the block, tore across someone's unkempt front lawn and found himself on an unfamiliar street. The adrenaline coursing through his body was tapering off, making it hard to breathe. He was hell and gone from the police station.

Keep going. Just run until you fall down and die.

He didn't look behind him because he already knew what chased him, he could hear it echoing in the air, could smell it washing over him like a tsunami.

He reached the end of this block, took another right, calculating how he might get to the police station by the way the crow flies. He needed to head north west, stay off the roads.

Over the fences and through the yards, to grandmother's house we go.

He spotted a group of twenty-somethings in the street up ahead, hovering around a car. One of them held a beer. They stood like statues watching him advance. Did they see the massive crowd of flesh-eaters behind him? They must have, it was their in their eyes, in the way one of them had his beer can halfway to his mouth, just hovering there. They were bigger than Connor, stronger, could maybe help him. No, somehow they had not met Castor's newest problem yet.

But they sure as hell would in ten more seconds.

He yelled for help anyway, told them to start the car, let him in, but his voice was gone. His mouth dedicated itself to the sole task of sucking in gulping breaths as he fought through the cramps in his sides.

A hisser lunged at him. He didn't see the man attack, merely saw the body go flying by his left side as he cut up a driveway. The body rolled into a bush and got tangled inside it. The others ran up the driveway after him, some bouncing off the side of the house. Somewhere behind him he heard a challenge, then a scream. He could see the bloody beer can rolling in the street in his mind's eye.

We're all gonna die. They won't stop. We need guns.

There was a swing set in the back yard, but in the dark he almost didn't see it until it was too late. He leapt over the swing, saw the black outline of the five-foot wooden fence ahead of him, its pointed slats like teeth jutting up from the earth. He judged the crossbeams, knew by the time he stopped to step on the lower one they'd get him. He could practically feel their fingertips on his shoulders.

This is it. The end. Please let it be quick.

Instead of going for the cross beam he leapt for the top and wrapped his hands around the points. The wood cut into his hands, but he paid it no mind. He let his momentum carry him up, pushed up to the top. Behind him he heard the massive collision with the swing set. Chains rattled, a metal slide groaned. He got one leg over the top, turned himself around, caught sight of the pile up in the back-yard. Thirty to forty upset flesh-eaters, hissing and flailing and twist-ing to get up on their feet the way cats do when placed on their backs. It was a reprieve, maybe enough to get far enough ahead to hide, but he knew he couldn't stop and find out.

He hit the ground in the next yard and ran. Behind him, he heard the fence shaking as his hunters did their best to scale it.

Saturday, 11:21pm

"Turn here." Seth read the street sign as they drove by it. "I think it said Junger. Anyone know Junger?"

"Yeah," Nicole answered. "We're near Swanson's Liquors."

She knew it because Amanita knew it, had talked about standing out front and asking some of the men in town to buy them wine. Nicole had argued they'd get reported and go to jail. Amanita had told her not to worry, that guys like young girls. *Put on a wife beater and don't wear a bra underneath. Guys will do anything for you. Hell, the cops in this two-bit town will buy for us.*

In the end Nicole had talked Amanita out of such an idiotic plan. Partly because she didn't want a run in with the police marring her record and screwing up her chances of getting into a good college, and partly because she was too afraid to show her body. There were things she was not willing to expose to people.

She rubbed her thigh absentmindedly as she straightened the SUV out.

"Swanson's is on the north side of Farmers." Amanita climbed up into the front seat. "If we're near Farmers we're actually close by the police station."

On the radio, the news reporter confirmed that a plane had indeed crashed in Castor but that no reports had yet been filed and no authorities had issued a statement yet. The press may as well have been playing twenty questions for all they seemed to know.

"Connor better show up or I'll kill him," Nicole said, turning down the volume.

There was a silence as they continued on another two blocks and finally found the T-intersection to Farmers Road.

It was chaos.

A dozen cars were piled up in the middle, headlights stabbing up into treetops, onto the curbs, onto the upside down interiors of overturned cars. The other cars driving on the road did their best to circumvent the grim sculpture of vehicular death but only succeeded in causing a horn-blaring traffic jam. Everyone still alive was intent on getting to the Jefferson Bridge.

But that wasn't the worst part. Half the town, now hissers, climbed on the pileup like ants on a dead rodent. They leapt off and ran across the lanes attacking anyone who couldn't get around.

"There's so many of them," Seth said. "Who are these people?"

"I don't recognize anyone," Nicole said.

"At least there are real people driving," Seth continued, his voice slightly more hopeful. "We're not the only ones. We need to all get together or something. Strength in numbers and all that."

"But it's like they don't even know what they're seeing," Amanita replied. "Why are they still trying to drive by? They need to get off the road *now*, not try to squeeze around."

Nicole turned off the headlights. The undead hadn't paid them any mind yet, no doubt too focused on the cars right in front of them. "This is panic, madness. Where are the cops?"

In front of them a man and his small son were being dragged from their car. The father reached for his little boy, yelled, "Close your eyes, Travis. Close your—" and was slashed and bitten by four men and a woman with half-eaten faces. Travis's young screams made everyone's hair stand up, the sound like nails on a chalkboard. His innocent eyes were still open when the first bearded face swooped in and bit his lips off. In seconds the little boy's body was torn in two, one pack of flesh-eaters running off with his legs, the other group running away with his tiny head and torso.

Nicole slowly backed the SUV up. "No way. We can't get through this."

In front of them, the father rose from the ground, his throat opened wide, his severed left arm still lying near his feet. He opened his yellow eyes and hissed at the line of cars backed up to the south. With a jump he launched himself at them. When he landed, he bent down over a collection of severed abandoned appendages, rolled in the meat and gristle like a dog in a pile of trash, and then rose again.

Where his arm had been ripped off at the shoulder there was now a new "arm." A woman's leg, chewed in half just a few inches above the knee, had attached itself. He studied it for a brief moment. He looked dumbfounded, as if questioning his act, this new addition. It was not the look of a man who'd made a conscious choice, it was the look of an animal bewildered by its own instinctual movements. The leg bent up and down at the knee, the foot flapping its high-heeled shoe on the end as it responded to neural requests meant for a hand.

He paid it no more mind. He took off running, no longer a father, no longer human.

Saturday, 11:32pm

The street was empty, dark, abandoned. Somewhere behind him he heard an explosion, a siren. Were the cops fighting back? Was anybody?

And where the hell am I?

Connor risked a look back over his shoulder. He could hear the mobs of flesh-eaters on nearby streets, but he seemed to have outwit the giant pack that had been chasing him. Maybe they were still tangled in the swingset.

There will be more, he warned himself.

He stopped and bent over in the shadows of a small apartment complex. People were talking inside one of the units. Real people. Live people.

Correction: they weren't talking, they were pleading.

Then he heard the muffled pop and saw the flash of white in the window above him. There were more: *pop pop pop!* A bullet screamed out the window, raining glass to the lawn. Now Connor could hear the struggle going on inside.

A woman shouted: "Get it off! Get it off!"

Someone answered: *pop pop pop!*

There was hissing and the sounds of flimsy furniture shattering.

To his continual dismay, he saw loping silhouettes at the end of the road, coming his way.

"I can't run anymore. Please, God, I can't." He was not religious and only realized he was praying on a subconscious level. It was more the idea that wherever these inhuman creatures had come from must have an opposite pole, and if that pole existed it could only be the ultimate good.

Which meant it was either Santa Claus or God.

Unless God was the cause of this. Then where did that leave everybody? Praying to a savior who was upstairs right now sucking down suds and watching Castor tear itself apart like a lame reality show.

No, that was ridiculous, whatever was causing this mass transformation of the living into the dead was not supernatural. It was a viral or chemical reaction, something biological that could be transmitted and passed from human to human. It was the only way to explain the biting and sudden resurrections.

"Did we make this shit, God? This our doing? Because I didn't get a vote. And I can't run."

The faintest bit of moonlight fell on the silhouettes as they jogged closer. Maybe ten of them all together. A few old, a few young, a few fat, a few thin—a cross section of the town, except *normal* Castor folk didn't drag their intestines behind them. Even at this distance, their ravaged skin and gaping wounds were easily discernable.

From out of the window above him, a body fell to the complex's cement path, landed so hard on the back of its head that the front teeth knocked together and broke out. They bounced like little Legos in front of Connor's feet.

He looked up and saw the hisser leaning out the window. It was getting ready to jump out.

He launched himself off the complex's front wall and bolted across the street. Chances were the approaching mob saw him now, chances were even better the hisser in the window saw him.

It didn't matter. He had to keep going or die.

Legs pumping, chest burning, eyes watering, he sprinted down the road, hoping like hell he was going the right way.

He only registered the small white car out of the corner of his eye because of what was hanging from its door. He stopped short, ran back, stared in amazement. The keys were still in the door. He knew this because the hand holding the keys was still gripping them.

The hand's owner, however, was nowhere in sight.

Saturday, 11:38pm

The police station was across a major boulevard, a wide open field of green on one side of it and a large parking lot on the other. It offered almost no cover but presumably this was by design. Any perps making a run for it wouldn't have anywhere to hide and would have to be content with a major roadway.

And it had lights on!

Only a handful of cars passed them as they sped toward the beacon of safety. Seth cheered and the two girls followed suit. After all the time he'd spent with cops and detectives and criminalists when Joana was taken, all the times they'd asked him why he didn't scream, he never thought he'd be happy to see law enforcement again.

It looked like people were moving around inside. "Must be a backup generator," he said. "Something that kicks on in case of an emergency. They may even have phones and Internet."

Amanita nodded her head. "Well, I'd call this an emergency. And here I thought Castor was clearly run by retards."

Nicole turned the SUV into the parking lot, parked next to the only black and white car in view. "They'd better let me use their phone to call my mom. She always keeps her cell on her."

Seth merely nodded, once again not sure how to approach the subject of Nicole's mom. But she had a point. If they had phones in the police station maybe they could all find their parents. He'd been so scared about getting here alive that for a minute or two he'd actually forgotten about his missing mother and father. Did that mean he didn't care?

There were days when he felt that way, when he wanted to run away, because he knew they were still mad at him and it was like living underwater. They looked at him through a haze sometimes, didn't hear what he said.

The worst was two months ago, at the dinner table, when his mother had just gotten up from a nap. She had said, "Your grandmother wants to know what you want for your birthday, Jo." She had paused, looked at her food, then continued. "Seth. You should call her."

Seth had let it go. So had his father. Mom was on lots of antidepressants and he knew it. He knew he was the cause of it. He hated them for making it so obvious day after day how much their lives had been ruined by him.

"What if they ask me for a license," Nicole said.

The statement seemed so absurd it broke Seth from his black reverie. "Then I'll come visit you in the joint. You gotta throw the first punch in there or end up someone's bitch. You can shank some ho with a sharp spoon handle, too. Low and under the ribs."

Amanita spun around and glared. "What the hell are you talking about?"

"Just saying. You wanna run with bangers you gotta play the game straight up."

"You're an idiot."

"Whatever. It's from a video game."

"Again with the games."

"It's a good game. You can steal cars and have sex with hookers—"

Nicole opened her door. "Can we just go in already?"

The three of them exited the SUV and walked in the front door of the police station. The generator lights attached to the walls threw a sallow hue over all the desks and vending machines.

A female officer looked up from her cell phone when she saw the door open. She was standing behind the reception desk, sweating. Evidently the backup power did not control the AC. Behind her was an open hallway with six or seven offices off it. To her left was a large room with a collection of desks.

Seth waved, about to say hi.

She pulled her gun and aimed it. "Stay back! I'll shoot you!"

Nicole, Seth and Amanita threw their hands in the air and fell to their faces. "We're not those things," Nicole yelled. "We're okay. Don't shoot."

"How do I know you're not one of them?"

"Because we're talking, because I just drove here and I even stopped at the stop signs."

"She did," Seth said, "it drove me nuts."

"Would one of those things drive?" Nicole continued. "They just run and bite. Please put the gun away, I want to call my mom."

There was a tiny click as the gun's hammer fell back in place. *She actually cocked it*, Seth thought, *she was going to shoot us*. Suddenly all his video game achievements didn't seem so grand. It was one thing to be a marksman with pixilated characters, another thing to try and outrun bullets in real life.

The officer came around the desk, "I'm gonna frisk you just to be safe okay. Don't take it personal."

She ran her hands up and down Seth's legs and even patted his groin real quick. It was the first time a woman had touched him there. He blushed.

"Okay, stand up, all of you. How'd you get in the door?"

"We just opened it," Seth said.

The cop studied the station's front door. "Son-of-a-bitching back-up system's got everything screwed up. Only supposed to open when I buzz you in. And don't even say it. We obviously know about what's going on out there. We have no idea what it is. One second we're getting calls up the ass about some jackass kid having a party that's pissing off the neighbors and the next Castor is blind and deaf and under attack."

For the first time Seth noticed there were no phones ringing, no fingers tapping on keyboards. The lights were on, sure, but no one was home.

"Where is everybody?" He craned his neck to look into the room with all the desks. On the cop shows that room was always full of detectives making jokes with each other. Now it was a ghost town.

"Out there. Haven't heard a peep from the radios in about five minutes. The damn thing is on but no one's calling in."

"The phones aren't working?" Nicole asked.

"Not in here. And not my cell either. Complete power failure and phone silence. Goddamn plane must have taken out the cell towers somehow. I'm giving it another minute or two here and then I'm hopping in my cruiser and taking the bridge out for help."

"Just don't go down Farmers," Seth said. "It's like the apocalypse. Those things are everywhere. We just came from there and I can't even describe it."

"Figures. Farmers is the only way to the bridge, too. You didn't see any other jockeys out there, did you?"

"You mean on horses," Amanita asked.

Even Seth was confused at that one.

"No, jockeys, cruiser jockeys. Cops. Sorry, inside joke. My ex boyfriend is a cop, he's out there somewhere and I can't really think too straight not knowing where he is. I'm trying to work things out with him, you know? He has a mustache. See anyone like that?"

"None," Nicole answered. "We didn't see any cops where we were. But we were still about a mile from the bridge . Maybe that's where he is. Couldn't see it from where we were. We'd have died if I'd tried to get to it."

Seth sat in one of the waiting chairs against the wall. "So what do we do now? Can't you protect us, take us somewhere? We have to get out of town, find our parents."

"Look, they don't train us for this. We're just people, you know. We're not prepared for . . . whatever the hell this is. I'd call SWAT in from Jefferson but as we already covered there's no phone working here. I can put you all in the back of my car and take you with me but if something happens you'll be trapped back there. I don't know if that's a good idea, to be honest."

Nicole held up the keys to her mom's SUV. "It's cool, we have a car. We just don't know if we can get out on the roads the way they are. Plus I still want to find my mom."

"Me too," Seth said.

The cop looked Nicole up and down. "You look a little young to drive."

"I'm legal. I just, um, left my license at home."

"You don't have to lie, honey, I'm not gonna arrest you. Not in the middle of all this insanity. But if you're saying you wanna drive out of here then I want you to be careful. How old are you anyway?"

"Fourteen."

"We're all fourteen," Amanita said. "And let me get this straight, you're turning us away? The police are turning away people in need? Fucking fantastic."

"I'm not turning you away and I'll thank you not to mouth off to me. I'm telling you there's nothing I can do. I need to go to Jefferson and see if the phones are working. If you want to stay here I can lock you in the jail cell but there are seven people in there already, one of whom I wouldn't put anywhere near a young teenage girl so I advise you to find someplace better to hide until we can fix this situation."

"Leave us here, lock the doors."

"I'm not leaving kids or anyone else alone here."

"What about a gun?" Seth asked. "Can you give us a gun then?"

"Let me think about it. Nope."

Behind them, the door opened.

Saturday, 11:45pm

The SUV was parked in the police station parking lot. Only one other police cruiser filled the empty spaces next to it. Castor had something like twenty-two officers, Connor knew, which was not a whole lot, but even still the precinct looked completely desolate.

But, it had lights and that was a big plus. He imagined his friends inside, sipping warm tea, listening to police scanners. Or maybe they were huddled together crying through the pain of losing everything. That's what he felt like doing, just curling up in a ball and crying his eyes out.

The overwhelming need to lash out and hit something came over him but he fought it down. If he survived he would have time to curse the world, curse God, curse the town of Castor.

He parked the car, left the blood-stained keys in the ignition, and entered the police station.

His three friends, sitting near the reception desk, turned and for a second didn't seem to recognize him. Then Nicole broke free of the group and rushed at him, threw her arms around him and buried her face in his neck. "I didn't think you'd make it. Oh my God, I feel like I'm going to throw up."

"That a good or bad thing?"

She backed off him as Amanita and Seth crowded around him. "Sorry. I just can't lose anyone else right now."

"It's okay. I'm here." The idea of being wanted and needed helped numb some of the pain, helped him keep thoughts of his mother and father at bay. It almost felt good, except that there was nothing to feel good about this night.

Seth laid a hand on his shoulder and squeezed. "Damn, you run fast. I saw you take off down the street and those things were on your tail but I knew you'd make it. That's why you play front line. You can be in the shit and survive, man."

"It wasn't easy. When I buy my first house remind me to get a swing set." With a nod of his head he indicated the female police officer studying him with caution. "So what's going on with the cops?"

The officer stepped forward and cocked her head. "The cops are in the shit, too, as I was telling you're friends. There's not much I can do because we have no phone contact with Jefferson, and we need their SWAT team. Your friends say Farmers road is under attack but

I'm willing to risk getting to the bridge to get some real help. And you're bleeding pretty badly from your shin there. Come on back here. I'll get a first aid kit."

All four teens followed the officer back into a lime green room with a giant table ringed by metal fold up chairs. Connor ran his finger over an unintelligible name that had been carved in the table top. If he squinted just right it looked like it read *Maynard*.

The officer left them and returned with the first aid kit and opened it on the table, removed gauze and iodine. "Let me see that gash."

Connor put his leg up on the table, listened as his three friends commented on the deepness of the cut. He had pretty much forgotten about it during his escape from the hissers, but evidently the running had torn the gash wider.

"This needs serious stitches, but maybe I can at least stave off infection." The officer poured the iodine on it and wrapped it up, doing her best to hide the fact she was grossed out. The iodine bled through the bandages, turning them brown. "Better?"

"I guess."

"Well I'm not a doctor so it'll have to do. Now, I want names. You first."

"Amanita."

"Good name. You, you and you?"

Seth, Nicole and Connor revealed their names.

"I'm officer Whitaker, or Natalie, but when the shield is on—" she tapped the badge on her chest, "it's officer Whitaker. Now here's the plan. I want you all to pile into that car you drove up in, the SUV, and drive quickly and quietly back to your houses. When you get there, I want you to hide in a basement, hide in an attic, hide under the sink, I don't care, just hide, until I return with help or the fucking army shows up. Hopefully I can have this place swarming with sharpshooters in the next hour or two."

"But this place has lights," Connor said. "You want us to go back to places that have no power."

"This place is also a police station, Connor, and there's sensitive stuff in here, confidential stuff, not to mention weapons that, no, you can't have, and yes I'm looking at you, Seth. I can't leave you alone in this place. I went over this with your friends."

"I can't go home," Connor said. "My parents are dead. I'm never going back there again."

"I'm sorry, Connor, I have no words to make you feel better. And

I'm sure it stings that I'm making you go but my hands are tied. I can't turn the station over to kids."

Amanita leaned back in her chair. "I said we were fourteen. And besides, what about the men in the jail cell?"

Officer Whitaker pinched the bridge of her nose and let out a long sigh. "Honestly, I don't care. They screwed up. Drunks, troublemakers, and two guys who tried to have their way with an eleven-year-old in Wallington. Caught 'em speeding near the high school. Chief was waiting to reveal that one to local news tomorrow. At least it's something print-worthy for Castor. The arrest I mean, not the . . . Look, as far as I'm concerned they can all burn in hell. I realize that makes me sound like a bitch, but you work this job everyday and see how much sympathy you have for idiots who make these choices in life. Chances are they'll be fine and dandy anyway, locked up tightly behind those bars. Probably the safest people in town. I wouldn't worry too much about it."

"So that's it," Nicole said. "We're on our own again?"

"Sorry, kid. Like I said, they didn't train us for this. I have my own problems now. And I still have no idea where Ross is. That's my ex. Grew a mustache after we broke up. I hate it, think he did it just to piss me off. God, I can't stand him."

Sunday, 12:00am

When the police station was locked up, and Officer Whitaker had driven away in her cruiser, everybody piled back into the SUV. The vehicle was smeared with tacky blood and chunks of meat no one wanted to look at. The windshield had a lightning bolt crack stabbing straight down the middle.

Nicole let Connor take the wheel again while Seth and Amanita sat in the back. She still couldn't get over the fact that Connor had shown up, just like he said he would. It almost made her feel pathetic to know he'd lost both his parents and was still willing to fight. Part of her was ready to give up. Part of her was happy the officer had told her to go home, since that's where she wanted to be. Mom would be so disappointed if she just left.

She was getting upset and realized she was pinching her leg like she always did when stress set in. The sharp pain felt good, necessary, providing a moment of reprieve from her thoughts, a way to focus on something else. *Name all the Metalloids on the Periodic Table: Boron, Arsenic, Polonium, silicon, Germanium, Tellurium . . . You're missing one. Think harder. Got it: Antimony.*

She felt a little calmer, but not much. Instead she began to feel lost, hollow, defeated, a familiar twisted knot of a mood that was like an old friend. The same sense of inadequacy and worthlessness she'd woken up to the morning her mom told her Dad had left. Just got out of bed in the middle of the night, started the car, and never looked back.

She'd been five, and the depression had soon turned to anger, but back to depression again at some point. "We don't need him." Mom's battle cry for the next several years. Do your work, get into a good college, make *me* proud. Fuck that bastard.

There were times when she hated her father for leaving, times such as the Father/Daughter dances at the grade school when she had to ask Uncle Clive to take her. The man didn't want to be there and she didn't want him there either. It didn't really feel like family.

Other times, she wondered if her father might not be living a better life without them. A mansion in Florida, two Ferraris in the garage, a young model wife that never yelled. Could she blame him? Mom got angry so easily. God knew she would be pissed if Nicole didn't go home and organize a search party for her.

She felt the skin under her jeans break, an old cut opening up. With this new searing pain, she finally relaxed.

Connor turned the radio on and listened for updates but the DJ was still reporting that, despite the knowledge of a crash, no one had any firm details.

"I don't understand why we haven't seen helicopters," Seth said. "Every time there's a crash somewhere it's on the news in minutes. They always have aerial footage. Anybody else find that strange?"

"The whole night is strange, Super Mario." Amanita took out her pack of cigarettes and looked inside. "And I don't think it's a great idea to sit here like morons. What do we think of officer Witless's idea?"

"I think it's dumb," Connor said. "And I have no intention of going back to those streets."

"But what about our parents?" Seth asked.

There it is, Nicole thought. *Someone else wants to go back as well.* But she held back from commenting. Things felt too confusing at the moment. Maybe right now Connor was what she needed. She looked over at him, wondered what it would be like to put her lips on his, just stay there for a while.

Connor started up the SUV and backed out of the police station parking lot. "I'll take you somewhere close if you want to go, Seth. It's up to you. But I think it's suicide. And I know this sounds mean but I saw the group of freaks surrounding your house . . . and if you're parents were in the area then—"

"Don't say it! You don't know! They could still be hiding somewhere!"

Connor sighed. "Let's face reality here. These things attacked without warning and whatever they're spreading it's lightning fast. No one was prepared. We've been lucky to get away so far but it won't last forever. It certainly won't last on dark streets with roving mobs of undead."

"Well, what do you propose?" Seth was looking out the side window, perhaps to hide fresh tears. Nicole could see him in her rear view mirror but chose not to watch him. It was obvious he, like the rest of them, was on the verge of a nervous breakdown.

"The cop said you were on Farmers near the bridge?" Connor posed the question to anyone.

"It's bad," Amanita said. "Real bad. But I can't say what it's like near the bridge itself. Could be we were at the heart of the shitstorm."

The SUV pulled onto the main boulevard and headed east. "Well if that cop says she can make it to the bridge I say we try too. If we stay here those things will find us eventually. We already know they break into people's houses. All in favor say, 'aye.'"

Amanita said aye. Seth fingered the power lock button on is door for a few seconds then reluctantly said aye as well.

Nicole turned and looked out the window at the evergreens lining the road. She didn't want to go to the bridge, she wanted to go home. She wanted to go somewhere and let Connor hold her. She wanted to go back in time. She felt like a mess.

"Sure, why not," she finally said.

Sunday, 12:08am

They took the only back road any of them knew to skirt the traffic jam and flesh feast on Farmers Road. It was riddled with pot holes and had once been a trail for tractors. The older teens in town called it the Jumping Bean, rode their pickups over it as fast as possible, seeing which was stronger: the truck's will to throw them through the windshield or the seatbelts' will to break their collar bones.

Either way it was supposedly fun as shit.

The access road not only had no street lights, but was completely neglected by the roadways commission, which was in charge of trimming tree tops away from power lines and low hanging branches from over sidewalks and roads. Here the trees and bushes grew wild in the summer. It was like driving through a jungle.

A general consensus was met that Connor should turn off the headlights but keep the mud lights on. The illumination this provided was about the same as striking a match in space. Only once did the faint orange lights catch the reflective orbs of a raccoon or possum.

"*Tapetum lucidum,*" Nicole said.

"What?" Connor asked.

"From the biology test just before summer. The mirror-like tissue at the back of a nocturnal animal's eyes. It was one of the bonus questions."

"Oh, right. I got that one wrong." He'd only scored a 73 on the test. Science was not his strong point, not like history and health and, well, let's face it, phys-ed class. He wondered briefly if the animals were being attacked as well, and suddenly thought of a ragged golden retriever with yellow eyes and snapping jaws chasing down victims. Old Yeller come to get his revenge.

Sunday, 12:11am

The Jumping Bean let out onto Farmers Road just a few hundred feet from Jefferson Bridge. The tops of its arched trusses were visible over the small hill in front of them. The lights over the entrance to the bridge, that normally lit up the sign reading, TO JEFFERSON, were out. Abandoned cars were lined along the sides of Farmers Road.

There was no movement of any kind on the road. No people, no hissers, not even smoke or fire from the couple of overturned vehicles. There had been one hell of a party, it seemed, but they were too late to join in the festivities.

It was one time in Seth's life he felt okay not being invited.

Connor turned left, eased the SUV onto the road. Outside Seth's window everything felt wrong. It was all too dark, too black, too separated from reality. Even the woods around the gorge and the moon in the sky felt like a video game mod done by some amateur designer who'd goofed up the color palette. He'd been expecting either a scene of blazing fires or flashing sirens, police and firefighters ushering people out over the bridge into Jefferson. This was too quiet, too dead.

Inside the car, everyone remained silent, all eyes scanning the darkness around them.

Seth stuck his head into the front. "Turn off the radio. If those things are hiding outside we might be able to crack a window and hear them."

"Not a bad plan," Connor said.

The SUV crested the small hill and they all saw the entrance to the bridge. A handful of overturned cars blocked the way.

"Shit," Nicole said.

"I think I can get around those cars," Connor said. He steered the SUV through a small gap between a charred sedan and a pickup truck with one head light still on, its beam shooting into the gorge, just barely illuminating the distant rock wall on the other side.

Nicole's voice rose: "Watch it, you're gonna hit—"

Too late. The SUV scraped along the grill of the truck and snapped the rear view mirror off of the passenger door.

"Sorry," Connor said.

What are we apologizing for, Seth wondered. *It's not as if any of this matters anymore. It's not like Nicole's mom is around to ground her.* It wasn't like any of their parents could do anything anymore. Not punish them, not save them, not call him by his sister's name after two Zoloft and five glasses of wine.

The SUV finally made its way onto the bridge and began the trek across. Here, smoke from several ruined cars created a fog that threw even the wan mud light beams back at them. Connor crept to the right to avoid a downed motorcycle. The proximity to the guard rail of the bridge gave Seth a brief moonlit view of the dark, dry river bed some ten stories beneath them.

They'd all learned about the Jefferson River in school. The town's founder, Abraham Castor, saw the abundant amount of quartz in the wooded hills surrounding the valley they called home. The Jefferson River had served as his sole source of energy during the construction of the mining facilities, long since gone. Two massive water wheels, driven by the rushing rapids, gave light and other technological wonders to the budding community. Slats from the wheels were still hanging on the wall of the town armory, now a makeshift museum to Castor and his quartz empire. The slanderous story of how Castor impregnated two local squaws and had the children killed to save the sanctity of his marriage had been conveniently omitted, though it was easily found in any history book concerning the area.

Once a mighty gushing body of water, the Jefferson River had been reduced over two centuries of industry to a mere trickle of brown sludge that meandered pathetically through small boulders and weeds. Damming from logging companies and chemical spills from factories in the next state all but ensured its impending demise. The local press never failed to kibbitz about the proposed death date of the river—since journalists always rally around semantics and will fight about the color blue if given the chance—but all agreed it would not be more than five years before the riverbed was dry as a bone. At which point, someone would no doubt fill it in and put a strip mall on top of it.

As they approached the middle of the bridge, Seth thought he saw something move down below in the riverbed, a glint of pale skin among the dark black weeds. He squinted again to be sure but saw nothing. *A boulder,* he wondered. Or maybe just a momentary reflection of the silver dollar moon off the turgid rivulet that was the mighty Jefferson.

The SUV stopped. Connor cursed God, Nicole and Amanita each expressed frustration with expletives. Seth turned his attention from the river bed, glanced out the windshield, and saw the wall of cars blocking their way. A small fire licked the very bottom of the pile up. Connor let the vehicle drive right up to the façade, let the bumper tap the twisted metal before them.

All of them looked through the windshield of a small Honda Accord that was standing upright on its front bumper.

A woman was staring back at them, face pressed to the glass, her bottom jaw hanging down, a seatbelt still wound around her shoulder. She was frozen in a state of surprise, and Seth almost thought she would burst out laughing but for the fact bits of her brain had oozed out of her ears and stuck to the sides of her face.

Crushed upon impact, he thought. *It's almost better than what we're dealing with.*

Nicole turned away. "Please back up, Connor."

"Sorry." He backed the car up until the mud lights no longer cast their orange glow over the woman.

"Now what?" Amanita asked. She rolled the window down a crack and lit a cigarette. Seth looked at her, wanted to tell her where to stick those damn smokes, but caught the glimmer of tears in her eyes and decided to let it go. She wouldn't let the tears fall, kept fighting them back. She was a tough girl, and in the sickly light from the tiny fire, a very attractive one. It was too bad he wanted to punch her in the mouth all the time.

"We can either get out and climb over it," Connor suggested, "or we go back into town, try to get out on the state road. I honestly don't know which one is safer."

Seth knew. Knew because he'd played enough horror games in his time to know you took your chances with a vehicle. The SUV may not have had a gun turret attached to the top, but it was big and had weight and could run people down. It had already saved them enough as it is.

"We could climb over and find a car on the other side," Amanita suggested.

"I'm not walking around out there," Nicole said. "All of these cars are done for and what if we don't find one that works? Then we'll be toast. Not to mention anything could be waiting for us on the other side."

"We could send someone over to check real fast. If there's nothing there then come right back."

"No offence, Am," Seth said, realizing it was the first time he'd called her by her nickname, "but unless you want to be the volunteer, I think that's a shitty plan."

"You're a shitty plan."

"Good comeback."

"Eat a dick."

"I thought you two were done fighting," Nicole said.

"I'm done when he eats a dick."

"Fine," Seth said, "I'll eat anything to get you to shut up."

"I'll go over," Connor said. He was looking up through the windshield as if gauging how fast he could scale the cars.

Nicole shook her head. "No way. You are not going off on your own again. Nobody is. If we have to go back to get the state road then we go back."

Seth knew, as he presumed everyone did, that Nicole wanted one more chance to look for her mother. And while Seth was on board for this as well, he certainly didn't like the idea of going back into the wasps nest.

"Okay," Connor said, backing up, "We'll try 134. Let's pray we even make it there to check."

Sunday, 12:18am

The drive back toward town was like viewing a time lapse photograph in a museum. What had once been small town USA was now a kinetically crumbling ghost town: car headlights burning out in front of twisted bumpers, cracked storefront windows falling from their frames, burning paper skipping across roads to light small patches of weeds on fire. *Entropy in motion*, Nicole thought. *A town succumbing to a virus.*

She risked a look at Connor, saw his eyes on her before they darted away. What would have happened between them had this night not gone the way it had? Would he have come to Jason Drake's party? Would they have kissed?

He looked at her again, their eyes definitely meeting this time, but he looked away embarrassed.

"Is there an easier way around the crash site?" She hoped having something real to discuss would ameliorate the awkward connection they were creating in the front seat. "I don't think driving near the plane is a good idea."

He shook his head. "Maybe. Only way onto 134 is by the supermarket. I can maybe cut across the soccer fields and go wide of the plane, cut through the parking lot and back onto the road. Sort of how we came down from the fort."

"If we go into the fields we'll be sitting ducks," Seth said. "Unless this thing has good traction on grass."

"I'll kill all the lights, stay away from the road, go real slow. Maybe we can get across it without being seen."

"We're almost on E," Amanita said. "Do we want to waste the gas?"

"Going slow actually preserves the gas," Nicole said. "Its burning time is exponentially linked to the car's speed. The faster you go the quicker you burn through the gas, and vice versa. That's why my mom always drives so slow." She caught that familiar look in Amanita's eye, the one that said *thanks for making me look stupid, Brainiac.* "Or we could go fast," she added, desperate as always to not be the smart one, "and just worry about it once we're on the state road."

Just then the orange gas light came on, catching everyone's attention. Nicole thought there ought to be a laugh track accompanying it.

"Cars have reserve tanks, right? I mean they last like another ten miles or something?" Connor asked. At first he looked at Seth but the boy just shrugged, a silent acknowledgment that video game designers had not thought of that little detail in their racing games. Which left Nicole once again providing answers. "Typical SUV tanks can go near twenty miles once the reserve light is on. Maybe a few more on just fumes."

He thinks I'm just brains. He doesn't look at me the way the boys look at Am.

"Good enough. I'm going to get off this main road, try to stay hidden. I can hear those things somewhere up ahead."

Nicole could too. They all could.

Sunday, 12:23am

The park's fields were so black they looked like giant holes in the earth, pits descending into the Satan's War Room. Perhaps this was where the creatures had come from, clawing their way up a rock-faced fissure in the Earth's crust that opened when the plane impacted. Maybe more were still on their way?

Connor closed his eyes and let them readjust to reality. The dark pits were just grass, nothing more.

He killed the mud lights and dimmed the interior dash lights upon Nicole's suggestion. She was acting weird, like she was afraid to talk. Still worried about her mom, he figured. They all were. They hadn't run theirs over.

He drove the SUV into the dirt parking lot and then up over the small curb onto the nearest field. The low crunch of gravel became a shallow swish as the tires cut across the grass. He followed the edge out toward the second smaller field, this one for the pee wee players.

"Holy crap, look at that," Amanita said.

Back beyond the parking lot, they could see the dark gray smoke of the crash climbing over the trees into the purple sky. A small fire still burned low to the ground. The emergency lights of several dozen abandoned police cruisers and fire trucks cut through the trees with intense purpose, a bright fireworks show for the new independence of the living dead.

"Lookout!" Nicole yelled.

Connor saw the creature crawling on the ground in front of them, like a giant black slug. He accelerated to run it over.

It yelled in challenge. "C'mon!"

Connor spun the wheel at the last second, realizing this was not a hisser. The SUV's tires slid in the grass and the vehicle fishtailed to the right, narrowly missing the shadowy form on the ground by inches.

"You heard him, right?" Nicole asked. "Not one of those things."

"Yeah. He looks hurt. Maybe we can get him in the back. Do the seats fold down?"

"It could be a trick," Seth offered. He was holding a large kitchen knife now. Next to him, Amanita wielded a meat cleaver. Jesus, they needed guns.

"How so?"

"Maybe those things can talk. Maybe they've known how to all along. Or maybe they're learning. Think about it, we haven't discussed the idea yet but we shouldn't ignore the possibility."

"He's got a point." Amanita picked at the cut on her forehead. "I can't believe I'm agreeing with him but it could be true."

Connor looked back out the windshield at the form on the ground, now ten yards away. The man's faint moans were audible over the SUV's running engine. "Take a picture, why don't ya." This was followed by a dramatic and loud moan, like a man who wants attention in an ER. But in this case Connor knew it had to be true. There was no denying what they'd witnessed so far.

"Okay, we all go," he said. "Seth, you and Amanita flank him on the left, Nicole and I will take him on the right. If he makes one funny move we bash him and get back in the car. I'll leave it running just in case."

"Leave the door open, too," Seth added.

All four teens stepped out of the SUV, each one brandishing a homemade weapon. Seth and Am still carrying their cutlery, Connor now carrying a table leg, and Nicole a short metal pipe that had once been part of a broken heating vent in her living room.

They strode forward with arms raised, each one poised to strike at the slightest nefarious motion.

"What you gonna do," the slithering man said, rolling over onto his back, revealing a chest wound large enough to put a fist in, "break my bones? You see these legs, I'm not gonna run anywhere, least of all at you. You see this arm? Limp like a whiskey drinker's dick. And in case you didn't notice the hole here . . . Put down those fucking things and c'mere. Hurry."

Sunday, 12:25am

Lieutenant General Winston W. Davis did not fear much of anything in life, least of all death. He had served in The Gulf War, fought insurgents in Somalia, had taken two AK47 rounds in the calf in Bosnia—both passing straight through the muscle, thank God—and led four strategic raids on arms caches of known Al-Qaeda supporters in Iraq during the first of his two tours in that sand pit of hell.

In every engagement he'd killed a man, watched as pure shock and terror twisted their faces just before his bullets entered their hearts. He learned a lesson not taught in any manuals or training exercises, but in the field—you overcome death by *becoming* it.

The powers that be had taken him out of action in 2003, against his request, and stuck him back in the real world where his wife now proudly showed off her cell phone skills by calling him every hour on the hour. After twenty five years of marriage he still loved her, but not unlike the way he loved a perfect crease in his slacks. You admired it for a second, touched it for good measure, and then moved on with your day. There was no need to tell it where you were having lunch.

In the stack of notes he'd been keeping since his training at Paris Island, his memoirs as it were, there was but one mention of ever succumbing to the ultimate fear of possible death.

In Bosnia, along the Drina River on a routine information collection run which put him in charge of seven young men, a bullet came out of the woods and hit the young boy from Indiana they called Swig, coring a hole through the middle of his neck. The boy fell immediately to the ground, pleading for Winston to save him, but there was no hope and even the boy knew this. Winston ordered his men into the woods to find the gunman, himself following behind six adrenaline-charged marines that snuck from skinny, bare tree to skinny, bare tree. Dead leaves crunched underfoot, his breath steamed in front of him, he could smell the fuzzy, gray moss growing on the weathered tree trunks surrounding him. Visibility through the frosted pines and barren fruit trees was still good as the pink sun fell behind the hill they maneuvered up, ushering in the cold Bosnian night.

He would never recall exactly how he strayed too far from his men for those few seconds. Perhaps they were too intent on attacking their aggressors and sprinted forward, forgetting about maintaining a line of sight. He was suddenly all alone.

A man walked out from a nearby tree, dressed in rags. His beard was frosted like the pine needles of the trees. Some kind of broken bone jutted out from his neck, yet the skin looked to have grown back around it. His gaunt face looked at Winston curiously with solid, jet black eyes, and disappeared behind the next tree in his path. Winston trained his gun and waited for the man to appear on the other side of the trunk. It was only a foot in diameter. The man should have showed on the next side almost immediately, before his shoulders even passed out of sight. But the man never returned. Like in those old cartoons where an elephant hides behind an umbrella. Winston ran to the trunk and swung his gun around. There was no one there. *No one anywhere.*

He looked at the frost on the ground, saw only his own footprints leading back toward the river, a sign of real physical properties, height and weight. A human trace. The man had left no footprints. Nothing.

He would have checked every tree for this potential assassin had he not been shaken to his very core by those solid, jet black eyes. No whites, no pupils, as if something far more sinister was moving about the woods wearing the skin of a slain farmer. Winston Davis did not believe in ghosts or demons, but he knew that a real man would have shot him, would have circled back around and killed his troops. What he had seen was not a man. He sat on the cold forest floor and shook.

Winston never spoke of this, and sometimes still saw those black orbs staring at him in those dead woods while he slept. He'd written down the events of that night merely to get it out of his head, and never read the journal entry again. Better to chalk it all up to fatigue.

As Lieutenant General Winston Davis lay on the grass in some field in some puny Midwest town, his lower extremities jagged from a myriad bone fractures, his lungs exposed to the open night air, he realized he'd now seen something even worse than that entity in the woods surrounding the Drina River. In the last few hours he had seen the birth of a new race that should not exist, a virus of killing machines spreading faster than any biology should allow. He had come to see the end of the world.

And what really bit his ass was that he knew he was part of the problem. He'd said his Hail Marys already for what good it would do him in the afterlife. Part of him was fine with this turn of events, don't get him wrong. Something like this was bound to happen sometime, and if it was written on the wind then who was he to interfere. He was just a pawn in the end.

But the other half, well, the other half was just tired and finally realizing he couldn't win them all. Now it was a matter of *how* he would go out, not when.

When he'd seen the SUV coming at him he knew this was his chance to have his last wish granted. Of course, he hadn't expected punk kids with kitchen utensils to come out like some new aged Lord of the Flies.

They couldn't be more than, what, fifteen? Hell, they didn't even look old enough to drive let alone fight anything other than their own teddy bears. He'd served with young men in battle but they were at least trained with weapons, at least muscular, at least primed to kill, and they definitely knew when to obey orders they might not find morally sound. These idiots looked like they still pissed in their pants every night in bed. *Thanks, God. Way to go.*

" . . . c'mere. Hurry."

Sunday, 12:26am

Connor took a knee near the wounded man. It was true what he said, his legs were shattered and Connor could see the man's ribs poking through the hole in his chest. He had no idea how the man was still alive.

"Sorry, we didn't see you on the ground. I didn't hit you did I?"

"You came close, but no."

"We can put you in the car but I don't know if the hospital is still there or not."

"Forget the hospital," the man said. "Hospital isn't going to cure anything you see here. Besides, I think if I move anymore that'll be it. Lights out for good. I need to talk to you."

"Did those things get you? Why haven't you changed?"

"Kid, if I was attacked by those things, I'd be ripping your throat out right now. I've been laying here for a while watching the far streets, watching those fucked-up people attack anyone in their path, timing how long it takes the victims to turn bad. Figure it's an average of about seven seconds."

"I know. My mother was bit in front of me."

"Aw hell, my apologies, kid. Your first time in combat, I assume? Yeah, that can be rough. Tell you what I always told my troops: you think about it after you're sitting on your enemy's corpse."

"If you weren't bit, what happened?"

"I was on the fucking plane. Strapped in, gripping my knees—"

"You were on the plane!"

"You don't interrupt a superior, son. Now let me talk. I was gripping my knees. At some point I was flying through the air with a hunk of metal in my torso. Figured the impact would have killed me. I mean, it sure should have. Must have been launched out of the fuselage somehow. Some damn lucky way that you always read about in the papers where people swear they have guardian angels. Landed here, crawled a few feet, decided that was far enough. Mostly realized that it hurts way too much to move. Good view of the stars in this town, where ever the hell I am."

"Castor."

"Boring name. You got strip clubs?"

Connor wasn't sure. If they did he had never seen them. "I don't think so. I'm only fourteen."

"Well shit, that's a shame. Every good town needs a strip club. It's American like Coca Cola and Jay Leno and Marlboro cigarettes. Wife made me quit smoking ages ago, but now that I lay here . . . Wait, this ain't some Mormon area or anything, is it?"

"No. Pretty much your average town, I guess."

"Without a strip club? We call that below average. Look—" the man coughed and blood bubbled out over his chin "—what's your name, private?"

"Connor."

"Okay, Connor, I'm Lieutenant General Winston W. Davis of the Special Projects Division, USMC. I've got a request for you. It isn't hard and considering the predicament we're all in you'd best take it to heart anyway because it's a good skill to have."

"OK. What?"

"I want you to kill me."

"What!"

Nicole took a step closer to the man. "Sir, we can't kill you. Isn't there anything else we can do? We can try to find help, take you with us maybe—"

"Now listen here, you jackasses, I will not be turned into one of those things and I've been waiting patiently for death but God seems to have other plans for me. So fucking kill me already and spare me this other fate. I'd do it for you!"

As much as Connor understood the man's willingness to die rather than become one of those monsters, and as much as he realized he and his friends had been exposed outside the SUV for a good minute now, there was something else bugging him. "If you were on the plane, then you know what this is all about."

"Hey yeah, that's true," Amanita said. "What the fuck was on that plane?"

General Davis coughed up more blood. "Stupid kids. What, you think you can understand what was on that plane? Hell, *I* don't even know what it was. But fuck if it wasn't the perfect new weapon, right. I mean, just look around. Took out this town in a couple of hours."

"You made the people like this?" Seth asked. All four teens were squatting near the Lieutenant General now. "Why?"

"Shit, son, I didn't make anything. And if you think the United States Marine Corps is dumb enough to engineer something this uncontrollable you're as stupid as you look."

Connor had had enough of this man's attitude. Authority or not he wanted to know what was going on. Besides, right now authority was granted to whomever could outrun the hissers. "Didn't you hear me say my parents were killed, you sonofabitch? What was on the plane?"

"Slinging insults, now, kid? Good for you. Make you a deal. I tell you, you kill me. Sound good?"

"I might kill you anyway. My mind is starting to drift that way. What was on the plane?"

"That's it. Get tough." The wounded man chuckled, looked up at the stars. There was a pause. Then: "You know, when we first went to Iraq they told us we'd be welcomed as saviors. Like we'd get big bear hugs everywhere we went. Yeah, some places that happened. In others, they wanted us dead. In even other places, they just didn't know. And neither did we. There's the rub. You're in some foreign town, little kids are smiling at you, old men are glaring at you, and in your gut you know something is wrong, you know you could walk around the next corner and take a round to the face. See, with that enemy, it's rarely a guy with a gun. Nah, it's a landmine, or bombs, or some fucked up trap that goes boom and the next thing you know you're picking up your own arm or leg in a daze and trying too damn hard to reattach it but it won't go back. The looks on those poor soldiers' faces when they realize they won't play ball with their kids, won't ride a bike again, won't even walk . . .

"So we got tired of it, said lets come up with a way to combat those effects. The powers that be say we can't play God but you tell that to the good boys doing their best to kick Al-Qaeda's butt, who just happen to have the bad luck to walk by a suicide bomber and see their own body parts flying through the air. They get a free ride home, sure, but they still have to look in the mirror everyday and feel that phantom limb where there's nothing but empty space now."

"I'm getting bored," Amanita said.

"Getting to my point, private. We contracted out to the best geneticists we could find, told them to do whatever they had to do to make it possible to put Humpty Dumpty back together again. Reattach arms, reattach legs. Attach somebody else's legs and arms to someone in need. They gave us some gene drug, which was explained to me in chemical terms only moon men would understand but shit if it wasn't getting damn close to working the way we wanted. Or maybe it worked too good. There's a test subject in the lab in California whose body accepted foreign tissue with only minimal infection. A third arm.

You believe that? They used snake toxins to combat the rejection process, least that's what I heard on the plane ride. Fucking kid can move that arm too. Amazing stuff."

Connor thought about the hissers he'd seen with extra limbs. It was starting to make sense now if you believed in science fiction and the Devil—whose face he was pretty sure he was looking at. "So what was on the plane?"

"That's just it, Connor. I don't know. Cute blonde lady, Dr. Haley, was being flown to DC and she had lots of different samples all packed up in little freezers and bio-transport suitcases. Said she had some new strains of her wonder drug but I'd talked to her this morning so I figured I'd *seen* the newest strains. Said something about finding an error in the chemistry while we were flying, too, but fuck if I know what she meant. She could have told me she had Adam and Eve's bones in those cases for all I knew about how to verify her work. Wasn't my job to know, just to make sure she got it done and that it worked the way we wanted."

"What made the plane crash?" Nicole asked. Connor didn't look at her face but could tell she was getting angry.

"What made the plane crash? Let me explain it this way, private. That plane doesn't crash. It's tended to by the highest paid engineers in the country. It flies the top brass back and forth across the country on a daily basis and can do a full barrel roll at thirty-thousand feet while spitting out chaff and flares. Question is what *could* make the plane crash?"

"I don't get it," Connor said.

"Hell, Connor, I don't know. That's what's to get. An Act of God? A black-market anti-aircraft gun. One minute I'm having a highball and the next the pilot starts instructing us on an emergency landing. After that, the lights go out, the plane drops. I had my seatbelt on. Dr. Haley was across from me. She didn't have hers on. She flew up and hit her head so hard on the ceiling I saw her skull cave in. Only thing I remember after that was my stomach in my throat and then the sound of God screaming. I woke up here, like this, and my gun is over there. See that black thing in the grass? Pretty sure that's it but I can't move to it. So I watch the plane and see the stewards running around biting people like they haven't been fed in years. And I know that they're really dead because nobody can survive that kind of crash."

"You did."

"Like I said, this isn't survival, this is my punishment. To sit and wait for my turn to become one of those things. To know it's coming, it's always the waiting that's the worst torture. But I know a bullet to the brain will stop it because I watched a cop take down two of those things with two headshots before he got tackled and shredded alive. *Bam bam!* And they both fell. Dead again. Headshots will do it. At least it's a gamble I'm willing to take. Anyway, I can't tell you what happened. Fate didn't want that plane to reach D.C. Now, that's what I know. You gonna keep your end of the bargain?"

The first drops of warm summer rain hit the ground.

Connor rose and looked at his friends, saw the disbelief and anger in their faces. Despite the inconclusiveness of everyone else's parents' fates, it was reasonable enough to assume the four of them were all now orphans, and the man on the ground was part of the reason for it. Maybe a day ago he would have ignored this man's request and taken him to the hospital. A day ago he wasn't driving underage. A day ago he hadn't kicked, punched, stabbed, and run over other humans. A day ago he had dinner with his parents and played video games with Seth. A day ago Mom gave him ten dollars to go buy some pens and notebooks at the local Rite Aid. A day ago was another life.

He was about to propose a vote on what to do, but it never even got that far. It was decided with a simple nod from Nicole, whose once soft face was now caked in dirt and blood, whose hair had been done up hours ago in anticipation of a real high school party but was now matted with other people's flesh.

Just hours ago, in the fort, he'd hoped to end this night with a kiss. He'd never had a real girlfriend before, and Nicole was so much more sure of herself than he was. He had no idea how to make the first move with a girl but she seemed to always find a way to push herself into what she wanted. He'd been eager for that moment.

It was a slight nod, but the meaning was clear. And he knew now that the two of them were on the same wavelength.

He looked at Am and Seth for good measure. There was no nodding, but there was no suggestion of benevolence either. They hated this man.

"Who's got the flashlight?" Connor asked.

Amanita took it out of her waistband. "Here."

"Thanks." Connor took it and addressed the dying man on the grass once more. "Where'd you say your gun was?"

"That black spot in the grass. Over there. See it? If that ain't it then just find a rock and bash my skull in. Doesn't matter to me. Hurry up, private."

Connor walked to the point in question, swept the flashlight around as the rain started to come down harder, running water into his eyes. The Lieutenant General must have had the best eyesight in the whole damn military, because he was right, the gun was there. Connor picked it up and walked back, held it up to show he'd found it.

"There you go, private. Now cock that chamber and put one round in my forehead. Put the next one through the middle of my skull. We call that a double tap kill. Hurry up, now."

Connor put the gun in his waistband. The sound of hissing was drawing close. The Lieutenant General's voice was carrying into the streets. Dark shadows were appearing at the edge of the park, moving quickly. "No."

Lieutenant General Winston W. Davis' eyes went wide. "What do you mean *no*? Shoot me! Or give it to me and I'll do it myself. I can hear them coming already. Hey! You listening! We had a deal!"

Connor, Am, Seth and Nicole turned and made their way back to the SUV. As the vehicle started to move, as the rain finally began to wash the dried blood off the windshield, the first of the hissers came sprinting across the park lawn, making a beeline for the screaming man on the grass.

"It's not a good enough death for him," Amanita said.

Connor continued his drive around the perimeter with the lights off, the wipers on low, heading for the road, listening to the fading screams of a man being torn apart and eaten alive.

Sunday, 12:30am

The rain was really coming down now, dousing any remaining flames on the mangled fuselage that blocked the middle of the street. Abandoned police cars and fire trucks continued to throw their lights across the surrounding homes and businesses. A massive river from a ruptured fire hose had formed around the plane. Water was still flowing out in a steady stream, supplied by a bloodied fire hydrant.

Amanita pressed her face against the SUV's cool window and stared at the wreckage. A handful of bodies littered the ground. One of them missing a head, another lay in the water, lifeless. Two more hung from inside the fuselage, their flesh burned to a crispy black. *Had they turned into hissers,* she wondered. *Or had the fire killed them?*

They had seen a hisser go down in flames, hadn't they? Isn't that why they'd brought the lamp oil? She was having trouble remembering as she tried to take in the destruction around her. Wouldn't matter now anyway with the way the rain was coming down torrentially. It beat the roof of the SUV almost as hard as the hissers had earlier. The entire moment was too surreal, too removed from reality. The *swish swish* of the wipers was hypnotizing her, making her sleepy. She never thought she'd be tired enough to sleep while being chased by killers, but she was jonesing for her bed right now.

"I can't see anything," Connor said. "The rain is amazing. It never rains this hard."

Nicole squinted up at the sky. "Summer storm. The heat's been high and the roads are finally kicking it back into the air. I read last week the Gulf of Mexico was having some massive heat wave as well. We're sucking the moisture from the Deep South back over Castor."

Amanita wished Nicole would just read a *Seventeen Magazine* instead of textbooks and educational websites. The girl had been nervous about seeing Connor earlier and now she was going to ruin her chances by being a brain in front of the guy. Am wanted to hit her and tell her to knock it off.

Or maybe you're just cranky, Am. Maybe Connor likes smart girls. Some guys actually do.

"What are you gonna do with the gun?" Seth asked. "Did you see how many bullets are in it?"

Connor kept his eyes on the road, tried to steer through the wall of water coming from the sky. "I don't know. We'll just keep it as a last resort, I guess."

"Looks like a .45. They usually have fifteen shots."

Am kept her face to the cool glass and watched the ruined plane disappear behind them. "Let me guess, you played a video game with one?"

"Quite a few, your highness."

"Oh great, *Star Trek* references again."

"*Star Wars.*"

"Same dif. Connor, do you even know how to shoot it? Does anyone?"

Nobody spoke up.

Am continued: "Then let's make sure it gets put somewhere safe. I don't want to get shot because we drive over a speed bump. And I don't need baby Huey over here getting his hands on it because he kills space men on Nintendo."

"Connor plays Halo, too, you know."

"I don't know what Halo is, and don't care. Just please put the gun somewhere safe."

"I did," Connor said.

They were passing by the hill leading up to the fort, on the road that would become State Road 134, the road that wound through the dark woods for almost an hour before reaching the next town.

Nicole tried her cell phone again. "I still have no service. Unbelievable."

"Could just be the rain now," Seth said.

He might be right, but Am doubted it. There'd been something weird about the phone service since the plane crashed. Cell towers did not shut down because one plane took a nose dive. Not unless everyone in town was bogging down the system trying to call the police at the same time, but considering everyone in town was too busy eating each other's faces off, she was disinclined to believe that theory.

Thoughts of cell towers and phones were abruptly cut off as Connor hit the brakes and they were all flung forward, seatbelts slamming them back into their seats.

Connor shouted: "Are you kidding me?"

Instantly, Amanita's adrenaline pumped, anticipating another attack, wondering what window it was going to come from. The rain was so heavy now she couldn't see squat outside.

"Look at that," Connor said. "I can't get around that."

She let her eyes adjust to looking past the cascading water on the windshield, could see the several dozen crashed cars blocking the road. Just like the bridge. Like it was planned. She was at once extremely annoyed and absolutely terrified, because whatever had caused that destruction couldn't be far away.

"Drive off the road and go through the trees," Seth said.

"Are you nuts?" Connor replied. "The car's sliding all over. We'll end up in a ditch, overturned, and if those things are out there we're toast. Plus if I drive in there I'll have to turn the lights back on and anything hiding in those woods will see us in a second."

"Just keep them on low and drive real careful," Seth said. "We have the gun now—"

"Which no one can shoot," Am interrupted.

"Well, look, it can't take that long to get around that and we have to get out of here. I'm tired of all this. I know I sound like a baby but I want to get help and find my parents, Connor. So just do it."

"He's right." Once again Am couldn't believe she was coming to Seth's rescue. "We have to risk it. Going back is suicide. And my head hurts and your leg is busted and probably infected. I can see the blood seeping through the bandages again. We need to find help."

"I'm not talking about going back. I just can't go forward any-more. This rain isn't going to let up anytime soon and there's no way we'll make it around those trees, even with lights. You know it and I know it. Maybe if it wasn't pouring like I've never seen in this fucking town! Why is it raining so fucking fuck ass hard!"

Am winced. Connor was losing it.

"The high school," Nicole said. "We can go there until the rain lets up. It's got a bomb shelter. They built it back in the fifties when the Russians were supposed to attack. My mom told me all about it. There's probably tons of canned foods in it and maybe a radio. Plus we need a place with an infirmary that's got thick walls and locks on the doors. It's perfect. It's just back a little ways, closer than our homes."

"The high school is gonna have an alarm," Seth said. "If we break in it'll sound like the Enterprise getting fired on."

Nicole shook her head. "Most alarm systems shut off after a minute. And no one is at the police station, we already know that. If any cops out there are still alive they'll assume those things broke into it. Besides, the power's off all over town, anyway. It's probably not even on."

Connor drummed his fingers on the wheel. "I don't know, it could have a back up generator, like the police station. That scares me. What if it doesn't turn off and this loud ass siren goes off? It'll be like a giant announcement to every undead bastard in town."

"Oh for fuck's sake," Am said. "I doubt every window is rigged with an alarm. The damn school is ancient. Maynard Drake and that idiot Jared from the 7-Eleven broke in last summer and stole a computer. Remember? It was in the paper. They had to pay for it and do community service. That's why Maynard was always hanging around the super market smoking his crappy menthols. He was supposed to be handing out flyers for community fundraisers or something stupid like that."

"I remember that," Nicole said. "They really got in through a window? I don't remember hearing that part."

"I didn't hear anything about a window. I just know how stupid boys think. They had to have smashed a window because it's not like they're gonna hack an alarm system. Jared can barely tie his shoes. And where my dad works they have alarms on the doors and ground floor windows but not the second story ones because they know no one is going to scale the building to a higher level when they can break in on the ground floor, grab what they want real fast, and take off."

"I don't want to go back," Seth moaned.

"Okay," Connor said. "It's worth a shot. But just until the rain lets up."

The first flash of lightning lit up the road ahead of them. Lit up the interior of the SUV and highlighted the blood on everyone's face. Lit up the crashed cars and the miles of woods on either side of them.

And outside Am's window, lit up the two yellow-eyed figures in the woods just a stone's throw away.

They were running.

Am jumped into Seth's lap. "Hit fucking Reverse, Connor, and drive!"

Sunday, 12:36am

The lightning cut to black. The undead disappeared in the maze of dark tree trunks. But the heavens roared again and another bolt ripped across the sky, brighter than before. The zombies were closer, as if they'd jumped across time and space. Running around the trees, arms outstretched and mouths open wide.

The SUV peeled out and shot backward, drifting close to a speed limit sign which scraped its way down the door. The two zombies cut into the street and angled for the vehicle.

"Go forward!" Nicole yelled.

"What!?" Connor shouted back. "Why?"

Amanita pushed back into Seth's soft belly, felt his arm around her waist, heard him shouting in her ear. He was overweight, but he was also big and she wanted to get behind him and use him as a shield.

You're cruel, Am, this is why people don't like you.

Screw those people.

"Go forward!" Nicole insisted. "Hit them!"

Obliging, Connor shifted, sped forward. The SUV hit the two nearest hissers and sent them flying toward the side of the road. They immediately tried to get up but fell over with broken bones.

They all watched as the two zombies writhed and twitched on the ground.

"They're still moving," Connor said, his foot on the brake.

"Bullet in the head will kill them." Nicole added. "Somebody go do it. We're gonna have to try it sooner or later, right?"

Connor took out the gun from the center console, made sure to keep it pointed out the windshield. *There's something scary about the way he holds it,* Am thought. It was too big in his hands. It was too powerful for a boy his age, too powerful for anyone. And yet Nicole was right, it might be the best option.

Connor cleared his throat. "Anybody?"

After a moment of silence Connor swore and exited the SUV. He was lost in the rain almost immediately, and the ensuing seconds seemed to drag on for an eternity with nobody daring to breathe, but Am saw the two flashes of white through the windshield a moment later. Then the door opened and Connor was back, his hair soaking wet, his t-shirt stuck to his chest. For the first time she noticed that he had pretty good muscles for a fourteen year old. *He'll be naturally fit when he's older,* she thought, and not for the first time she was a little jealous of Nicole.

Connor said nothing, he didn't need to. They knew he'd killed the creatures. If it hadn't worked he'd have told them. Am saw him shaking as he started the SUV. She knew it had nothing to do with cold rain and his thousand-yard-stare confirmed it.

Sunday, 12:44am

They drove the SUV around the back of the school and parked it in the teachers' parking lot. Inside the school, the emergency backup system was providing dim lighting throughout the hallways.

"Alarms will probably be on," Connor said. He felt miserable in his wet clothes. The images of the two hissers still lingered in is mind's eye. The way their brains and blood had shot up out of the bullet holes in their foreheads and plopped on the road. The way the gun had kicked back and shocked him. The incredible loudness of the shots. The way the hissers lay still with their eyes wide open. Two men, mid-twenties. Somebody's fathers or brothers or sons or boyfriends, both of them. But when they'd stopped moving, he didn't feel a whole lot of remorse. He just felt betrayed.

Please don't make me do that again, he prayed.

Seth said, "Yeah, alarms could be on but maybe the phones are on, too. That would be a blessing."

Nicole took out her cell for good measure and tried to get service. She got bupkis.

All four of them grabbed a weapon from the SUV and followed Connor to the school windows. The rain was coming down in full sheets and they were all soaked the moment they stepped outside. Connor shined his flashlight around the windows of the ground floor, into the classrooms where teachers had already hung up posters and arranged shelves for the incoming classes. They all inspected the window edges for wires. Some had them, others did not, but it was too hard to tell if they were just not seeing things properly in the rain.

"Would it be so obvious," Nicole asked. "I mean, do we just break the ones without the wires?"

Connor took a moment to assess the building. "I can't tell. How about . . . look, I'll climb up to the roof over that door, get up on the landing on the second floor. I think I can get up from that fence there. If nothing else I can get to that window ledge over there."

Nicole shook her head, her sopping wet hair whipping back and forth. "In this rain? Are you nuts? You can't—"

"Yeah, 'scuse me, Nicole," Seth cut her off, "you saw him run down the street in front of those things, right? Connor is nuts, but he knows his limits. Just let him do it."

"You'll fall," Nicole continued, ignoring Seth. "You'll fall and then what? We'll have to carry you."

The thought of falling was almost appealing to Connor. To fall and hit his head and just lay there and die. Such a relaxing wish.

"It's either me or one of you," he said. "If we're going then we need to be stealth about it. All in favor of me?"

It was like the moment with the gun, he didn't expect them to answer, but he knew they wouldn't object. In the last couple of hours they had come to adopt him as a de facto leader. Which was fine for moments like this when he didn't want to argue, but it was not what he wanted to be. He was unfit for leadership, unfit for saving anyone from trouble. If he'd had any ounce of bravery and leadership then his parents would still be alive. He would not have let his dad stand by the door alone, would not have abandoned his mom in the bedroom.

"If I can get in and open a door I will. If not, I'll just get a window open and we'll have to crawl in that way. Maybe you should all get back in the car just in case."

"Fine by me," Seth said. He went back to the SUV and got in the backseat.

"Such the white knight," Amanita said. "A white knight fifty pounds overweight." She pulled her wet shirt off her stomach and let it slap back again. Connor could see the white bra underneath, and could swear he saw a faint circle of pink through the bra. He turned away embarrassed.

"Be nice to Seth, Am," Nicole said. "He's got a weight problem. Not everyone can be a twiggy like you."

"It's the end of the world, Nicole, I don't have to be nice. Besides, I'm fucking soaked and I'm miserable and I'm scared and on the verge of a nervous breakdown."

Nicole and Am shared a moment of unspoken words through a glance only girls can produce. It said *you are the bitchiest bitch I've ever known and I love you to death but you need to take a chill pill and stop before the claws come out.*

"Fine," Amanita said reluctantly, "I'll go apologize. He was kind of cushy after all. Maybe I can use him as a pillow."

She got back in the SUV as well, leaving Connor and Nicole in the pouring rain together. They were far enough away from the SUV that he felt alone with her for the first time. He knew this was one of those moments when he was supposed to say something nice, or romantic, or just funny, but he could think of nothing. He wished he could blame it on the rain, but he knew he was just too much of a wuss to ever tell her she was kind of cute and he wanted to kiss her.

Instead, she took the reins, as she always did. "I like you, Connor. If you weren't here right now I'd be crying in a corner somewhere."

"Nah. You wouldn't, you're too smart. You'd have already gotten out of town."

"No, for real. I'd be at home, waiting for my mom. I'm not stupid and I know that, I know I'm the straight-A girl, but I wouldn't have had the strength to leave. I'm worried about her and I know she's probably dead but I don't know how to go on just wondering what happened. So I'd still be there, crying, and probably getting attacked by now. You made sure that didn't happen. Just be careful up there. It's gonna be slippery."

She leaned in and kissed him on the mouth. She pressed into him and opened his mouth with hers, as if she'd been kissing men this way her whole life. He felt her tongue slip into his mouth for the briefest of moments before it darted away. He felt her arms slip around his back as she pulled him close. Somehow his own body ignored any rational thought and he found his hands moving up to her cheeks and cradling her face, then he let them slip around her neck.

They pulled each other tight as if they were trying to become one person. It was the first time he'd felt a girl's breasts against his chest. It made him flush. Finally, their lips parted and they pulled back from each other.

They uttered no words in the moment that followed, as she looked into his eyes, wet strings of hair dividing her face. They just stared at each other for a heartbeat, and then she was gone, back to the SUV.

It took a minute for Connor to regain his composure, to force his legs to stop shaking. He'd pecked girls before, in the way that young boys will, as a dare, as part of a game, but not like that. That was a first for him. For the first time in his life, he felt like a man.

Getting up on the fence was no problem. Getting up to the window proved a bit harder but he found footing on a water pipe and used it to launch himself up. He grabbed the edge and rolled onto the thin landing that ran around the building just below the windows. He lay on his back resting for a second, letting the rain pound him in the face. He could still taste Nicole's breath in his mouth and he never wanted it to go away.

As he sat up he realized he had an erection. *Oh great, please tell me I didn't pop that while she was kissing me. If she saw it she'll think I'm some kind of creep.*

He stood and walked around the windows, checking them each in turn. Amanita must know her shit because none of them were wired. When he reached the corner he stopped, looked out over the school's property, a square of grass connected to a half basketball court. Through the rain he saw a crowd on one of the near streets, excitedly racing this way and that, like children on a playground. But they did not move the way humans did—they were hissers. His heart raced as he watched them leap and scurry. So fast, so deadly. More than a few of them were sporting extra limbs now.

Freaks.

Undead, psychopathic freaks.

And then, way off in the distance, almost lost in the shadows, something hulking and monstrous lumbered into view like a tank on spider legs. *What the hell is that,* he wondered. The massive form walked slowly on its many legs, letting hissers run beneath its belly as it stalked something. It spun in a circle, then charged off into the darkness and was gone.

Every hair on Connor's body was standing up.

What the hell was that!?

He turned to the window behind him, raised his good leg, and kicked through the glass. There was no alarm.

Sunday, 12:50am

Seth had never been inside the school before. It felt weird wandering the hallways alone. It felt almost invasive. And yet, being in a place where authority normally reigned supreme, there was a strange sense of freedom that accompanied it. He wanted to run down the halls shouting as loud as he could. He wanted to go into the principal's office and rummage through his desk. He wanted to be the bad boy for once.

But he had absolutely no idea where they were.

Connor shined his flashlight on the wall. The gun was tucked into his waistband now, there'd been no squabbling about who would hold it, even though Seth was pretty sure his aim was better than Connor's. Something was written over the lockers. WELCOME TO C WING. "Anybody know what's in C wing?" he asked.

Amanita looked around her. "Four of the wettest losers the world has ever seen."

"Doesn't really matter," Nicole said. "The bomb shelter will be in the basement so we need to find a stairwell. And I assume the nurse's station will be near the offices."

They continued on and turned right down another hallway. Either no one had thought to install emergency lighting here or the bulbs had never been tested because it was darker than a serial rapist's thoughts. To avoid any Jack-in-the-box surprises they all huddled a bit closer together, ready to swing fists and weapons in unison should it come to that. They read posters on the walls declaring the benefits of saying no to drugs and studying hard. The graffiti on the lockers declared just the opposite.

Seth stopped in front of a poster with a small girl on it. It was an ad for depression. You could tell because she had a tear sliding down her cheek and was staring at her feet. Also because it said *Defeat Depression: Talk To Someone.* Connor's flashlight had illuminated it only briefly but long enough to see the girl's face. She looked as Jo would have looked, had she grown up.

Are you still alive, he wondered, staring at the dark wall, barely seeing the edge of the poster. *Is it my fault? I'm sorry.*

The poster lit up. The girl still stared at her feet, but he waited for her to say something.

No, the *poster* wasn't lighting up, Connor had swung the flashlight beam back to find him. He moved it again and hit Seth in the eye. "Hurry it up, man. We found the nurse's station."

Sunday, 1:00am

As they checked the cabinets and drawers for supplies, Nicole risked eye contact with Connor. Even though they'd just walked the halls together, they had yet to speak since the kiss. She felt awkward, almost ashamed, but she was glad she'd done it. He hadn't resisted, which would have made her want to crawl in a hole and die. No, he'd kissed her back, wrapped his arms around her. She didn't know if that made them boyfriend and girlfriend exactly, but it was a good sign.

Or maybe he just felt bad for you, she thought. *Maybe he was just too embarrassed to tell you no.* God she hoped not. For once in her life she needed something beyond grades, something to make her feel there was more to life than school and her mom's constant warning that all men were evil.

Connor stood the flashlight on its end on the counter. It threw light up to the ceiling like a dim lamp. He was still limping, with his clothing soaked and his skin slick with rain he looked like a lost and wounded dog. How she wanted to kiss him again right now. Tell him she needed him, that she'd been watching him since they were six, that she had dreams about him.

"Ook ab all dis spuff," Seth said. He had two tongue depressors in his mouth, clicking them together like mandibles. He took them out and tossed them into a small metal trash can. He reached into a drawer and extracted a small device that looked like an outdated MP3 player, held it up to his ear. "What's this?"

"Diabetes meter," Amanita said. "My father uses one. When he remembers."

"Oh." Seth put it back where he'd found it.

They found gauze and iodine in the other cupboards, along with various ointments, Band Aids, cotton balls, a defibrillator, cold and hot packs, CPR masks, lice products, feminine hygiene products, and a collection of medical tapes and bandages.

"I guess they don't keep butterfly sutures in the school," Nicole said, taking out the gauze and bandages. She pointed to Connor's leg. "But maybe if we pull the bandages tight enough . . . "

She unwrapped the dressing Officer Whitaker had applied. The blood had completely seeped through and the gauze was already shredded.

Connor ran his hand down his wound. "It actually doesn't hurt that bad anymore. I mean it hurts, but it's more itchy than anything else."

"That could be infection setting in and you don't want that. It could turn gangrenous and they'd have to cut it off. What? I'm serious. My mom's a nurse, remember. Sit on the table. I'll clean it up."

Connor hopped on the table. She realized she'd mentioned her mother again as if she were still alive and well, still out there somewhere hiding, looking for her daughter. Such an ugly habit to try and break, speaking of your mother as anything but the loving pain in the butt she was. As she swabbed the dried blood and dirt off of Connor's leg she felt herself starting to cry again. But this time, she stopped herself.

No more tears. Not until we're all out of this. You're still on the defensive and you need your wits about you.

Amanita picked up the phone near the door. "Well, big surprise. It's dead."

"Welcome to Castor," Seth said.

Sunday, 1:10am

It took them another ten minutes to find the bomb shelter, which thankfully wasn't hidden at all. A sign that looked like it was ripped from a 1950's atomic-age creature feature—a small radioactive symbol with an arrow on it—was posted on the doors to the indoor gymnasium. They followed the arrow to another door at the far end of a hallway lined with trophy cases. This door was locked. Next to the door was a laminated certificate of occupancy so old the actual number of allowed persons had faded out.

"What now?" Amanita asked. "Without the key this plan goes to shit."

"Shoot the lock," Seth suggested.

Connor considered it, but was still hesitant to make unnecessary noise and/or waste bullets. He stared at Nicole, hoping she might have a solution. If their archetypal parts in this survival story were being drawn, she was clearly the brain. Not to mention the only one skilled in medicine. She'd cleaned his wound up and wrapped it up so tightly it felt like the blood wasn't getting from his heart to his toes but it still felt a hell of a lot better than it had before. Her mother may be a nurse but where she learned to actually treat deep wounds was another mystery.

She shrugged.

"This door's open," Amanita said, pushing open the door marked Teacher's Lounge just a few feet away. "Must be for the gym coaches." She stepped inside and stepped out a second later. "There's a microwave and fridge and coffee pot and even a TV."

"Sounds like home," Connor said. And led the gang inside.

Sunday, 1:21am

They dined for the second time that night. A collection of single serve potato chip bags, crackers, pretzels, and a fridge full of warm soda. "Cool gig. Teachers get free drinks," Seth said, taking a Diet Coke and sitting on the floor beneath the sink. He preferred regular Coke but he'd been trying in his own little way to lose some weight, even though he knew it was a hopeless task. He was fat, and would always be the fat kid.

Connor would become popular and he, Seth, would drift into the shadows, soon to be forgotten. It was happening already, the way the girls looked at Connor as if he was Shia LaBeouf or something. He'd seen the kiss, what looked like a kiss, in the rain outside the school. It had made him angry, but mostly because it made him jealous.

They moved the tables and chairs against to door in case someone tried to get in. There was no window in here, so it was the only entrance to defend.

Then they all sat on the ground, the flashlight in the middle, just eating, drinking, refueling. Nicole leaned close to Connor and for a moment they shared a look. Seth felt abandoned. He knew he should be happy for his best friend, but he had never had to compete for his friend's attention with a girl before.

He glanced at Amanita, saw the way her wet shirt clung to her body, saw the bra clear as day beneath it. Just seeing the lace outline made him excited. It wasn't that he had never seen a bra before, but you didn't generally see them through a girl's shirt in person. It was weird how such a flimsy piece of material could create a mental barrier between plain old clothing and a forbidden piece of adolescent heaven.

She was thinner than Nicole, he observed not for the first time, but had a slightly bigger chest. Mostly it was her willingness to show skin that made her scary to him. She would be the girl the seniors wanted to date, and she made no bones about the fact she *wanted* to be that girl. Her snarkiness would be ignored because guys would want to fuck her. And she might just do it.

"Are you staring at my tits?" she said.

"What? No."

"Yes, you were. Perv."

He turned away, blushing. "I wasn't. I just . . ."

"Dude, your eyes were locked on my chest. They get hot when

people look at them. They swell and burn. Don't you boys know that?"

"What? They get hot? Are you . . . *seriously?*"

Amanita laughed and threw a cracker at him. "No, retard. Of course not. But don't lie, I saw you staring."

"Sorry, I wasn't meaning to. I just—"

"It's okay. I'm too fucking tired and hungry and wet to care. Besides, I'm used to it."

"Maybe you should put them away once in a while," Nicole said jokingly.

"Whatever. Boys like them. They buy me shit because of them." She cupped her own breasts. "Right, girls?"

"Like what?" Seth asked.

"I dunno. Like beer. Cigarettes. Stupid shit like candy. This guy my dad works with bought me a subscription to *Rolling Stone Magazine*. He said I look like Britney Spears or something and wanted me to read it and see what she was wearing, which was mostly a g-string."

"That's pretty creepy," Nicole said.

"Tell me about it. That guy stares at my tits all the time. He comes by my house sometimes to see my dad. Always looks at me. Just like Seth did."

Seth threw a cracker back at her. "I said I was sorry."

"Are you sorry plus infinity?"

"I'm not six, you know."

Amanita was giggling, giddy from the soda. Seth couldn't help but notice the way her chest jiggled up and down now. *Oh God, I'm staring again!*

"Swear on never watching another *Star Wars* movie that you're sorry."

"For the love of God. Yes, I swear I will never watch another movie—"

"*Star Wars* movie!"

"—*Star Wars* movie again if I am not utterly sincere. There, I said it."

She held her hand out to him, pinky curled like a hook. "Now pinky swear."

"What?"

"Pinky swear, bitch." She was laughing so hard cracker was flying out of her mouth.

He wrapped his pinky around hers and they snapped them apart. He liked the way her hand felt in his, soft and slightly cold. He felt himself blushing the same way he had in the SUV when she'd jumped on him. He hated her attitude, hated how she was laughing like a loon right now, but she was very attractive and he couldn't deny his own blossoming urges. He would give anything to just kiss her. He knew he was going to grow up to be fat, and that he'd never kiss a girl even half this attractive. His only consolation was that she'd grow up to be some man's nightmare.

"So what did your dad do?" Connor asked. "About the guy who told you to dress like Britney."

Amanita shrugged, finally stopped laughing, looked at her cracker. A moment of silence passed. "Nothing. He don't care. Typical day at my house. These crackers suck." She tossed them on the ground behind her.

It was awkward, yet somehow characteristic Amanita. The sudden onset of a bad mood. And for some unknown reason Seth felt like he'd started the whole thing, brought her to this place she was in now, feeling depressed and unloved. He felt like he needed to make good on it.

So he threw a chip at her.

She watched it land on her leg but made no move to brush it away.

He threw another. This one hit her in the head.

She looked up, not really smiling but maybe not so angry anymore.

Then something hit *him* in the head. And he turned just in time to see Connor throw a Dorito at his face. Seth threw a chip back. Nicole threw one at Seth. Amanita threw one at Connor. Dozens of chips suddenly cut the air.

And before they knew it their first high school food fight had erupted.

Sunday, 1:26am

They were laughing, rolling in a sea of nacho crumbs and plastic wrappers when Seth felt the first tear pool in the corner of his eye. He just couldn't stop it. It was a need he'd been withholding all night. Without warning the floodgates opened and he was suddenly crying into his lap, his breath catching between sobs. He knew it was due to the sudden emotional upswing. Letting the happiness in for a moment had opened his emotional doors; the secrets he kept buried in the dark places of his mind saw the daylight and ran for it.

I am having a nervous breakdown at fourteen, he thought as his mouth hung open, collecting tears.

The food fight ended. Nicole, Connor, and Amanita were suddenly speechless.

"Seth?" It was Connor. "Are you okay?"

No, Seth was not okay. He was as far from okay as anyone could be. He was tormented, lost, alone, and at fault for the greatest crime he'd ever known. "I didn't scream because I was scared. Really fucking scared. I couldn't even move. It was like being covered in cement. Why didn't I at least scream? Why didn't I at least get out bed and run to Mom and Dad's room?"

"What's he talking about?" Nicole whispered to Connor.

Seth cut off any reply. "That!" He pointed to the poster on the wall near the fridge. The same one he'd seen in the hallway. He'd tried to ignore it since coming in here but it just kept staring back at him, the one with the Joana look-a-like on it. "For all I know that's her. She looks young enough to be her."

"Oh crap," Connor whispered.

"Who?" Amanita asked. "What's wrong, Seth? You're scaring me."

And then it just came out, torrential, like the rainstorm outside. "Joana."

"Who?"

"Joana was my sister. Is my sister. I don't know. She must be dead. Oh God."

"I'm still not following," Nicole said.

Connor filled them in on the short version. "Seth's little sister was kidnapped. They never found her." The way he said it, it was like he was betraying his friend.

"Oh my God," Amanita said. She put her hand up over her

mouth. "I'm sorry."

"Don't be," Seth snapped. "It's not your fault. I was too fucking scared to save her."

"You were just a kid," Connor said.

"You know what, Connor, enough. I have to own up to this. I was a kid but I could have saved her. I was a fucking coward and I let my stupid fear overpower me. If I'd just gotten out of bed they would have had time to chase the guy. Joana might be here today, instead of . . . wherever she ended up."

"How old were you?" Nicole asked.

"Six."

"Well, shit, Seth, no six-year-old would be able to do anything. Connor's right, you were too young."

"A six-year-old should at least cry. At least make some noise. You should see the looks I still get from my parents. Not a day goes by all three of us don't think of her, but only I get the accusatory looks. My parents want her back and they want me dead."

"I'm sure they don't blame you," Nicole said, trying her best to sound maternal. She scooted closer to Connor and put her knees against his thigh.

"Yeah," Connor said. He quickly looked at her knees then back at Seth. "Your parents are nice to you. I think you just dwell on it."

"I dunno. Sometimes they deal with me. They started getting a little nicer since we moved here. I mean, Mom still checks the abducted child websites everyday, but we actually have conversations now and then."

"They're always buying you video games. It's not like they don't pay attention to your wants."

"But is it just to get me out of their hair, or do they care about my happiness?"

"That's why you were upset about the sword and the video game thingy," Amanita said. "You think the gifts mean they like you now or something, but I bet they never hated you. It's got to be hell on earth to have a child kidnapped, I'd be scatterbrained too."

"Oh, they hated me. They missed my tenth birthday because they were at some rally for missing children. You know how that made me feel? To be alone on my birthday because of something I did to my parents? To be completely ignored for years?"

"Yeah, I kind of do."

"Really. You know? I bet! You know, you don't have to be a know-it-all bitch about everything."

Amanita's lips curled into a snarl. "*What?!* Guess what, Seth, you're not the only one with problems. I DO know what it feels like because I'm ignored every day of my damn life. My parents pay way more attention to their kind bud and microbrews than they do to me."

"Your parents smoke pot?" Connor asked, as if it were taboo to even say the word.

"Smoke it?" Amanita replied. "They *grow* it. In our backyard. And not a day goes by that it's not made clear to me what's more important to them. They come home from work, they get high, they wake up, they get high. The weekend rolls around and they sit in front of the TV, get high and get drunk. Meanwhile their dirty old friends swing by for a bag and look me up and down like they're gonna offer me money for a blowjob. I'm their fucking daughter and they don't give a shit who looks at me like that. They don't give two shits about me, so yes, Seth, I do know how it feels."

"Then why do you dress like that?" Seth asked. "If you don't like people looking at you."

Amanita looked down at her wet shirt, saw her bra showing through it. When she looked up again she was crying. "I don't know. Because I can. Because . . . I guess it's better to get someone, anyone, to pay attention to me than be completely forgotten. I just want . . . someone . . . to . . . to say something nice to me for once. I don't want to keep hearing about how I was a mistake. That's what they say: *'a mistake.'* They told me the truth one night when they were drunk and high, how I was the product of a broken condom and failed birth control. How they never wanted kids." She stopped to wipe tears from her face, but more kept coming. "Fuck! I . . . I want to feel like love exists, you know. All day long I do what I want—I smoke and drink to show them it's fucked up—and no one tells me no, and so I just do it now to feel numb. And I walk around dressed like this hoping someone will just whisk me away to a better place. And right now all I have to offer is my body."

Nicole blanched. *"Am!"*

"Well it's true. I figure if this can get me somewhere better in life then I'll do it. I hate living there. I hate being around them. You know why they weren't at home tonight? I bet they were at their friend's house smoking it up. I want to be somewhere where people care. Like when I was little, and Dad bought me this dollhouse with these princess dolls. One of the only nice things he ever bought me. And I would just sit and play with that thing all day because it was better than my real house, better than my real life. In the dollhouse everyone loved everyone else. I had this weird OCD thing where all the princesses had to do everything together. If one ate, they all ate, if one went on a date with a prince, they all went. Like a real family. Not like mine, where I needed Dad to open a can of Spaghetti-Os for me so I could make my own dinner when I was seven, but he couldn't because he was passed out drunk and Mom was asleep on the floor from smoking her brains out. Where I had to eat slices of Wonder Bread for dinner with patches of fuzzy green on them. I don't even know how they maintain their fucking jobs, the loser stoners. I fucking hate them." She put her head in her hands and continued to cry.

For once, Seth didn't feel so alone. He felt bad for Amanita, and wanted to apologize for mocking her but also let her know that he understood. If there was ever a scenario he could empathize with, it was feeling invisible in front of one's parents.

"That's why I always go to your house, Nicole. I love your mom better. I wish she were mine."

"She's not all she's cracked up to be."

"Oh please. She's a saint compared to my mom."

"She's okay. But she's bitter and angry most of the day. She puts on a happy face for company, but behind closed doors she's just pissed all the time. Why do you think she loves that dog so much? She hates my father for leaving, and she won't date because she's too bitter. So the dog is my new dad. And the dog is a girl."

Amanita pushed her hair out of her eyes. Her face was puffy and red. "Well, you're dad was a dick for leaving. I can sympathize with her."

Nicole nodded. "Yeah. He was a dick. But I have good memories of him. That's what sucks the most. The guy I remember was a good dad. I wish I knew why he left. I still have this crazy fantasy he'll come see me someday, like drive up and say hi and have a legitimate explanation for leaving. Makes me hate my life too sometimes."

"You're life is better than mine, Nic. Deadbeat dads aside I'd trade with you in a heartbeat. Trade for your brains and normalcy, for your money."

Nicole was looking into her own lap now. "I don't want brains. And I only get spoiled because Mom feels bad she had to raise me alone. I would give that up to have my dad back. Sometimes I wish I had what you have, a good body, something men would notice about me."

"What are you talking about? You have a good look, you just need to maybe show a little more leg here and there. Those boys at the park today, they were kinda cute. Older and creepy, yes, but cute. You could have at least rolled your shorts up or bought a higher pair."

"Actually I can't."

"Sure you can. You just gotta try it."

"No. I can't. Can we drop it?"

"I'm just saying, Nic, you're a hottie. Right, Connor?"

Connor stuttered, subconsciously shifted his position. "Um, yeah. I mean, yes, I think you're very attractive."

"Girls don't want to hear the word 'attractive,' Connor. Tell her she's sexy."

"Am!" Nicole threw a chip at her friend.

Connor stammered again but then got out a somewhat coherent string of words. "Sure, you're totally sexy."

Seth could feel his best friend blushing. He was blushing as well. Using the word 'sexy' was just awkward for them. It felt almost pornographic.

Am was almost giggling, but opting for a sly sneer instead. "Don't you want to see her legs, Connor?"

"Am, knock it off!" Another chip hit Amanita in the shoulder.

Connor was smiling out of sheer embarrassment. The poor boy looked like he might run through a wall just to get out of this situation.

"Come on, show Connor your leg. I saw you guys kiss. He's bound to see it sooner or later."

"Am, seriously." Nicole's demeanor shifted. She was genuinely getting angry.

Finally Amanita relented. "Fine. It's just a leg. I was just trying to tell you you're a sexy bitch. You should flaunt it instead of covering up all the time."

"I cover up for a reason."

"Which is?"

And then Nicole was crying.

Jesus Christ we all need therapy, Seth thought.

Sunday, 1:35am

This was the part Nicole had nightmares about, the reason she hated it when Am pushed her to dress a little skimpier. Even her own mother questioned her choice of frumpy clothing. She began to sweat.

Maybe if it were just she and Am she would come clean about her legs. But Connor was here, and Connor was a different story. She wanted to keep him close. If he saw what was on her thighs he'd run to the hills. She needed a distraction to change the subject.

But then she felt Connor's arm around her, and he pulled her close to him, like he'd done at her house. He was obviously nervous judging by the awkward way he moved closer, but he was good at putting just the right amount of weight against her to make her feel safe. "It's okay, guys. Let's just change the subject. She doesn't need to talk about her legs or anything else she doesn't want to."

She appreciated that, wanted to kiss him again for his concern; he was here for her.

But will he be here for you if you lie to him. If you keep secrets. Things are different now. Now we have to be our true selves. It's the only way to survive.

She knew her conscience was right, that Connor deserved to know all her secrets. But this felt like the wrong place. Seth and Amanita didn't need to know. Then again, she was surprised Amanita didn't know all ready. Keeping her habit from her friend for so long had grown exhausting.

And Seth. Seth was Seth. Harmless and just as fucked up.

She stood up and unbuttoned her jeans. She pulled them down to her knees, exposing her panties. She saw Seth's eyes go wide, but as much as the boy looked embarrassed he did not turn away.

Connor looked as well, but she could tell he did not know what he was supposed to be seeing.

It was Amanita who picked up the flashlight and shined it on Nicole's thighs. Nicole took a breath and waited for the comments.

"Jesus Christ, Nic."

Connor shifted around to get a better look. "Are those . . . scars?"

Nicole looked down now, took in her legs. Scars criss-crossed her thighs, stitched back and forth like lightning. Some were old, some were fresh. Half moon fingernail gouges and thin purple vines still gooey with blood.

Am got up close. "Did you do this?"

Nicole finally managed to stop crying. There was no use anymore. All three of her friend's wore the same astonished look. "I cut myself," she said.

"But why?" Connor asked. He seemed sincerely confused.

"I don't know. Because it feels good. Because it feels like anything. Because there's no grade involved. Because I don't have to impress anyone with it or see looks of disappointment if it doesn't meet anyone's expectations. Because it's kills my inner monologue and the pain is better than depression. Because I'm fucked up, that's why."

Slowly, Connor got closer, put his fingers on the scars. "It's not that bad. Mine is worse." He stuck his leg out and showed her the bandage she'd wrapped around it. It made her smile, his attempt to comfort her, but she was still sickened by the sight of her own flesh and the guilt behind her own self mutilation.

"Why didn't you tell me?" Am asked.

"I don't know. How was I supposed to tell you? I can't stop. It . . . it makes me able to sleep at night, you know. I don't know why or how."

Suddenly Am was up and was hugging Nicole. Her arms carried a weight different from Connor's but satisfying nonetheless. The weight of friendship. "I'm sorry, Am."

"Don't be sorry."

"I just. I don't know how to be normal. I'm just a brain. I want to be like you. Carefree, rebellious, okay with my body. Not worry about pleasing Mom and school and . . . "

"Nicole, you're my best friend. From now on when you feel like you need to do this you call me, okay? Look at me. Call me. We'll deal with this together."

"Do you think I'm weird, do you hate me?"

"Yes, but only because you refuse to watch Paul Walker movies with me, not because of this."

"He's not that hot."

"He's an Adonis and I want his children." Am hugged her hard enough to make her cough.

Nicole spoke over her friend's shoulder. "Do you hate me, Connor?"

Connor stood up and put his arm around her as well. "No. And you can call me too."

Am nodded. "See, you can call your BF as well. Now pull up your pants before Batman and Robin here explode."

"I'm not even looking," Seth said from somewhere outside the huddle. "Wait, am I Batman or Robin?"

When Nicole sat back down, Connor was sitting next to her, his arms still around her. "You really don't think I'm a freak?" she asked.

"I think you may need to talk to someone, but I will help you. I really like you, Nic."

"You're too sweet. You really are."

This time when she leaned in to kiss him, there was no hesitation on either part.

Sunday, 1:34am

They pulled apart and Connor felt a little scared. Nicole's legs looked pretty bad. She needed someone with good credentials to figure out where her problems stemmed from, although it was pretty obvious—since they'd just all shared their inner most demons—where her problem lay.

On a strange level it also made him feel needed and right now, strangely, he wasn't having such a hard time accepting that.

"And what about you, Connor," Amanita asked. "You're last. Spill the beans. How are you fucked up?"

Seth and Amanita both chuckled. Nicole squeezed him a little harder around the waist. Connor knew it was coming but had hoped he be able to dodge the bullet. Everyone's face was slick with drying tears but his own.

"Actually my folks and I got along great. My dad was encouraging and funny, and my mom told me she loved me just about every day. And then they died.

"And I ran my mom over in a car."

And that was the end of their therapy session.

Sunday, 2:12am

For the next several hours the storm grew worse, but none of the teens inside the school knew this; the teachers' lounge had been built in the middle of the building. Outside gusts of wind whipped down the streets like runaway steeds, tearing branches off trees and knocking over empty garbage cans. The rain snubbed the last of the flames on the crashed plane and washed most of the blood off the streets and into the curbside drains. Cats hunted for mice, and mice hunted for crumbs, and the edacious hissers hunted for the last few remaining residents of Castor who had been stupid enough to hide in their houses. Doors were kicked down, windows were smashed, rain sprayed inside living rooms and bedrooms as the undead wrenched their friends and family from under beds and out of closets and tore them limb from limb. Those who caught the virus before death took them were reborn in seconds, others were simply left to rot as rare hamburger in the bellies of demons.

At some point in the night two Jeeps rolled into town, each carrying scouts from the United States Marine Corp. They did not expect the townsfolk to rush from the dark yards and open doorways and attack in almost infinite numbers. They did not expect the townsfolk to swarm the Jeeps, hissing like steam pipes, stab claret-stained fingernails beneath their chins and necks and cheeks, and pull back long strips of skin and muscle, rip it clean off and then fight for it like hungry jackals.

There was nothing the scouts could do against the voracious flesh-eaters who wanted to eat them alive. There were gunshots and SOS calls over radios as the men went down, but they were ignored by the Marine Commander who had set up his new HQ at a farmhouse just on the other side of the Jefferson River ravine. He stared at a direct order from his superiors instructing him to assess the crash site of a plane carrying a known mutating pathogen. Should the area show signs of infection, he was to institute a Code 72.

So, as he listened to the screams of his men dying over the radio, he shifted his gaze from the orders to a map of Castor, sipped a coffee, and began drawing red circles around various hotspots where his soldiers were dying as they scouted for trouble.

The entire map was now one red circle.

Inside the school, the four teens made a decision to catnap, give the storm another hour and then try for State Road 134, maybe find a smaller car that could weave around the trees beside the pileup.

Connor and Nicole slumped at the north end of the room, near the fridge. They were asleep in minutes, arms around each other.

Seth lay on his back near the sink, staring at the ceiling, wondering where his parents were. Wondering where Jo was, and what he could have done differently that horrific night. At some point, just before he fell asleep, he felt another body crawl next to him. A head fell to his chest.

"I'm cold. You mind?" Amanita said.

"Um . . . no."

"Thanks. You're not so bad, you know," she said.

"Neither are you," Seth replied.

"I know."

Seth smiled in the dark.

Amanita lifted her head, looked at him. "I've never done more than kiss a boy, despite what Mandy Robinson says. And I never got naked with my cousin's friend. I just lied. I don't know why. I'm waiting for someone special."

"I didn't hear anything."

"Oh. Well, I heard from Danielle that she told Alicia that I was messing with some guy . . . you know what, it doesn't matter. I just wanted to tell you I'm sorry. And you're soft . . . I like that."

She put her head back down on his stomach and was soon drifting off to sleep. *Weird girl*, Seth thought. *I think I may be in love with her.* He slowly put his arm around her, closed his eyes, and found his own peace and quiet as well.

PART II:
SUNDAY BLOODY SUNDAY

Sunday, 9:00am

The ground rumbled as if giants were walking through Castor. Connor opened his eyes, groped for the flashlight and found it, snapped it on. He saw Nicole lying next to him, still asleep. The first time he'd slept with a girl, he realized. Well, slept next to one anyway. She looked peaceful despite the anguishing revelation she'd made a short while ago. He still hadn't digested that one as much as he needed to, but right now it was unimportant.

Across the room Seth was sleeping with Amanita, her head on his chest. His position looked forced, propped uncomfortably against the wall, an art student's sculpture of a man with no spine. Must have stayed stock still all night for Am's comfort.

How strange, he thought, *that in all this horror we each find ourselves in the arms of girls. Is that what they mean by life being a circle? You're down then you're up in just minutes? No, this isn't up, we're still too far through the looking glass for any of this to be positive, girls or not.*

A crack of light was spilling in under the door, probably from the windows in the hallway beyond. It was a new day; they'd slept through the night.

The ground shook again. Dust fell from the ceiling. He shook Nicole. "Hey, wake up. Something's going on?"

She grunted and sat up, picked sleep from her eyes. "What?"

"Something's happening. You feel that shaking?"

"I feel it," Seth said, his eyes now open. "Feels like an earthquake."

"We don't have earthquakes here," Nicole pointed out. "We're nowhere near a fault line."

Amanita woke now as well. "Don't suppose anyone brought a toothbrush?"

This time the walls shook, and plastic cups fell out of the cupboards over the sink.

"C'mon," Connor said. He began clearing the table and chairs from the door. "Something's going on outside."

Sunday, 9:12am

The morning air was humid, yet still chilly. The rain had seeped into the soil of the school's front lawn, turning most of it to mud. Plants and bushes had been weighted down under the downpour and remained slanted sideways. The grass was sparkling with beads of water.

Out on the road past the lawn, there was a military Jeep. A plume of black smoke rose from its hood.

Beyond that lay a strip of businesses, CLOSED signs still hanging in the doors and windows. A line of trees ran behind them, extending back for miles of undeveloped land.

Out of the sky, a tiny object fell in a line of gray into the trees. There was an explosion, followed by a snaking trail of smoke that rose up and dissipated.

"That was a mortar round," Seth said. He'd played enough war games to know what they looked like. He also knew that if one came close to them there would be no surviving it. He stood with his three friends just outside the school, constantly scanning his surroundings for the undead. It was bright out and he felt exposed. He wanted to get back in the school or in the SUV. There was no telling where those things were hiding.

"Hang on, I want to check out the Jeep," Connor said. "If the Army is here then we're saved. We just have to find them and let them take us out."

"Officer Whitaker must have gotten word out," Amanita said. "Which means she could have taken us with her, the bitch."

Connor wasn't listening, he was already moving toward the lawn.

Next to Seth, Amanita stood a little closer than normal. What do I say to her now, he wondered. Did last night even mean anything?

Nicole started following Connor. "I'm not letting him go alone."

Walking out into the open street was a stupid move, Seth knew, but he had to admit he was curious as well. When he took a step, Amanita started walking with him.

The four teens moved slowly across the lawn. They all swiveled their heads, anticipating an attack, but they made it to the Jeep without incident.

The Jeep was wet with rain drops. In the front seat was a mound of red and gray meat. The smell was enough to make one's eyes water even in the open air. A head lay in the back seat, its lower jaw ripped off. Two M16 machine guns were on the ground near the back tire. A collection of bullet holes riddled the dash board and steering column.

"Jesus," Nicole said. "They lost the fight. What does that mean? If the Army can't even—"

"They're SOCOM," Seth said, pointing out the spear logo on the Jeep. "Or MARSOC, a branch of the Marines." He bent down and picked up one of the machine guns. He waited for Amanita to tell him to drop it but this time she said nothing.

It took him a second to find the release for the magazine and let it drop out. Empty. He pulled back the slide, exposing the chamber. There was no bullet inside.

"He shot the whole thing off."

He examined the other gun in the same way. It was also empty. "They fired every round they had and still died."

"Strength in numbers," Connor said. "They must have been overwhelmed. We've already seen how they work."

"We were right inside the school, so close," Nicole said. "Thank God whatever did this didn't come looking."

Another mortar round exploded in the trees, further away than before. "They're still fighting," Connor said. "We should get out of here."

"To the SUV?"

"First I want to check the phones," Connor replied. "If the marines are here they may have restored the connection."

Sunday 9:23am

The school's reception area was open to the hallway, situated directly across from the room marked DETENTION. On the wall next to the door was a white porcelain water fountain that coughed up the most heavily-chlorinated warm water they'd ever tasted, but it didn't stop each one from satiating their morning thirst. Connor hoped it would wash away the stale taste of defeat in his mouth.

The reception area already showed signs of an administrative work force——coffee mugs and family photos, papers and pens and staplers with people's names written on them in whiteout. Connor checked the phones again for a signal but they were still as dead as the lumps of marine meat in the Jeep outside.

"It's too dark." Seth pulled the leads for the floor-to-ceiling Venetian blinds just enough to get a view of the outdoors. The school's front lawn stretched twenty yards to the road. The Jeep was visible. To the left the school's flag pole swayed in the morning breeze.

Connor put the phone back in its carriage. "Still out. We're gonna have to drive toward where they're firing the mortars from and see if we can't find any more troops."

"They're firing the mortars from the other side of Jefferson River," Seth said. "There's no direct route unless you want to climb down a rock cliff into the ravine and then up the other side."

"So then we'll go out the way we were planning. Take the State Road out and swing around till we find the cavalry."

"Hey, look what I found," Amanita said, stepping off a chair she'd used to explore the tops of nearby filing cabinets. "It's an old police scanner."

Seth squinted his eyes. "A what?"

"Police scanner. My mom had one when I was little. You use it to listen to the cops talking to each other over their radios." She brought the device over to the front desk and plugged it in to the outlet in the wall beside it. The red bulbs on the front lit up.

"Thank you, backup power," she said.

"You know how to use it?" Nicole asked.

"Yeah. It ain't hard. Each of these switches is a frequency. You just flip them around until you hear some talking. We can get a better idea of what the situation is if we can find what frequency the cops are on." Amanita flipped the switches up and down but they heard nothing.

"Cops are either dead or too busy to talk," Connor said. "Not to mention this thing looks ancient. Don't they have ways to get around this nowadays?"

"Maybe. I'm not on the force, you know. But it used to work when I was young. Mom would sit for hours stoned out of her mind, paranoid the cops were coming to arrest her. All you mostly hear about is asshole guys beating their wives and drunk drivers and shit like that."

They stood around as Amanita flipped the switches in different patterns, hoping they might hear someone talking about Castor's predicament, but no chatter came. Finally Connor took the car keys from his pocket and jingled them.

"Alright. This is just wasting time. Let's just get going. We'll drive fast. Stay off main roads. Try to—"

"This is General Ryan to Team Six. I need SITREP now." The static-laden voice came through clear as day.

A second voice responded, quivering, but with the same static-heavy effect: "Quadrant one beyond saving, sir. Those things are everywhere. We found Team Nine's truck. It's empty, covered in blood. Nothing left but their guns. We thought we saw them in a pack of those things on another street, running all fucking wild like the rest of the town. These things are zeroing in on anything that moves, sir, especially our Jeeps. We're making too much noise in this thing and they can spot us from down the road. Permission to get the fuck outta here, sir?"

"In a sec. What about the plane?"

"Plane is empty, sir. No Dr. Haley, no General Davis."

"And the data disks? You find them?"

"Negative, sir. Could not stay around the plane long enough. They started coming for us. We shot down a handful but . . . sir . . . they're not right anymore. They have legs and arms and more legs and Jesus God they're just not human—"

"Alright. Calm down. Shit. Without the data we have no idea what we're dealing with."

"Should we return to the plane, sir?"

In the background someone yelled, "Don't ask that!"

There was a pause. Then: "Negative. Negative. You tried and I can't risk more men, we'll have to do this the easy way. Where are you now?"

"Passing Myers and Newcomb."

"Visual report. Quickly!"

"Sir, we've got a group of those fuckers at the tip of the street. Sir, they just saw us, they're heading our way."

Someone else yelled: "Go for the heads! Shoot them in the head!"

In the background there was the sound of marines yelling and crackling gunfire. When the radio man spoke again he was screaming.

"Sir, there's too many of them. Permission to return, sir? Please."

"Affirmative, private. Yes. Haul ass and get back here now. The town is dusted and we're sealing off the exits STAT. Anything tries to get out of the town we shoot first and worry about it later. I'm not risking this thing getting out, I don't care how human they may look or sound. We're moving into Code 72 Containment. One hour."

"Roger, sir. Heading back."

Connor expected the line to go dead but the gunfire and yelling remained. The private who'd been on the radio was still holding his thumb on the button for some reason.

"What's a Code 72?" came a new voice.

"They're gonna firebomb the whole town?"

"You mean . . . ?"

"Burn it down from the outside. Blow up every nook and cranny where those things could be hiding. We've got one hour, then Castor is gone."

"What about survivors?"

"Do I look like I fucking care? It's Code 72, there will be no survivors!" There was more gunfire, then: "Ours is not to question why, Tin Man. Just follow the fucking orders and get us back to Kansas."

"Still say they should turn the phones back on."

"You're not listening. National emergency. Contain and diffuse. This never happened. Remember?"

"Yeah, I hear. Thank fucking God I don't live here. Shoot that one! Oh shit, get that one and—"

" . . . motherfucker . . . "

" . . . get him off me, get him off . . . "

More gunshots. Hissing. Screaming.

Finally the line went dead.

Connor exchanged glances with his friends. "They turned the phones off."

"How?" Amanita asked. She took out her cell phone again.

"Armed Forces can jam that shit," Seth said. "It's a radio wave, goes out over the whole town and causes interference. Few years ago there was a game on Xbox—*Spy War IV*—that supposedly used the

176

same equipment the real army uses. They made a big deal out of it on the gaming blogs. You could get this Tactical Response Jammer that would stop the enemies from calling into their base. Supposedly it was real at the time. And that was five years ago. Probably they can just do it from a satellite now. Bigger question is why aren't they transmitting on encrypted frequencies. Special Ops—all military units—transmit with encryption."

"Maybe they don't care," Connor suggested. "Or maybe . . . they did it on purpose in hopes someone was listening."

"Who?" Seth asked. "Who would even know enough to scan for it?"

"The jerkoff we left in the field," Amanita said. "That Davis dickhead who's to blame for all this. Bet you that's who. They knew he was on the plane. It makes sense."

"I still don't get why they're blocking the phones," Nicole added.

"Because someone called in a Mayday," Connor said. "And someone on the other end knew what they were dealing with, so when the plane went down they cut communication into and out of Castor. Think about it. The plane had a top secret bio weapon on it, right? Look what it did to everyone. They want this all contained."

"Assholes." Amanita turned the scanner off.

"They know something," Nicole said. "Not everything. They don't have the data they need to really figure out what happened. Maybe it can be stopped."

"Stopped? You can't reverse this," Seth said. "These people got killed and came back as something else. They're not human anymore. All you could do is return them to . . . being dead."

"Doesn't matter," Connor said. "You heard what they said. They're gonna fire bomb the town in the next hour. We have to get the hell outta here."

"Couldn't we just, like, go up on the roof and paint 'We're Alive' on top?" Nicole asked.

"Sure," Connor said, "if they plan on flying planes overhead first. But we don't know that. They could be launching missiles at us for all we know."

"What about my parents," Seth asked. "I mean, we still don't know what happened to them. To Nicole's, to Am's. We can't just let them bomb this place. There have to still be people alive."

"You heard them talking. There's nobody left. We saw what was happening before anybody else. We kept running. Nobody else knew so they just got attacked."

"I'm telling ya I think my parents might be alive," Seth said, a hint of anger in his eyes. "I'm not gonna leave until I find them."

Amanita turned to him. "Seth, I have to tell you something."

Sunday, 9:30am

Normally, Amanita didn't mind being the bearer of bad news, because usually she didn't give two shits about the person she was bringing it to. Telling some stupid boy he was ugly, telling some dumb bitch she was fat, and a day ago she wouldn't have minded too terribly telling Seth about his parents. Now she found herself suddenly hesitant to explain what she'd seen outside of Seth's house the previous night.

The way he looked at her—already guessing at her words, already expecting bad news—made her want to shrivel up and die. Maybe it was because of the way he stayed still all night while she slept on him, maybe it was the way he had revealed himself to be a little smarter and quicker on the draw than she'd expected, or maybe it was just that she knew these people were all she had left right now and to cause them pain might cause them to turn their backs on her. Any way you cut it, she was not looking forward to this.

Yet she had to tell him. He deserved to know.

"I saw your parents. When we were at your house. They were outside, near that guy with the gun. They were . . . they'd been changed. I'm sorry."

Seth took a step back, leaned against the wall. His eyes met hers but she knew he was not looking at her so much as through her, trying to comprehend what he'd been told.

She walked up to him and put a hand on his chest. It was the first time she'd just let herself feel another person breathing, knowing she could take his breath away with words.

Slowly, she leaned closer and hugged him. "Sorry."

Seth said nothing in return.

She backed up. "I couldn't tell you. I figured you'd break down and we'd be screwed. I mean, we were in a pretty bad spot right then."

"You knew the whole time?" he asked rhetorically.

Reluctantly, she nodded.

"Maybe you just saw them wrong. Maybe they were running away from—"

"They were eating someone, Seth. Did you want to hear that? Do you want to hear it now? I couldn't tell you. I don't want to tell you now."

"Then I have no one left," he said. "I let Jo get taken and my parents are dead. What am I supposed to do?"

Connor squeezed his friend's shoulder. "Just keep doing what you're doing right now, just worry about getting out of here alive. It's what I've been doing since last night. It's about the only way to stay sane. Trust me."

Soon, Nicole threw her arms around him as well. Amanita found herself hugging the group before she even knew what she was doing.

They stood there in the empty school, arms forming a ring around themselves like some magical protective spell, trying hard to understand the new family they had become.

Eventually someone started crying and Amanita wasn't sure who it was until she tasted her own tears.

Sunday, 9:33am

"Seth, you good?" Connor asked. He let his arms fall away from the group.

Seth shook his head no, because rightfully who would be okay with such news.

"Well you're gonna have to suck it up right now because we have to get the hell outta here fast. C'mon, man up. Like Master Chief would do."

"I'm only level 18."

"In the game. Be a level 50 in real life, man."

Seth finally nodded. Arched his back and stood straight.

The circle broke and Nicole wiped the tears from her eyes. Like everyone else, she'd joined in the collective crying session. It didn't make things better per se, but at least she knew she wasn't alone. "They said they're blocking the exits, shooting anything that comes close. How the hell do we get out now?"

"We have to convince them we're human." Connor scratched his head. "We could put a white shirt on the car's antenna or something. You know, like a truce flag. Those undead things wouldn't do that."

"What if they think it's a trick?" Amanita said. "I think they kinda *want* to shoot at stuff. They sound like they mean business and I don't feel like getting shot."

"We could try to bust into the shelter again," Seth said, no signs of his grief-stricken trance remaining. "We can see in here now with the sun. There's got to be a key somewhere in the school."

"We're forgetting something else important," Nicole said.

"What?"

"There's data in that plane wreck. Somebody is gonna need it to figure out what they're dealing with."

Amanita shook her head in protest. "What are you, Spiderman? Who cares?"

"She can't be Spiderman," Seth said, "she's a girl."

"Well I don't know any superhero girls, Seth."

"*D'oy!* Wonder Woman. Batgirl. Elektra. Harbinger. Actually . . . there is a Spider-Girl, now that I think of it—"

"Ohmygod! I don't care. My point is who gives a crap about their data. They must have backed it up wherever they created it anyway. Let's just get going!"

Nicole felt her hand reaching toward her thigh and quickly curled it into a fist instead. She squeezed until her knuckles were pearl white and she could feel her nails digging tiny smiles into her palm. It was no better than cutting herself, the pain was still necessary to relieve the stress, but it was an easier way to hide the affliction. "No, that General guy said the bio-geneticist lady realized the error of the formula on the plane. Remember? It might still be there, in one of those cases she carried on board."

"Are you crazy," Seth said. "Nothing survived that crash. Any data they had is burned to a crisp."

"The general survived."

"Through the act of a sadistic god. And besides, the Army can deal with digging through that crash site. We're frigging teenagers for Christ's sake."

Way to be myopic, Nicole thought. How the hell did she explain to them that even if they got out of here it meant nothing if the virus could still find a carrier beyond the containment zone? If that happened every town would become Castor in a few days.

Her mother was surely dead, her town was under attack, her high school career was pretty much postponed. This was the new course life had handed her. This was what she needed to do. Solving problems was what she excelled at.

She turned to Connor. "I'm going to the plane. I'm at least going to see if I can get close. If I can't, then fine, I'll head to the bridge. But think about it. What if the only answer to this whole problem is in that wreckage?"

She watched his eyes as they glazed over, no doubt thinking about a future where man fought wars against entire continents of hissers. A world engulfed in flame or tainted with radiation from nuclear bombs.

Okay, it was a tad theatrical to assume this was the end of the world, but she knew it was serious enough to warrant reflection.

"Ah, crap," Connor said. "I'll go with you. Seth and Am, get to the bridge and don't get shot and tell them we're not far behind."

Seth threw his hands in the air. "Are you fucking nuts? Has everyone gone insane?"

"Well she has a point. It's not like I'm thrilled about it."

"Hold up," Amanita said. "First things first. I'm not going to the bridge. We already discussed this . . . they're gonna shoot us. They said so on the radio: anything they see moving is getting shot first and questioned later. They've written off the whole town. We need another way over the riverbed. Then you two can play superhero or whatever it is you want to do."

"That's just it," Seth said.

"What's it?" Amanita asked.

"Over the riverbed. We're trying to get around it on roads but we just need to get over it. We can just climb down the cliffs, cut across the bottom of the Jefferson River ravine, and climb up the other side. Like I joked about earlier. *Voilà.* We're out of Castor."

"We could cut up over the mountains to the West, too," Connor said.

Seth shook his head emphatically. "No way. The Marine HQ is across the river bed. If we cut across it, circle around the back of their HQ they'll just assume we came from Victorville. We saunter in safe and sound."

"I can't scale a cliff wall," Nicole said. "Sorry. Girl."

"Ditto here," Amanita said.

"Yeah," Seth added. "Me, too. I mean the climbing the wall thing . . . not the girl part."

All three of them looked at Connor, the athlete of the group.

"Don't look at me. I'm not a rock climber. And even if I was I can barely stand on this leg. I suppose we could just get some rope, tie it around a tree and climb down. How hard can it be?"

"We don't have any rope," Nicole said.

Amanita snapped her fingers. "The hardware store, next to Jefferson Liquors on Adams street. They've got to have rope."

"Okay," Nicole said. "Then we split up. Connor and I hit the plane, you get the rope."

"We'll meet at the fort," Connor said, "before the hour is done."

"I kind of feel like a Jedi," Seth said.

"Don't forget all the Jedi were killed."

"Yeah, in *Revenge of the Sith*, but I don't count that movie . . . it sucked."

"We are so dead." Amanita took out her cigarettes. There was one left. She said fuck it and lit it up inside.

Sunday, 9:40am

They stood outside the school, shaking hands like combatants off to war. Nobody actually said the word goodbye, but Amanita and Nicole hugged and Connor and Seth bumped fists. Now was not the time to go soft.

Another mortar fell into the woods east of the park and made the ground tremble.

"I hope they keep their aim where it is," Nicole said.

It was agreed that taking the SUV now would be a bad idea. There were no cars on the street still moving besides possible military Jeeps, and they'd heard what happened to those guys. Any roving cars in the open would alert the town's undead, who were currently—eerily—nowhere to be seen.

But they *were* out there, waiting and hungry. They all knew it. The screams from the dying marines still echoed in their heads. The four friends could feel the weight of the undead's numbers even if they couldn't see them.

They were hiding, ensconced, geared up for an ambush.

Connor readjusted the bandages on his leg. The blood had seeped through and his ankle was severely swollen. Nicole thought infection had definitely set in and was currently eating away at his cells, but that was something to worry about after they got away.

The wind carried subtle hints of smoke and decay, most likely from the plane and numerous car accidents, but also the fresh summer aromas of dandelions and dewy grass. On any other day the latter scents would make it a marvelous morning to be living in Castor. But not today. Maybe not ever again.

A dog barked from the yard of a nearby house, low and guttural. Could have been a warning bark, the kind to ward off an intruder. Could just be that the poor mutt was hungry and wanted someone to fill its bowl.

It'll die in the bombings, thought Nicole. *They'll all die. All the dogs, all the cats, all the people in hiding who had no idea what was coming.* She could try and stop it when they got across the river, but she had little hope of convincing the authorities to hold off. And so, like the way they'd left the general in the park to die, she once again faced her own culpability in other people's deaths, and cursed herself for her lack of a soul.

She didn't deserve this, nobody deserved this.

Seth and Amanita broke away from the group and began jogging toward the running track, intent to cut across it and into the back yards of the adjacent street, which would spill them out one block from Adams.

Connor leaned in and kissed her. The first move he'd made on his own since this mess began.

"Thanks," she said.

"My pleasure."

"I mean it. Especially for understanding my . . . " She looked down at her thighs. "Fucked up issues."

"Don't sweat it. We'll talk later. Besides, that's not fucked up. That can be mended. What's fucked up is that we have forty-five minutes to get to the plane crash, look for something we have no description of, and then scale up and down the sheer rock cliffs of a ravine without any rock-climbing experience . . . all without getting eaten alive or blown to bits."

"No problem, we just let Aunt Sally guide us."

"Huh?"

"Please Excuse My Dear Aunt Sally, the basis for solving any variable equation. Certain parts of a problem must be solved before others. Parentheses, exponents, multiplication—"

"Right, I remember, from Pre-algebra."

"We just go in the proper order, which in this case if fairly linear. Right now Aunt Sally is on the plane."

"Well, I hope she has a bazooka, because we're gonna need one to get out of this whole mess by 10:30."

"After you." They took off running, staying behind trees and bushes and fences and whatever else concealed them.

Sunday, 9:44am

And now we're back to the running, thought Seth. *I hate this part. Always have, always will. Running is as much fun as getting smashed in the nuts with the claw end of a hammer. Racing around in the car was pretty messed up, but at least we had wheels. This? This sucks.*

Ahead of him, Amanita hopped over some railroad ties that had been erected as a barrier separating the field from a strip of dirt that ran along the back side of some fences. Beyond the fences were the backyards of the houses on Felton Street.

He hopped the railroad ties, caught up with Amanita. He had to stop to catch his breath. "Hold up. I'm fat. I can't run unless there's a Twinkie at the end of the race."

"What?"

"Nothing. A funny joke. Something the soccer team used to say about me."

"We can't stay here. We're exposed. We can get over that fence there to that house."

"I know. I see it." He sucked in a big breath. "Okay. I'm good, let's go."

They jogged to the small chain-link fence and looked into the yard beyond. An above ground pool, a ten speed bike, a barbecue grill, lawn chairs, flower pots. *Pretty nice place,* he thought.

They both got over the fence without too much trouble.

The familiar dog bark kicked up once again, a few yards away, across Felton Street.

"Maybe it sees someone nearby," Amanita said. "Maybe we should go a different way?"

"I don't know another way from here. All we have to do is get across the street and cut through those yards onto Adams."

They ducked down as they walked, scanning the windows of the house before them. Seth expected a bloodied visage to appear at any second and roar at him. It would be followed by a wave of undead spilling out from a mid-morning tea party to feast on his intestines.

Thankfully no faces appeared.

Amanita reached the gate to the driveway, reached up for the latch and began to push it open.

Seth grabbed her hand. "Hang on, Leeroy Jenkins."

"Leeroy who?"

"Do you even own a computer?"

"Yes. I mean, my dad does. Did."

"Never mind. I'm just saying we can't run out there like this. The street's too open."

"Then what's your suggestion?"

"I dunno. In Halo I'd throw a plasma grenade or something. See if it got anybody to move. Wait for their red dot to pop up on my radar."

She titled her head and went tight lipped.

"Okay, sorry. I know, you hate games. Tell you what, we get out of this, I'll teach you to play. You'll dig it. You get to kill lots of stupid boys online."

Her lips loosened. "Well, maybe I'll give it a shot for the sake of hurting men, but for now, there's no way out without opening the gate."

"Fine. Just do it slowly."

She undid the latch and pushed the gate. It screeched a record scratch across the cement driveway, loud enough to get the dog across the street barking again.

"Son of a bitch!" Amanita whispered emphatically.

Seth felt a rush of adrenaline surge through him. "Well, it's open now. Let's go."

They hugged the side of the house and snuck down to the front bushes.

Seth peered out around them, scanned the street.

Empty but for two cars abandoned in the middle, both of their windshields broken. Chips of vehicular glass glinted like gemstones around the tires, twinkling in the morning sun. Almost looked like a head-on collision, but there was no way to be sure.

He shifted his gaze to the houses across the street. Some front doors were wide open, what looked like clothing was scattered on one front lawn. The now all-too-familiar undead graffiti—bloody hand prints—branded front doors and picture windows.

He took a tentative step out into the open, looked up and down the street but saw no one moving. No undead, no military, no survivors. Only the dog's lonely barking serenade let him know civilization once existed here.

"Okay, run to the cars and stay down. Then we'll jet to the house across the street, go around it and cut through the backyard. Sound good?"

"No, a grilled chicken salad sounds good, but it sounds familiar so I'm not gonna complain."

"Hardy har. Okay, on three. Ready?"

Amanita flexed on the balls of her feet, ready to take off.

"One. Two. Three!"

Together they sped out past the front yard, hunched down as low as they could go and still run. Their feet slapped the pavement of the road, too loud for comfort. Seth spun in a three-sixty, tried to get a panoramic view of their surroundings. Still alone.

They were at the cars in two seconds flat, squatting down beside the dented sides of the vehicles. Seth was huffing and puffing again. Amanita leaned up and looked through the driver's side window, then sat back down. "I don't see anyone."

"Me either."

"Shit, I gotta stop smoking. I can't breathe."

"Join the club."

The damn dog was still barking.

"So far so good," Amanita said. "Ready to go again?"

"Yeah. On Three. One. Two—"

The dog yelped in pain.

Sunday, 9:51am

If he hadn't already known the way to the crash site, Connor was confident he could follow the smell of fire and be there in minutes. As it was, he and Nicole raced out toward the main road, staying low, gunning for the strips of local businesses lining the sides. Their plan was to get into the alley behind them, take that all the way down toward the public park and then haul ass to the plane.

Connor kept the gun in his hand as they went, his index finger pointed straight out along the barrel to avoid accidentally pulling the trigger—like he'd seen in so many movies. He'd checked the clip just seconds ago. Thirteen bullets.

Do I save two for us, he wondered.

The main road was dead. Not a car moved. Not a person ambled. The stores were all closed, the absence of ambient noise was unsettling.

Gone were the rushes of car engines and rolling tires on blacktop. Gone were the buzzing tones of cheap neon signs outside of diners. Gone were strident footfalls of joggers and the laughter of children riding bicycles. The traffic light at the far corner was off, swaying ever so gently in the light breeze, a grim reminder of a society that once had laws.

They reached the sidewalk and turned right, toward Hanson's Rx, one of the remaining private pharmacies in town and a local institution. Connor used to spend his allowance there when he was younger, in the dollar toy aisle. Knock off Transformers, Lord of the Rings toys that had defects. To a collector it was garbage, to a kid it was treasure. He wanted to slink in now and grab handfuls Tylenol and Advil to help the pain in his leg, but knew they could not afford to get sidetracked.

The road ahead stretched out for a good mile. Nothing but silence and a handful of cars parked sideways across the lanes. There should be police handing out tickets to crazy drivers like that.

The small parking lot of the drug store was empty, a Styrofoam cup rolling lonesome across the white parking lines.

"Back here," he said, reaching the edge of the building and turning down toward the alley in back. They tiptoed by the giant blue dumpster set in a small fenced in square. A small mouse darted away into a drain pipe on the adjacent building, a coin-operated laundry.

It would be so easy for someone to bottleneck us in here, he thought. *Hissers at both ends, running toward us. We'd have nowhere to go. Only thirteen bullets to shoot. We'd be dead in seconds.*

They stepped over an oily puddle into the alley, the backs of the buildings on one side, a drainage ditch and small incline on the other. At the top of the incline was another chain link fence protecting the far edge of the school's fields and any other private properties.

"You still want to do this?" he asked. He already knew what her answer was going to be but a man could hope, couldn't he.

They moved deftly for a few more yards, passing rusted back doors with EMPLOYEES ONLY stenciled on them.

"Here's the thing, Connor," Nicole said. "When my dad left, my mom started going to church. She didn't want to go but one of her friends from work convinced her to go, you know. Some God-fearing woman who swore the Almighty would save us or bring my dad back or whatever. My mom was pretty devastated at the time so she went. I mean, we both were, devastated that is, but I was younger so I don't think I even understood what was happening."

"Mmm." Connor was trying to listen but was also busy scanning the alley ahead of them. He wasn't exactly sure what she was getting at.

"She took me of course, because she didn't have money at the time for daycare and I was too young to be home alone. I only remember one sermon very clearly and it was about Jesus coming back from the dead, you know. It was Easter Sunday and I remember all the kids getting a little basket with a small prayer book in it. I think I was just happy to have a gift. I wasn't paying a whole lot of attention at first to the service, but I started listening eventually.

"It was the only time the story of Jesus' resurrection had been preached to me and the priest was getting sorta worked up about it. He said that guards were put outside Jesus' tomb to make sure no one would steal the body. These guards were so conditioned to obey orders by fear of death that there was no way they'd leave. I guess in that day any guard who went on a coffee break without permission was immediately killed, but the guards outside the tomb *did* move away at some point and no one knows why. Also the big two-ton stone out in front of the tomb had been rolled pretty far away, and Jesus' burial clothes were still in the shape of a body, but his body was gone, like it had just disappeared. The priest said the clothes looked like a moth's cocoon, which I thought was pretty creepy. And because of all that there is irrefutable proof that Jesus came back from the dead and was

God's son.

"The priest said the only way all of that could have been accomplished was by divine intervention."

"Yeah. It's a weird story."

"Anyway, I said to my mom, rather loudly right there in the middle of the service, maybe they just made the whole story up. Everyone looked at me and Mom was mad."

"My parents weren't religious. We never went to church. I kinda think the *Bible* is a lot of nonsense."

"But the dead *are* back, Connor. Only it wasn't God, it was us. *We* made this happen. Humans."

Connor stopped. He still wasn't following her point. "What's that got to do with the story?"

"If Jesus came back then, maybe it was divine intervention. We'll probably never know for sure either way. *We* did this, but we're not God, nor are we gods. We just think we are. We tried to do something we weren't meant to do, that we shouldn't do. No one has gone on record as having come back from the dead since Jesus. And so we just made it up. We made up this fucking story. And it went wrong. And now a town is going to be eradicated. And it'll continue to go wrong until we set it right. If one of these things gets out alive . . . dead . . . you know what I mean . . . it'll get worse. We've fought wars for two thousand years over stories that were possibly made up, but at least those stories gave some people hope and made others kind. Now we've taken God out of the story and proven we can play His part without Him. If this thing spreads, what are they gonna do? Firebomb the country? Firebomb the continent? Think of how crazy the whole world is going to get."

Connor sort of saw her point now, disjointed as it may be. It wasn't that she wanted to get the data, she *had* to. The data proved man could raise the dead, and only God—whether you bought into religion or not—should be the one to do it. He knew she was smart but he hadn't seen the true method behind her madness until now.

"This isn't just about getting the data to find a cure," he said.

"Part of it is, yes, but what if they burn the town, it survives, and someone finds it. It's the power to beat death, Connor. And it shouldn't *be*. It's a power that belongs to God, not us. It'll be the end of all civilization."

"Yeah but . . . it's a double edged sword. They'll need it for a cure. Somebody has to get it. "

"I know. But if the military gets it, who knows what they'll do with it. It was just supposed to help repair wounded soldiers, right? Instead they made a virus that replicates and brings hell on earth. The data needs to be given to the *right* person."

"Who's that?"

She finally stopped walking, reached down to her thigh and pinched it. He walked to her, reached down and took her hand, lifted it away from her leg. She was shaking. "I need the pain," she said.

"No, you need to hug me. C'mere."

He put his arms around her and squeezed. She squeezed back.

"I know where my father is," she said. "I found him."

He held her tightly, his nose in her hair. "Where?" he whispered.

"He's in San Diego. He's a network administrator for Aminodyne."

"What the hell is that?"

She pulled away from him, her hands still clenched but no longer seeking to be injurious to herself. "They make drugs. Mostly for cancers. They're geneticists. The whole city is one big biotech hub. He's just an IT guy but he'll know who to give this data to."

"Are you sure?"

"No. But it's the best option."

"Is it? He left you."

"I know, but I remember him singing me lullabies, bouncing me on his knee. I think he's still a good person. If I can just talk to him in person."

Connor wanted to ask if she was thinking of her father like this because she couldn't stand not having any parents. Was she just transferring her hopes to a man that had screwed her over in the worst possible way? He decided to give her the benefit of the doubt. "And you're sure he's there?"

"That's where he was last time I checked. A couple of weeks ago. I paid an online company to find him. Used Mom's credit card. The bill hasn't come yet but I figured she'd kill me when she found out."

"You've talked to him?"

"Sort of. I emailed him a few days ago and said I want to speak with him, told him who I was."

"And?"

"And he said okay."

Sunday, 9:58am

The hisser broke through the fence across the street, exploding wooden slats out like dynamite. A dead Jack Russel terrier hung limp in its mouth, canine blood cascading down the creature's torn shirt.

That sight alone might have been enough to illicit a fearful yelp from Seth and Amanita, but what really made their hair stand on end was the third arm jutting straight out from the undead abomination's chest. Like a wily snake it whipped back and forth, grasping at air, searching for prey.

Seth and Amanita, peeking out from around the bumper of the cars, each swallowed lumps in their throats.

"That's fucked up," Seth whispered.

Amanita put a hand to her mouth, stifled a cry. "Oh, my God, I know him!"

It was Jason Drake, his greasy blond hair hanging down in his face like a California surfer. The boy she'd wanted to so badly to talk to last night. The boy she'd thought could finally piss off her parents enough to get a real rise out of them for once. The boy she thought she might even bother to spend some real time with. He was a jerk, sure, but he was hot, and it's not like she planned on marrying him. She just wanted to know what made him tick, what his arm would feel like around her. As she looked at him now, watching his head swivel from side the side, the dead dog whipping back and forth in his jaws, she cursed God that she would never get to kiss him just once.

Such a waste.

But then she looked at Seth, huddled nearby, saw the way his fists were balled up already, remembered how content she'd felt as she lay with him last night, and thought that it was probably a blessing this bad boy Jason had joined the dead. He'd just annoy her in the end, because he wouldn't be genuine. He'd use her, because that's what assholes did. They used you and ignored you. He was nothing but real trouble, hot or not.

"It's that asshole Jason Drake," Seth said, as if reading her thoughts. "I hate that prick."

"Well, he's dead now so the universe worked out, I guess. Should we wait until he . . . it . . . leaves?"

Seth shrugged. "Figure we got about forty-five minutes still. If he leaves we'll be okay."

But Jason didn't leave. He put all three hands on the small dog and ripped it out of his mouth, bursting canine entrails onto his Nike sneakers. He slurped down the dog's intestines as if they were giant noodles.

He tossed the dog away. The carcass did a Frisbee spin and landed on the hood of the car.

He opened his mouth and hissed, ran straight for the cars as if he were playing catch with himself.

Am felt the hot hand of paralysis grip her.

Seth, likewise, had gone completely still.

Jason leapt up on the hood of the car, picked up the dog carcass, and tore another chunk out. Only this time, he looked down and saw human meat cowering below him.

"Ah shit," said Am.

Sunday, 9:59am

The alley ended at an intersection, just across the street from the south side of the park. The quickest route to the plane would be to cut across the open fields. Almost the same route they took last night when they found General Davis.

Only problem was there was absolutely nowhere to hide besides some flimsy bleachers.

"Do we run or walk?" Nicole asked. "That's a long way out in the open."

Connor wanted to say run, because he just wanted to get across the open space as fast as possible, but truth be told walking slowly and staying behind the bleachers was probably the better option.

Then again . . . the Lieutenant General had been right. It's the anticipation that kills you. Screw it. "I say run."

"Yeah, I agree. How's your leg?"

"Going pretty numb, but I'm betting on that being a sort of blessing."

"If you fall—"

"I won't fall. But if I ever do . . . just keep running. You know how to get to the fort. Just get this stuff from the plane and get there."

"Hey, none of that talk. This is a team effort, remember? If you fall then I fall."

"Yeah, but I won't jump off a bridge if you do so don't even think about it."

"Not following you there, sport."

"Nothing. Something my mom used to say. You ready?"

"As I'll ever be."

Hunched down, they scooted across twenty yards of open grass to the first set of metal bleachers, grasshoppers leaping out of their way as they went. They stayed behind the back, hoping the criss-crossing supports might camouflage them a bit.

When they came to the edge of the baseball field, Connor opened the gate to the dugout and slinked inside. Across the field he could see the hills ringing Jefferson River, could almost make out the exact spot where the fort was.

At least if they encountered trouble they'd be near the rendezvous point. Whether or not they could run there in time was another story.

"We're gonna have to cut straight across," he said, looking toward the street where the fuselage lay like a beached leviathan.

Nicole laughed. "I've never run on a baseball field. How dumb is that?"

"Well here's your chance to impress the scouts. And lucky for you there's no need to hit every base."

They hightailed it as fast as they could, kicking up clods of sod in their wake. Every time Connor landed on his left leg searing pain from his wound shot up his body. They reached the waist high chain-link fence at the back of center field and climbed over. Connor had never been able to hit a home run over this fence, but he figured he would someday. Now, if he made it out alive he had no intentions of coming back to Castor.

Just one hundred yards of open grass between them and the road, then a hop jump and skip to the plane crash.

"You hear something?" Nicole grabbed him and yanked him down behind some metal trash cans. Bees swooped in and out, probably dining on discarded soda cans.

Connor did hear something, a sound that made his stomach go tight. He turned back and looked at the field they'd just crossed.

A dozen hissers were charging at them, and they looked right pissed off.

Sunday, 9:59am

Seth didn't think, he just grabbed Jason's feet and yanked as hard as he could. The creature went down on his back on the hood of the car, cracking its skull against the windshield.

"Run!" Amanita shouted, already twisting and cutting around the back of the car.

Seth wished she hadn't screamed, but he probably would have too were it not for the fact his voice was caught in his throat.

The hisser that was once Jason sat up, his extra arm reaching out and grabbing Seth's T-shirt. The fingers were strong, the arm covered in wiry dark hair, like it had once belonged to a beefy Italian man.

Seth pulled back and his shirt tore down the middle, ripped right off of him. The hisser put the shirt in its mouth. It was still holding the dog in its left hand.

Enraged, hungry and wild, the creature spit the shirt out and lunged at Seth just as a flagstone came down on its head so forcefully the heavy rock broke in half. Both of Jason's yellow eyes bulged out, blood seeping from behind them. The flagstone came down again, the jagged corner stabbing into the top of Jason's undead head, wedging in and cracking it open. Again it slammed down, and again. Brain and chunks of cranium landed on the street.

Jason Drake fell forward, landed on his extra arm, looked for a minute like he might do some kind of break dancing hand spin, and remained still.

Where he'd been standing, Amanita remained, the bloody flagstone down at her side. Her face was awash in bits of gray meat. *Brains.*

"Get up," she said. She was shaking. "Let's go before more come."

Seth stood up, felt the breeze kiss his bare chest. Even though he'd just survived a near-death experience, he was embarrassed to be shirtless in front to Amanita. His body was flabby, pasty white. She would laugh, like the boys on the soccer team did when they played shirts against skins.

"Come on!" she urged.

He rose, covering his chest with his arms, and followed her across the street toward the nearest house. He saw the path to the front door missing one of its flagstones, and finally said thank you to Amanita. She shrugged it off.

They entered the backyard, ran around the in-ground pool.

Something or someone in the house behind them was banging at the back door. Seth risked a look back and saw an old woman with curlers in her hair and dark yellow eyes tugging at the door from the inside. The mesh screen had been ripped off but the metal latticework, like jail cell bars, was still in tact. *Stupid lady locked herself in*, he thought. *They can break through glass and wood but they still don't know how to undo a deadbolt.*

Finally they reached the fence separating them from Felton Street.

"Climb up and check," Am said. "And stop covering yourself like that. It's weird."

"I'm fat. I have bigger tits than you. I have man boobs."

"I don't care about your *moobs* right now. See if the street is clear."

He climbed up and peeked over the top of the fence. Jefferson Liquors was a stone's throw away, and next to it . . . the hardware store.

In the middle of the street was an overturned motorcycle. The rider was still on the seat, his face bashed to a pulp. *Must have destroyed the brain*, thought Seth. Everything else was still and quiet.

If a tumbleweed had drifted across the road right then, it would have seemed all too appropriate.

Sunday, 10:30am

There was no time to even shout about running, they just had to do it. Nicole pushed as hard as she could, willing her legs to move faster than her body would allow. A nauseating sickness filled her belly, fire burned in her chest. Beside her, Connor was running just as fast on his wounded leg.

She looked back and saw that their speed was not enough. The things were fast, too fast to outrun. Her only hope was that the fence around the baseball field would slow them down. But when the creatures reached it, they leapt over it like a hurdle. The couple that got tripped up on it jumped to their feet and joined in the chase again.

She could see the plane ahead on the street , the fire trucks and police cars still where they were last night. Some of the lights had died out, but most still spun and flashed. Two Marine Jeeps had joined the impromptu vehicle graveyard.

Connor looked over his shoulder as he ran. "I count eleven!"

"Who fucking cares!"

They hit the street, their sneakers sloshing through the deep, oily puddles from the fire hoses. The water slowed them down just enough that they had to take high steps as they ran.

Connor stopped. Spun around.

Nicole, now ahead of him, turned back and called to him.

She saw him raise the gun, aim, and fire. In the near distance, the top of a hisser's head erupted in a mist of red. The body fell in a tumbling heap, tripping up two creatures on its heels.

Like a natural, she thought.

He spun back and raced past her.

She went after him, still processing the sight of one of the hissers behind them, the one with the hand growing out of its neck.

They were running so fast they each slammed into the plane, palms out, to stop themselves. A hole the size of a pickup truck had been ripped in its side, just above knee level.

"Get in!" Connor shouted, climbing up into the charred cavity of the fuselage. He reached out for her hand. She gave it. He hauled her up.

He leaned out and fired off another shot.

She didn't see if it hit its target. She was too confused.

"Find it!" he yelled, sighting down the gun's barrel.

Even if he hits every attacking monster, she thought, *the gunshots will bring out more.*

"I don't know what I'm looking for," she said, spinning in a circle. The inside of the plane was both soaking wet and hot as hell. Burned, wet leather seats were piled up in a pyramid. An overturned drink cart had spilled out cans of Coke and Sprite, V8 and Minute Maid orange juice. Luggage was tossed everywhere. The rest of the interior was a collection of wet ash that smelled like death.

She saw a bone at her feet. An arm bone, once human, now a memento of some geneticist's work gone wrong.

"Anything?" Connor asked.

"No!" She caught a glimpse of blue sky from out the front of the plane, where the nose had been ripped off, moved that way. Shoving aside piles of blackened debris and loose wall, she pushed toward first class. If she were a doctor, someone important on a trip to Washington D.C., she'd probably have sat up close to the cockpit; hopefully the geneticist who'd been on board had had the same ego. Nicole had only been on a plane twice but she knew that the desire to sit in first class was hard wired into most people.

"Here they come!"

The first of the hissers jumped toward the opening in the plane. Connor fired, caught the creature between the eyes. Brains blasted out the side of its head.

Another one reached in, grabbed Connor's leg and tried to yank him out. He pressed the gun to the creature's eye and pulled the trigger. *Bam!* The back of this one's head flew off in a pink disc.

Nicole instinctively counted the bullets. One on the field, one as they'd climbed in, two just now. *Four.*

She had to hurry.

She tore through more debris, trying desperately to ignore the angry grunts and spine chilling hisses coming from behind her.

Bam! Five.

Nothing, just ash and clothes, a fire extinguisher and bent metal from the seats. She jumped ahead.

Bam! Six.

More metal supports, a laptop computer burned beyond repair, indistinguishable bits of plane.

Bam! Seven.

The door to the bathroom, caved in almost to an L shape. She slid over it.

Bam! Eight.

The shot rang in her ear, closer to her now. The bathroom was open, something metallic inside, under the busted sink and toilet.

Bam! Nine.

Connor was retreating inward toward her. She threw herself into the bathroom, buried her hands in the flotsam and grabbed the shining object.

Bam! Ten.

Her ears rang. She pulled out the object, turned it over. A metallic briefcase, wrapped in a thin film of soot. Something vaguely readable etched into the dented cover: Prop rty f Dr. M ci Hal y. It was still warm. A single key lock was fastened tight under the handle.

She felt Connor's legs bump into her. "Time to go," he said.

"I think this is it but I can't tell."

"Drop it. Back away."

She dropped it. He spun and shot the lock. The damn thing actually popped open.

Eleven. Two bullets left.

The papers inside were brown and yellow, nearly destroyed from the heat. But there was enough visible writing she knew she had found something important. Chemical equations and various notes, scribbled in black pen, covered every page. Other documents mentioned DNA and chromosomes. Two USB flash drives were labeled *SEQUENCE DATA 1* and *SEQUENCE DATA 2*. Whoever designed this briefcase deserved an engineering award.

There were some printouts, what looked like x-rays, and a Polaroid picture bubbled from heat exposure. What little she could make out in the ruined photo showed a young military man, just a boy, with an extra arm growing out below his ribs. He was screaming in pain.

Bam! Bam! Twelve, thirteen.

She heard a thud. The last hisser was down.

Her ears were ringing.

Connor lifted her up and dragged her forward. She dropped the briefcase, yelled for him to wait, then saw there was still one creature left in the cabin, barreling up the fuselage toward them. She just had time to wrap her fingers around the two flash drives before Connor pulled her so hard she nearly lost her shoes.

She kicked out and caught the creature in the gut, tripping him backwards over debris.

"Get up! C'mon! No more bullets!"

She got up and chased Connor to the front of the plane, fighting her way through thick ash. Connor jumped out through the hole where the cockpit should be. She could see the fear in his eyes as he looked back at her. She could hear the hissing maniac behind her.

She slithered out like a snake, landed on her back in a puddle, rolled up onto her feet just as the creature, the one with the hand on its neck, fell out as well.

Connor grabbed a strip of metal near his feet, swung it at the undead man. The makeshift weapon was caught by the vestigial hand. Both Connor and the creature fought for control of it as the monster's other two flailing arms lunged for Nicole's head.

Her wet hair slipped between the hisser's hands as she leapt sideways, landing on something long and hard and metal. A piece of rebar. She grasped it and lunged at her attacker, drove it upward under its chin.

The rebar stabbed up through the creature's mouth, pinning it shut. Connor wrestled the metal bar back, beat the creature in the head until it fell backwards into the puddle, slimy bits of brain dancing in the shimmering rainbow oil slick. Finally it went still.

He fell to his knees and took deep breaths.

Nicole moved cautiously around the three-handed hisser and sat beside Connor, threw her arms over him. "That was close."

"Too close. Did you find it?"

She held up the flash drives. They were now wet, but maybe still useful. "I found these."

The open mouth of the fuselage sat before them. Within, a line of dead hissers lay motionless on the debris. The blackened interior cabin walls were wet with brain.

"You shot them all?"

"Yeah, tight spot. They couldn't get around each other. Let 'em get close then—blam. Headshots." He dropped the empty gun in the puddle.

"Thought you said there were eleven."

"I suck at math."

"I need to go back and get the briefcase. There're documents and other bits of information that might—"

"No time. We announced our arrival pretty good."

He was looking down the street. She followed his gaze and felt her stomach drop. Unlike Connor she was a whiz at math, and by her estimates about a hundred hissers were racing toward the plane.

"Shit," she said.

"Figure we got about a half hour left before the fire bombing begins."

"Double shit."

Sunday, 10:10am

The door to the hardware store was locked, so Seth picked up a trash-can and hurled it at the front window. It hit with a *BONG*, bounced off and rolled back onto the sidewalk.

"Bullet proof?" he asked.

It wasn't the glass that was the problem, Am realized, it was that Seth was too worried about covering up his body to use both hands. Okay yes, he was overweight, but it wasn't like that was such a big deal in the long run. She could stand for an overweight guy if his intentions were kind and he made her feel special. *When would guys learn that being able to listen and talk was just as appealing as a six pack stomach?*

"Not bulletproof," she said, "just backbone."

"Huh?"

"Put some into it. Forget about your damn body for a second. Use two arms."

She could see how uncomfortable it was for him to pick up the trashcan again and expose himself but this was not the time nor place for vanity. He heaved it with all his fourteen-year-old might. This time the window spider-webbed.

"Do it again. Hurry."

"I'm going, I'm going." Seth retrieved the trashcan and spun in a three-sixty, let it go when he was facing the window. The can burst through the glass and slid across the tile floor inside, knocking over a rack of batteries and crashing against the cash register counter. The din was sure to raise the dead, no pun intended.

Am held her breath and waited for the alarm to sound. Then she remembered the power was out. Aside from the crunch of their feet on shards of glass, the store was silent.

They stepped over the threshold into the store. Even with the sun-light coming in the broken window it was still relatively dark. A mix-ture of *PineSol*, rubber, oil, wood, and dust beat the olfactory senses dull. Goddamn if it didn't smell like a hardware store was supposed to smell.

"Where'd the rope be?" she asked.

"Down one of those aisles."

"I meant which one?"

"I don't know. Let's split up."

While Seth ran off to the right, Amanita started from the left of the store. She went up aisles of tools, aisles dedicated solely to nails, nuts, and bolts, aisles with rakes, shovels, and garden hoses, and an aisle full of nothing but doorknobs.

The next aisle was where the booty lay. Rope and twine of every color and size. Seth turned down the aisle at the exact same time, and they met in the middle.

"Fancy meeting you here."

Seth pointed up above them where a sign hung listing the items in that aisle. "Yeah, well, I finally saw the sign."

"How long?"

"Just a second ago. Would have saved us the trouble had we just looked up first."

"How long a rope, Einstein."

"Oh, I dunno. Figure the bottom of the riverbed is a good three or four stories down." He pulled a giant coil of solid braid rope from a hook. "This one is two hundred feet."

"Will that be enough?"

"Gonna have to be, it's the longest they have."

"Then get two."

"I can't carry two. They're heavy."

"You could if you stop covering up. Don't worry about impressing me, Seth. I don't care about your weight."

"Sure you do," he said. "I know what I look like. I know how gross it is."

This was getting ridiculous. She grabbed him by the back of the head and kissed him. The boy froze solid, leaned back out of fear and knocked over several spools of nylon twine. She pushed her head closer, whispered, "Relax," and kissed him again. This time he didn't move, though he was practically shaking.

When she pulled back he was staring at her half in fear and half in awe. "See," she said, "would I have done that if I found you hideous?"

"I guess not."

"Good. Now grab two spools and let's get out of here."

"Maybe you should take one, too, just to be safe."

"Can't, because I'm taking . . . " She walked back two aisles until she found the axes, selected the biggest one she could find, and returned. "This."

Sunday, 10:12am

With his bum leg and fatigue from the fight inside the plane, Connor knew they weren't going to outrun the approaching mob of undead. Their only hope was to stay down behind the police cars and fire trucks and make for the back of the supermarket.

Nicole followed closely at his heels as they darted from one vehicle to the next. Hisses and snarls carried on the light afternoon breeze.

"They're getting close!" Nicole whispered.

"Keep moving. C'mon."

The first of the creatures, an older man who looked too weathered to move as quickly as he was, reached the plane and leapt inside like an ape.

Connor moved to the last police cruiser offering any coverage. He squatted behind the wheel well, Nicole gripping his arm, and stared at the open road between himself and the supermarket. Maybe fifty feet to the other side. Nothing to hide behind.

He peeked up and looked into the car. A headless cop lay slumped in the driver's seat. The driver's side window was smashed. Blood covered the steering wheel and inside of the windshield. The car's radio was still in the corpse's hand.

"How many grasping fingers does it take to tear a head off?" he asked.

Nicole was looking at the body now as well, but the carnage no longer surprised her. She merely sat back down and rested against the side of the car.

The sounds of the undead grew steadily louder as the remaining hordes converged on the plane. The hissing reached a decibel level that was deafening.

"It's like a million snakes," Nicole said, hands over her ears. She peered up through the car windows once more, her terrified glance saying all that needed to be said, and then sat back down. "They're just running around the plane, looking for us. They move so damned fast I can't even focus on them. You don't think they can smell us, do you?"

"I have no idea. But sooner or later they're gonna wander over here. We need to jet across the street and get behind the market fast but we're gonna need serious luck on our side. Then we can get up to the fort and wait for Seth and Amanita."

"And if they don't show up?"

"We climb down the cliff, I guess. I don't see any other choice. We've got the flash drives, we've got to get out of here alive. Our parents would want that."

"I know. What if we distract them, those things, maybe throw something."

"I already thought of that but there's nothing to throw. Maybe these small rocks on the ground but I don't know that a noise like that will really get their attention. They make so much noise themselves that they must have hunter's ears. They're waiting for something distinctly human. If I were a ventriloquist I'd throw my voice but—"

Nicole grabbed his knee and squeezed. "Wait, if this is unlocked then I've got an idea." She gripped the handle of the police cruiser and lifted it. The door opened without any protest. *Thank God for small miracles*, thought Connor.

She slid up into the seat like a worm, slithered her way across the passenger seat and picked up the radio headset in the dead cop's hand. The key was still in the ignition, the battery still on. She pressed the thumb switch on the handset and whispered. "Testing. One, two three."

Her voice wafted out of another police cruiser, two vehicles down. The hissers near the plane began to spin in circles.

Connor realized her plan now and hoped the other cruisers near the plane were still running. "It's working," he said. "They can hear it. Keep talking."

Nicole pressed the button again. "Hey, you ugly bastards, I'm over here."

Connor peeked around the back of the car and smiled as the hissers raged and attacked a police cruiser on the far side of the fuselage. "Perfect! They ran around the other side. Let's go!"

Nicole slithered back out of the car and together they raced toward the supermarket. As they ran across the street, they each kept their eyes on the nearby fuselage. None of the undead took notice as they were too busy trying to break into the abandoned cruisers.

Sunday, 10:15am

The sun was cresting in the sky, a brilliant white pearl on blue satin. The temperature was heating up the roads, evaporating the morning dew. Insects were flitting on the awnings of buildings, butterflies were exploring rose gardens and flower boxes, squirrels collected seeds in the park and carried them into the hollows of trees. Seth and Amanita ran behind the hardware stores and record shops and bakeries of Castor, ropes and a new shiny ax bobbing their hands.

The first of the rapid, chasing footsteps began when they drew close to Frederick Street, which would lead them toward the back of the supermarket. At first, neither turned to look, too afraid of what they might see. But Seth couldn't contain himself anymore, he had to know what was behind them.

He turned and nearly tripped over his own feet. "Run!" he shouted.

Amanita screamed and moved as fast as her spindly legs would carry her.

The hissing reverberated off the backs of the buildings, like the swishing of a tidal wave.

"Here!" Seth shouted, and pulled her into a tight alley between two buildings. A cracked and bloody face appeared at once, arms reaching in for them. Without hesitation Amanita swung the axe, the blade coming down on top of the monster's head. The blade wedged in and spilt the skull down the middle, one half of a face falling left, the other half falling right. The hisser went down on its knees and crumpled in a ball. Immediately, more yellow eyes and groping hands filled the emptiness behind the dead creature. Amanita swung again, catching the closest monster in the teeth. Molars and gums whistled by Seth's ears and splattered against the brick walls on either side of him. Amanita pulled the axe back and swung again, hitting the next one in the sternum, knocking it backwards on its ass, the axe stuck tight in its chest.

More appeared, leaping over the unmoving bodies on the ground.

"This way," Seth shouted, sprinting toward the main road, his bare chest slick with sweat. His elbows scraped the brick walls as he ran, ripping the skin off to the bone. He didn't care, this was pain in the face of survival. This was what every gamer thought about when running around imaginary lands online, trying to outwit other humans in a game of life and death. But those who died online respawned in seconds to fight again. This was different. This was real. There was no coming back from this if they were caught. Just like Joana.

He'd lost that game, and she'd never returned. Losing Amanita was not an option.

Behind him, a gray arm snapped out and grabbed Amanita by the shoulder, began pulling her back to the rotund dead man it belonged to. She screamed and flailed but was too small to fight the large hisser.

"Seth! Seth!"

He turned and saw her go down on the ground.

"No!" He ran full speed toward the undead man trying to take this girl from him. He didn't see the man's bloody face or torn flesh, he only saw his parents, the cops who had questioned him, and the strange, bearded stick man that had stole into his bedroom when he was six.

He hit the beast in the chest, knocking it back into the bodies behind it. He swung the spools of rope and hit another hisser in the mouth, staggering it.

Amanita was up and running already, calling his name, screaming bloody murder.

He turned and ran, his belly rippling as he poured every ounce of energy into his legs.

They cleared the edge of the building, and ran into the parking lot that connected the small private businesses. Across the street, two wandering, undead women spotted them and came running.

"Down here," Am shouted, leading them down another alley toward the back of the buildings again. They ducked behind a dumpster and pressed up tight against it. The two ragged women sped down the alley and turned right behind the buildings, their anguished cry exploding into the air.

In the parking lot, hordes of undead ran by the alley. But the running began to slow, and soon they were milling about out front, spinning in circles, sniffing the air. Too many of them stood at the entrance to the alley for Seth and Am to get up and run.

"We're trapped," Amanita whispered. "I don't want to die, Seth. Oh God, it's gonna hurt. It's gonna hurt and I don't want it to."

Yeah, it's gonna hurt like hell, Seth thought. And what was worse, they would probably come back as those things. Then what? They'd get burned to a crisp when the military fried the town. They were so close to the market, so close to the woods on the other side and the fort where Connor and Nicole might be waiting for them.

Amanita grabbed his arm and hugged him close, buried her face in his puffy shoulder. "I'm sorry, I thought we could hide here."

"It's fine. We'd be dead out there. Least here they can't see us."

"They'll find us in minutes. Oh God, I don't want to be eaten like that. It's gonna hurt, Seth."

"Just don't think about it."

"Seth?"

"What?"

"Will you kiss me once more? Just in case. I just . . . I want to feel like someone cares when I die. I need to know someone loves me."

She was crying, squeezing his hand. He wanted to kiss her more than anything in the world. Wanted to show her he did care. Cared about her, cared about Jo, cared about every child neglected or forgotten, who died alone or lived alone, wondering why Mom and Dad had forsaken them. For the stolen, for the murdered, for the abandoned.

For the sister he should have protected, and the girl he hadn't realized he'd been protecting until now.

"I don't want to die alone," she continued. "When they come, hold my hand okay?"

She slipped her hand into his, their fingers intertwining. "Please kiss me."

He leaned forward and met her lips.

He tasted their sweat, tasted the salt of their fear. He felt her tongue rest against his. There was nothing sexual about it, just the fierce yearning of two young people attempting to share their love and fear, two people trying so hard to become one in the only way they knew how. He didn't want Amanita to hurt. She was the first girl who'd looked past his ugly body and geeky passions. Her toughness had broken down to reveal the same thing lurking inside that everyone his age must feel: fear. *She may be a bitch on the outside, but she is more human on the inside than most people I know.*

He let go of her, and dropped the ropes in her lap. "Get these to Connor. Tell him this makes me a level fifty, he'll know what I mean."

"What? What are you doing?"

"Am, I love you. I know I hardly know you, but I know I love you. And I'm tired of saying I'm gonna act but never actually acting. Now don't make me do this for nothing. Get going as soon as I run."

"Run? No! Seth, don't even do this to me."

"Just take the rope and run toward the market and don't stop until you get to the woods behind it."

"Oh my God Seth don't do—"

He kissed her once more, then stood up and ran out toward the parking lot.

Amanita shrieked: *"Seth!"*

But her voice was merely the trumpet summoning him to battle. It was better this way, he realized, as he ran into the bright sunlight, perfect cotton clouds lazing in the sky as if painted there by a cartoonist. It was better to know he was dying for something *real,* not made of pixels and computer code. It was better to know that when he saw Jo again, she would forgive him, would understand his six-year-old fear and his teenage redemption.

It was better for Amanita to live, because for the first time since his little sister's disappearance, he finally remembered what it felt like to live for someone else. And Amanita, for better or worse, deserved that.

The hissers rushed him, coming at him from every angle like an explosion played in reverse. He was a magnet and they were slivers of metal drawn in.

He fell to his knees.

The first hand gripped his left ear and ripped it off in a gout of blood. His lips tore from his face under blood-crusted fingernails. Teeth sank into his eyes and popped his vision. His nose was bitten off as more teeth worked into the top of his head. Somewhere there was screaming, and somewhere he knew his legs and arms were flailing, but inside his mind, there was only Jo and Am.

Ten seconds later, his head separated from his neck and he was with his sister once again.

Sunday, 10:21am

In the daylight it was easier to see what the wing of the plane had done to the trees around the fort. A wide path had been cut, like a reverse Mohawk in the woods. Everything that had stood in the way was now destroyed. Felled trees lay in random Xs over one another, dead birds lay broken in the debris, leaves and pine needles blanketed the ground like some kind of funeral shroud. The wing was still embedded in a tree a good hundred feet beyond the fort. Piles of embers crackled on the ground, only contained by patches of dirt and the morning's dampness.

Connor maneuvered his way over the logs and stumps and stared at the remains of the fort that had been a Castor institution for so many years. It felt like his childhood lay on the forest floor, broken, ruined, ready for Mother Nature to erase it from the earth.

From up here on the hill, he and Nicole had a good view over the entire town. The park before them was bright green, tire tracks running through the middle of the fields. The plane crash was still swarming with undead. The houses nearby, where Jason and Maynard Drake had gathered their classmates, were nothing but kindling. The nose of the plane had made short order of anything in its path. The streets were stagnant, cars sitting abandoned where their owners had fled them in panic or been yanked from them in terror. On the side streets, hissers ran about like remote-controlled toys being steered by infants. They scurried over parked cars, zoomed around trees, sprinted down the middle of the road wailing for blood. They were indifferent to one another, only moving out of each other's way lest it should impede their search.

"I can't believe this," Nicole said. "Of all the towns in the world for that plane to crash in . . . "

"If I did believe in God I'd sure as hell wonder what His plan for us was."

Nicole held up the two USB drives. "I think we're supposed to move the rock away from the tomb."

He didn't want to look at the scene below anymore, didn't want to pretend that he couldn't see his house from here. The house where his father had tried to save him and where he'd killed his mother, even though he knew she wasn't his mother anymore, by that time.

The view of Castor was a cheap painting of hell.

"C'mon," he waved her toward the riverbed. "Let's find a tree to tie the rope to when Seth gets back."

"If they get back."

"Don't think like that. Seth knows how to survive situations like this. It's a matter of preempting your opponent. You should see him play Call of Duty . . . he's a machine."

They moved through the woods until they reached the edge of the cliff overlooking the dried-up Jefferson River. The wind howled up the ravine like a heaving breath.

"This tree will work," Connor said, rubbing the bark of a slanted evergreen. He wrapped his arm around it, leaned out over the rock face and looked down, and figured it about sixty yards to the bottom. Hopefully Seth had found a good, long rope.

How they would get up the other side would be another matter all together, but he'd worry about that when the time came.

The howling in the river gorge grew louder. *Funny how the wind sweeps through it down there, but I barely feel it up here,* he thought.

Any further thought was cut off by footsteps, and he turned to give his best friend a hug.

Amanita walked up carrying two ropes, her shirt torn, her face awash in dirt. She dropped the ropes to the ground and sat on her feet, staring off into the distance.

"Oh my God, Am!" Nicole threw her arms around her friend and was practically crying.

Connor sat down next to her, saw blood on her face. "Where's Seth?"

Amanita didn't say anything, and Connor felt his stomach drop to his ankles.

What had happened to Seth was written in the girl's eyes.

"Tell me it was fast," Connor pleaded. Tears were running down his cheeks now as well. He had never cried so much as he had this last weekend. Maybe it would be enough crying to last him the rest of his life. It was pretty useless when you thought about it, tears did not bring back the dead, they did not undo God's errors, they did not turn back time.

If they did, he would have gone back and joined his father at the front door of the house and avoided the incredible pain and loss that now filled his heart.

"He left me," Amanita finally said, her voice just a whisper. "I asked him not to, but he did. And now he's dead and it's all my fault."

"It's not your fault, Am," Nicole said, brushing sweaty strands of hair out of her friend's face. "None of this is your fault or my fault or Connor's or Seth's. And we have these—" she showed her friend the flash drives "—to prove it."

"But, he just left me. He kissed me and told me to run and then . . . they just tore him apart."

Connor turned away, fighting the images that rose in his mind's eye. He didn't want to think of Seth that way, he wanted to think of the best friend who'd ridden bikes with him and played video games on lazy Saturday afternoons.

"You've got to get up, Am," Nicole said, helping her friend to her feet. You've got to help us tie this rope and get across the gorge, before they start the bombing and the fires."

Connor took Amanita's hand and held it tight. "Am, if Seth saved you he sure as shit didn't want us to get killed here, and he was my best friend so don't think I'm not as upset as you, but we've only got a few minutes left. We still have to get up the other side and then get through those woods before they start. Can you stand up?"

Amanita's eyes suddenly cleared, as though she snapped back from another world. She looked him in the eye and leaned in close to his ear. Her hot breath was quavering, and he was almost afraid of what she might say in her current state. But what she said not only let him know she was coming out of her shock, but made him smile.

"Yeah, I know," he replied, "Seth was always a fifty in my book."

Sunday, 10:25am

Connor tied the rope around the tree jutting out over the ravine. He dropped the loose end down and watched it unravel as it fell. End over end until it was completely unwound. The tip swung a few feet above the dry riverbed, so they'd have to jump down at the end but they wouldn't hurt themselves.

"I don't think I have enough muscles to do this," Nicole said.

Connor took up the rope and wrapped it around one leg, held the rest up in front of him. "Like this, see? You put one foot on top of the other, clamping the rope in between. They didn't make you do this in gym class?"

"They made us play volleyball," Amanita said. "Any gym teacher who makes a girl climb a rope is in for a class full of little bitches."

"And it ruins your nail polish," Nicole added.

"Well, trust me," Connor said, "this method works. Nicole you go first. I'll lower you down. Then you go, Am, and I'll follow up."

"Maybe we should have just tried to get across the bridge?" Nicole looked out over the rock face, grimaced at the height.

"You heard what they said. They're shooting anyone who gets close to it."

"Pretty un-American, if you ask me."

"Don't think patriotism comes into play when you've got a situation like Castor has. You ready?"

Nicole moved to the edge of the cliff, wrapped the rope around her leg the way Connor showed her, and began her descent. She moved in tiny increments at first, getting used to letting her feet slow her descent. "It's not that hard, Am," she yelled up as her head finally moved below the lip of the rock face.

Amanita went next, using Connor's hand as a safety handle until she had herself below the lip as well. Like Nicole, she started out slowly until she got the hang of it, then the two of them moved steadily toward the ground.

Connor went next, checking the knot on the tree one last time, making sure the bark hadn't frayed it. He then tossed the other spool of rope down into the riverbed in case they might need it later.

With a deep breath, he wrapped his foot around the rope like he'd shown the girls, and worked his way over the lip. He had climbed the rope to the top in gym class during their physical training week, rung the little bell someone had affixed to the crossbeam—which had felt triumphant at the time, before he realized it made the other boys feel weak and overweight. And by other boys he mostly meant Seth, who'd barely made it up a single foot.

By the time he was halfway down, Nicole was touching the ground. A minute later Amanita was down, and when he finally touched his feet to the dirt, they were ready to tackle the harder part—climbing up the other side.

The howling in the ravine grew louder, almost like a tea kettle heating up. It swam down the rock walls on either side of them and passed over their heads.

"What's that noise?" Amanita was spinning in circles, trying to get a bead on where it was coming from.

"It's wind," Connor said, not for the first time. But truth be told, it sure as hell didn't sound like wind from down here. Aside from a light breeze, there was no rush of air hitting them.

"It's not wind," Nicole said. She took a few steps forward, in the direction of Jefferson Bridge, which was just a black sketch in the distance. "It's those things."

No sooner had she spoken the words than the first one appeared, careening around the bend on the gorge, arms outstretched, mouth open, head tilted back, legs pumping like an Olympic runner.

Nicole screamed, Amanita swore and Connor scanned the opposite cliff, trying to find foot and handholds.

"Up the rocks! Up the rocks!" he shouted.

Both girls raced to the rock cliff, grabbed whatever crevices they could find and started climbing up toward the woods outside of Castor. Only because the cliff on this side was slanted were they able to ascend at all, but the moving was slow and the hisser sprinting at them was moving so fast he might be able to leap above their heads.

Need a weapon, thought Connor. *There, that branch.* About the same size as a baseball bat, fallen off from one of the trees that jutted out over the ravine. He hefted it as the girls climbed up, stood his ground on the riverbed floor.

"Connor, hurry!" Nicole shouted.

"Just go, I got this." A fourteen-year-old boy about to bludgeon a grown man with supernatural strength? Hah! Fat chance. But what option did he have?

The monster drew closer, blood-stained teeth snarling and strips of shredded cheeks whipping like tiny flags.

The hisser jumped.

Connor swung.

The branch caught the hisser in the head and sent it sideways into the rock wall. It stumbled, and Connor was on it, smashing as hard as he could, putting all his weight into breaking the skull and killing the brain. Again and again and again. The creature's neck snapped and the body fell backwards, the eyes fluttered and the undead thing opened its mouth wide and wailed in protest.

Connor drove the branch into its mouth, out the back of its neck and into the dirt, pinning it to the ground. Its arms slashed at anything and everything, its eyes spun in mad circles like a cartoon character.

"Hi, Maynard," Connor said, finally realizing who he was looking at. The older teen who'd tried to run him off his bike just two days ago. If there was a scourge in the town it was Maynard Drake and everybody knew it. Bully, thief, all around prick. Without hesitation, Connor picked up a boulder the size of a bowling ball and brought it down on Maynard's face with all his might. There was a mighty crack as the hisser's skull caved in, and pink ooze shot from the monster's ears.

The undead former-bully stopped moving. The boulder sat in the depression of its ruined face, a snug fit.

"Goodbye, Maynard."

Above him, the girls screamed louder and started climbing like they'd never climbed before as two FSX F-14 fighter jets roared overhead, close enough to shake loose chunks of rock from the cliff. Connor now finally realized why that howling was so loud.

Down the gorge, racing towards him at full speed, was just about the entire town of Castor, now abominations. But it wasn't the ones running through the dry riverbed that made him want to lie down and die, it was the ones running along the walls on either side.

Undead human spiders, he thought, mesmerized by the way their additional arms and legs allowed them to grip the crevices in the rock.

Big-ass undead hissing spiders.

Just fucking great.

Sunday, 10:30am

What made the human spiders even more terrifying than their multiple arms and legs, was that they were an amalgam of different residents sharing one new body. The larger ones were comprised of four torsos, and up to six human heads. From this distance the heads looked like the multiple eyes of a giant tarantula.

This wonder serum that was meant to help soldiers re-grow and reattach limbs, was like human superglue; as long as there was a brain attached somewhere, whatever form of body it picked up would obey its command.

There were *hundreds* of these spider monsters racing along the gorge walls.

There's no way to outrun them, he thought. He glanced up over his shoulder and saw that the girls had made it half way up. The rock face was slanted enough they could almost walk up, like ascending narrow stairs.

He picked up the branch he'd used to brain Maynard Drake with, leaned it against the rock wall. He quickly tied one end of the other spool of rope to it, then held it like a spear. When he threw it at the oncoming mayhem, he said a little prayer. *Mom, Dad, if there's a heaven and you're up there, now would be a good time to help.*

He turned and climbed up the rock face, digging his hands into the tiny crevices and fighting for a good spot to get a foothold. He climbed up two feet, three feet, four feet.

The roped spear landed in the middle of the hissers and was kicked up by thousands of running feet. It wrapped around their legs and pulled them to the ground in a great tangled mess. But the monsters on the walls kept coming, as did the thousands of hissers who merely ran over their fallen brethren.

"Hurry hurry hurry!" Amanita was already at the top, looking down at them.

The planes circled back and Connor looked up just in time to see the first missiles fire from their underbellies. Lightning fast streaks of explosives whistled through the air and hit the gorge cliff about a hundred yards from Connor, sending human spider zombie meat into the air like parade confetti. Then the planes passed overhead and banked left, circling around for another attack.

As if that wasn't enough, two AV-8B Harriers roared into view and made a beeline for the ravine. What looked like two canisters fell outward from under their wings and careened through the air.

Connor barely had time to register their impact before the napalm flames shot along the cliffs walls searing everything in its path. A vast majority of the undead were caught in the attack and fell instantly, the scent of burning meat and hair carried forward on the thermals. The human spiders tried to scurry up and over the rocks but were sucked into the flames where they burst apart like beans in a microwave.

Connor waited for the tsunami of flames to curl over him and burn him to a crisp but the line of fire did not reach him. The heat did, however, and he felt the hair on his legs curl up, felt the skin on his face blister. He heard the girls screaming overhead, saw Amanita fall sideways with her hands over her face, saw Nicole bury her head in her chest as her clothing rippled under the hot winds.

The burns were superficial, but they stung and when Connor slid his hand into another cranny, it felt like he was climbing up the inside of a giant oven.

"Connor!" Nicole lost her grip and fell, her feet kicking him in the head. Somehow, she got hold of the rocks beside of him and hung there. He grabbed her, steadied her until her feet found the slope again. Her face was beet red from the heat, her hands were bleeding from climbing.

Over her shoulder he saw a handful of flaming human spiders racing along the rock wall toward them. Even while dying they were hungry.

"Keep climbing!" he shouted.

The first two planes circled back and their missiles were streaking through the sky, impacting on the rock wall diagonally opposite them, taking out whatever monsters scurried there. Pebbles hit their backs like bullets from a machine gun. Both he and Nicole wailed in pain, but they held on. If they fell to the ground they were done for.

Together they scrambled further up, racing toward Amanita's voice: "They're coming back! Hurry!"

Connor didn't know if she meant the hissers or the napalm planes. It didn't really matter, either one was going to kill them if they didn't reach the top and get into the woods immediately.

He pulled himself up, his feet working along the inclined ridges of the cliff. The top was so close now, he thought he could reach it. Amanita was on her belly, reaching down with her hands to help.

"Conn—!" Nicole was yanked from Connor's side.

He reached for her, saw her stricken face as a monstrosity of conjoined undead humans enfolded her within five grasping multiracial, arms.

"Nicole!"

She fought the arms and legs, but there were too many and she was too small. The human spider's three heads hissed and sank their teeth into Nicole's neck. Blood spit out and splattered the cliff wall.

"*NO!*" Connor yelled, still reaching for her. Overhead, Amanita's cry of protest rose to the heavens.

The hissing spider beast looked at Connor with its six eyes and three mouths and started pulling Nicole back toward the flames. One of those heads was Lieutenant General Winston W. Davis, and it was his arm that gripped Nicole around the neck.

Connor tried in vain to move right, but he was too slow. The spider moved back quicker, its numerous arms and legs able to find more footing as it scurried.

The napalm planes banked into view again. There was no mistaking their trajectory this time.

Sunday, 10:34am

She had planned on attending medical school someday. Mom wanted her to, and her teachers always joked that she'd be a doctor. That was the kind of thing teachers said to the smart students to make sure they didn't waste their lives on drugs or unrealistic dreams like acting or writing or music.

The next four years of her life had seemed such a magical open road, where the transition from child to adult was paved with discovery. She had wondered if she'd be popular, what after school clubs she would join, what new friends she might make. She had wanted to have a boyfriend, and had spent long hours at night thinking that maybe she and Connor could give it a shot. Sure, she knew the way it would probably pan out, that they'd go to different colleges and end up as friends. That's the way high school was. You never married your high school boyfriend, unless by some twist of fate you both reconnected in your thirties or something. But mostly that was the stuff of movies.

She'd thought about who would be her first lover. That territory was so unknown, so confusing and scary, but with Connor it might have been safe.

Now she would never know. She'd never know the trepidation of a first date, she'd never know the fun of finding a prom dress, she'd never know the excitement of joining a punk band or cheering for the football team, she'd never partake in late night conversations in Denny's, she'd never greet customers at the local fast food chains where the other high school students worked. Worse, she'd never grow old and have kids and a career and look back on what she was able to leave on this earth. She would disappear and that was that.

Nicole felt the three mouths clamp down on her neck, felt all those teeth pierce her soft flesh and rip at her veins. The pain was glorious, far more stimulating than any razor blade across her thigh could be, more satisfying than her pinching fingernails at their sharpest moments. There was a transcendent release of endorphins in such pain. She felt ashamed, but it felt oh so good, because this was truly feeling . . . for once.

Immediately she felt herself go dizzy, felt something else enter her bloodstream. Along with her incredible fear of dying right now, she also felt an insatiable need for blood and meat coursing through her.

It's that fast, she realized. *The virus, whatever it is, passes that quickly.*

Already she was staring back at Connor, his arm outstretched to her, his mouth in a gaping *O* as he tried in vain to save her. She wanted one more kiss with him, but she also wanted to eat his face and dine on his insides.

Oh God, she thought, *I'm turning. I don't want to be one of these things. Please don't let me turn. I don't want the earth to remember me as some flesh-eating demon. Please just let me bask in this pain and ride it into darkness. Don't let me turn Connor into this. He doesn't deserve it.*

Then don't give in. Save him. Save them all.

She reached into her pocket and pulled out the flash drives. Once more the teeth sank into her flesh. She flung the drives toward the boy she would never kiss again. Then she was hauled backward, and the teeth found the top of her skull.

She let the pain roll over her, and in that final deluge of white hot light, she ceased to be human.

Sunday, 10:34am

Connor saw the two drives flipping through the air. His arm was outstretched, a futile attempt to save a girl he'd come to love, as if his fourteen-year-old muscles could fight off the furor of the raging undead. One drive flew past his head, arcing into the dry riverbed below. He snatched his hand out and caught the second drive before it could get past him. He saw Nicole's smile when he caught it. He wanted that to be enough, for Nicole to know her death wasn't wasted, but of course it never would be.

Her smile became a zigzag of anguish. He screamed as her body went limp and she was drawn under the spider's mutated abdomen of human torsos, where the three heads bent low and went to work on her flesh.

He wanted to die right then and there, but he felt fingertips brushing his head. Amanita was bending over the lip of the cliff and was trying to pull him up. "Fucking move, Connor!"

She was crying, bordering on hysterics, but she was maintaining whatever modicum of rational thought she could and he had to hand it to her, the girl was tough. "The planes are coming!"

Connor watched as Nicole's sneakers fell down to the winding line of dry dirt that had once been a mighty river. One of the sneakers still held her foot and calf.

"Connor! *Now!*" Amanita's fingers found a shock of his hair and pulled tight.

It was enough to snap him from his frozen stare. He shoved the flash drive in his pocket and dug his feet into the cliff, leapt up with all his might.

Amanita's finger's closed around the back of his shirt, then got a hold of his waistband and pulled.

He was at the lip, crawling up, his upper body on flat land now, his legs coming up next.

"Up up up!" Amanita yelled, her arms under his shoulders now.

He heard the thunder of the jets coming in, felt the air pressure around them change, whipping around like a vortex. He heard the cry of something destructive speeding to the earth above them.

Together, they ran for everything they were worth.

Sunday, 10:35am

The two canisters of napalm struck the edge of the cliff twenty feet from where Connor had been. The human spider feasting on Nicole's corpse disintegrated in a whoosh of ash. Nicole's bones were blown into the ravine, where thousands of hissers writhed in flame, slowly dying.

The wall of fire swelled up over the lip of the cliff and rushed at Amanita and Connor, who could feel the intense heat burning their backs.

This is it, thought Amanita. *We almost made it. We almost mattered.* She felt the hair on the back of her head catch fire.

And then she was falling, dragging Connor down with her. Water swallowed her, cold and dark, and it was just as well she couldn't breathe because they were dying anyway and she'd rather suffocate than burn.

She opened her eyes and saw shades of orange and red and brown. Connor's face was besides hers, his eyes closed, his mouth open in a scream that shot bubbles above their heads. *At least I didn't die alone*, she thought, and put her head against his.

The red glow above them flickered and danced, and then was gone.

He was up before she was, hauling her to her feet. She rose into hot air and smoke, the crackling of burning trees and bushes filling her ears. She looked down and saw she was knee deep in a water-filled hole. Leaves floated on the surface, camouflaging it. No wonder they hadn't seen it until they fell in.

"What the . . . ?"

"Some kind of ditch," Connor said, brushing his wet hair out of his eyes. "Thank God for the rains last night. You okay?"

All around them, the forest burned. Behind them, the hissing screams of the burning undead played like the soundtrack of hell.

She nodded yes, saw her own current condition reflected on Conner, who was soaking wet and red with burns.

"They're burning it down," Connor said. "They're burning Castor to the ground."

Up through the flaming trees, in between the clouds of smoke, they could see more planes, maybe twenty in all, circling their hometown like vultures.

Connor held up the flash drive. "Let's go. Before they drop more on us."

As they jogged through the woods, wet shirts over their mouths to filter smoke, they heard more missiles and fire bombs falling behind them, razing their homes, killing everyone they'd ever known.

Erasing a mistake.

Sunday, 10:47am

General Ryan scratched his chin as he watched the monitors in front of him. Cameras mounted under the various jets showed artillery falling to the earth. The chatter coming over the radios filled him in on the rest: "That's a direct hit." "Target acquired." "Got a group near the high school, coming back to clean house." "That river gorge is still crawling, making another pass."

Ryan sat back and told himself this was the right thing to do. The orders had come down from higher up, but he couldn't say he didn't agree with them. In war, there were casualties, and he doubted that every living thing in Castor was infected. But this was no ordinary outbreak. This was not SARS or Bubonic Plague or Cholera, this was potential Armageddon. If everything in that town was not contained and destroyed, then life on earth might never be the same.

Hell if he even understood how it happened, or what this wonder drug was they'd created, but it didn't matter anymore. Kill the virus, kill anything that moved, and hopefully, in the destruction, he'd destroy any data left behind.

That was the part he'd amended on his own. Special Projects Division was calling for retrieval of anything on the crashed plane, but he was in charge here and he knew how bad it was, so they'd have to deal with his final results. He'd allowed his men the initial try, but the hissers had cut them off. Perfect, the data was better off destroyed. God forbid anyone on this planet got their hands on such a deadly chemical equation ever again.

During his time in the military men had feared him, liberals had protested him, he'd ordered the deaths of thousands, and did his best to fall asleep at night. But always he kept his love of this country close to his heart. If killing this town would save the rest of the country then he was going to do it, if destroying that precious data would keep such a horrible incident from ever being repeated, then he was going to act first and deal with the nightmares later.

After all, it was himself he had to face every morning in the mirror while he shaved. It would be God whom he would face at the very end. He simply did not believe this was God's plan. This was human error, and he was going to set it right.

Please God, he thought as he watched the high school go up in a massive fireball, *let that evil data fry in this cleansing.*

Sunday, 11:02am

Never in Connor's life had his body hurt so badly. His bones creaked with every step, his skin—blistered and red—burned under the weakest breeze, his eyes itched and his head throbbed. Beside him, Amanita shuffled along like a zombie in an old B-movie. There were no smiles shared between them. Neither spoke a word.

Connor held the flash drive tightly in his clenched fist, trying hard to remember what Nicole's lips had felt like. It was no use, all he could taste was soot and mud from the watery ditch.

The woods grew denser, darker, the bugs grew hungrier. He didn't know how long they'd been walking for, but the sounds of explosions grew weaker and the earth didn't rattle so much.

They took a break and sat on a large stone covered in moss. Amanita sat next to him, then slowly lowered her head to his lap and rested there. She let out a single sigh and then closed her eyes and remained silent. He stroked her hair, but could find no words to comfort her.

There were no words for any of this.

How would the government explain this, he wondered. *You can't just destroy a town. There are going to be too many questions and accusations. There are going to be mass sympathizers and angry elected officials.*

Aren't there?

He gazed down at his leg and saw the skin turning gray. It no longer itched but it was certainly numb. Would he ever run again?

"I'm thirsty," Amanita said.

"Me too. We should keep moving. They might have food at the base."

"Don't want food. Don't want to eat ever again. Just want some water and maybe a coffin to take a long sleep in."

"Don't say that."

"Well, that's how I feel. I can't stop seeing Nicole getting bit when I close my eyes. I loved her. We were like sisters."

"Seth was like my brother. I don't know that it's hit me yet. I don't feel much of anything. Is that wrong?"

She lifted her head out of his lap. "Everything is wrong, so I wouldn't worry too much about it."

She's got a point, he thought, taking in the trees and briar bushes surrounding them. We shouldn't be sitting in the middle of the forest while planes blow up our homes. If there was ever anything more wrong, he couldn't think of it.

Then he remembered the flash drive in his fist and realized there was one thing that could make this wrong a right. He could honor Nicole's wish and see to it the correct people got their hands on this data, could make sure this sort of thing never happened again.

Together they dozed and let their bodies recharge. The birds sang lullabies to them as the occasional fighter jet flew overhead making its way toward Castor. At some point they awoke, the woods had grown darker.

Connor shook Amanita. "Okay, let's get going and get this over with. It's gonna be a while still before we make it all the way around."

They stood and resumed their trek through the dark green wilderness toward Victorville. Their pace was slow but they settled into a rhythm that was hypnotic. It was as if their bodies moved separate from their minds.

Sunday, 6:48pm

Soon the sun was setting, and the woods became so dark they couldn't see their hands in front of their faces. Amanita slipped her arm around Connor's and together they trudged forward over boulders, logs, stumps, thorn bushes and more.

The mosquitoes came out, and like a miniature army, swarmed the two teen's ears and stabbed their proboscises into red, welted flesh. It would have bothered any one in a normal state of mind, but Connor and Amanita were beyond caring about their bodies. All they wanted was to see . . .

. . . *lights*. There, through the trees, massive spotlights illuminated the flattened cornfield of a farm. In the center of the lights were two large tents made of canvas and steel. Military vehicles were spread across the field, men running to and fro among them.

Connor and Amanita stepped out of the tree line and shambled toward the vehicles.

A gun popped. A bullet whizzed by Connor's left ear, striking the tree behind him.

"Perimeter breach!" yelled some young private from his lookout station in the field. "Perimeter breach!"

"Wait!" Connor yelled as another bullet zinged by his shoulder. He fell to the ground, his arms around Amanita, thinking it couldn't be real. They'd made it all the way here and were going to get shot now. Of course they must look like the living dead, so it was understandable, but it was also infuriating.

"Don't shoot!" Amanita yelled.

Two more bullets struck the ground near their feet. They scrambled back behind the nearest tree and plastered their backs against it. A bullet hit the tree on the other side and spit bark into the woods.

Connor peeked out and saw a line of five or six Marines charging toward them.

"Perimeter breach! Shoot the fuckers!"

"We're human!" Connor shouted, trying in vain to yell over the startled men and popping gunfire. He turned to Amanita and saw the anger in her eyes. They were going to get shot, there was no doubt about it.

Then Amanita was up, rounding the tree, tugging at her shirt. Connor was screaming for her to stop but she kept walking. Bullets zipped by her head. Connor closed his eyes, not wanting to see her brains explode out the back of her skull.

The shooting stopped. A southern accent spoke: "Hold up, boys!"

Connor leaned out again and saw Amanita standing there with her shirt and bra up, exposing her chest. He couldn't see the expression on her face but he'd be afraid to right now. The men before her stared at her, perplexed, but also aroused.

One of the men lifted his hat and scratched his head. "Well dang, that is a nice pair of titties. Sorry, miss, we thought you was . . . "

Connor stepped from behind the tree and raised his hands up in surrender. "We're human, you jackasses."

"Well, we can see that now," the head-scratching idiot said. "Those things don't normally flash titties at people. We almost shot this fine young thing here. What a waste that would have been."

Amanita put her shirt down, stepped forward and slapped the man in the face. "Scumbag!"

Sunday, 7:00pm

General Ryan met them at his makeshift desk, a large table covered in maps and manila folders. He sipped his coffee one more time and thanked the young squad of officers for bringing him the two children.

They looked like hell. The boy would need medical attention on his leg. It was a wonder he could even walk. Both he and the girl had blistered, superficial burns.

"We have no reports of violence in Victorville. You're sure you didn't just come from Castor?"

"We already told you . . . " Amanita began. She gave up and just raised her hands to show she didn't want to go over the questions again.

Ryan played with the handle on his coffee mug. "I don't need to tell you I don't buy your story. I can see plain as day where you came from."

"So, then what?" Connor asked. "You kill us? Quarantine us?"

"Kill? No. Quarantine, absolutely. I'll need you to be examined. You have no idea what we're dealing with here. I don't know what you've been exposed to."

"Trust me," Amanita said. "I know damn well what we're dealing with. We just lost our friends to it, and our families. And you assholes didn't even try to save us."

"Save you? Little girl, I lost four squads of men in that town in the last twelve hours. There is no saving it or anyone in it. Anyone steps foot in that town they might as well be a steak in a lion's cage. I've never seen anything like this and I'm not letting it get out. You're too young to understand."

"Eat shit," she said.

"Nice mouth. You'll go far with that attitude."

"Don't you see that if we could get out there may be others?"

"I'm aware of that, little girl. I'm aware of much more than you concerning this whole situation and I will not be questioned by someone who hasn't even gotten a high school diploma."

"So you'd have shot us coming over the bridge?" Connor asked, no longer trying to hide the fact they weren't from Victorville. The cat was obviously out of the bag.

"Son, my men have orders. The rest is classified and I will not discuss it with you. Look, kids, you're lucky I don't have you tied down to metal tables with needles poking in and out of every pore of your body. For all we know you're contaminated and you're contaminating this entire camp. But since little miss nudist here and her big mouth have proven there's still a trace of human insolence in you, which those things couldn't care less about, I'm giving you the benefit of the doubt, despite your lies and tricks. Now, go with Lieutenant James here, he will show you to your new quarters until we get you all checked out. Don't make problems or I assure you it will not go well for you. I don't give a shit how young you are. You are considered tainted until I'm told otherwise."

Sunday, 7:15pm

Behind the bivouac were two white domes under which men and women in HAZMAT suits studied tissue samples under microscopes. Beyond that was a series of smaller tents ringed by a six-foot fence.

Lieutenant James led them through the gate and into the small camp. Four guards on heavy machine guns flanked the gate. Several more walked around the perimeter.

Inside men and women, children and even dogs, milled about. They all looked as if they had not slept in days. Bulletin boards had been erected in the middle of the tents, on which were posted hundreds of wallet-sized photos of people of all ages. Even now people were standing by it crying.

"What is this, a jail?" Amanita asked.

Lieutenant James locked the gate behind him. "No, it's not a jail. Just temporary housing. The locks are just a safety precaution."

"To keep infected people inside."

"There are no infected people. Anyone infected would be running around trying to eat you. No, the lock is just to stop anything from getting in."

"So then we can leave if we want to?" Connor asked.

"It's a little harder to explain than that, and anyway, Connor, we need you to talk to our doctors. But if you're wondering if we're going to hold you captive for ever, the answer is no."

"What happens when the news finds out?"

"Not my department. I'm sure there will be lots to explain but I'll let our qualified people handle it. Now, there are cots in the tents, you should get some rest. That big red tent has food and water if you're hungry. There's no cell service so you can't use any phones but if you sign one of the communiqué forms in the red tent we'll do our best to relay your message to whomever you want."

"You *are* blocking the calls," Amanita said.

"We're being practical and doing our best to contain this."

"Who are all these people?"

The Lieutenant sighed, seemingly annoyed with all the questions. "Friends, relatives, people who got out early enough, before the bridges and roads were clogged with those . . . things. I have to go."

With that he left, let himself out and locked the gate once again.

Connor and Amanita watched the people around them, their skin crawling at the way these people studied them. Everyone was thinking the same thought: Do I know these people? Are they my friends, acquaintances, anyone I've seen around town before?

Sadly, nobody recognized each other.

"I want water," Amanita said, and made her way to the red tent. Inside, people sat at picnic tables and dined on what looked like crackers and soup and small bottles of water. The food was all being eaten out of strange tan bags. A man in fatigues was showing a little girl of about six or seven how to put a small heat pack inside her bag to warm up her food.

"MREs," Connor said. "Never seen one in real life before."

"They look gross."

Amanita found a giant barrel full of the bottled water and took one out, downed a large gulp and wiped her lips.

"AM! *Oh my God, AM!*"

Two people came running across the picnic tables and grabbed her, threw their arms around her and began sobbing hysterically.

Connor took a step back, unsure whether he should try and save his friend. The man and woman squeezing Amanita were shaking so badly they almost all fell to the ground in a heap.

Finally, they let go and began rubbing dirt off her face, bending down and kissing her cheek. "We thought you were dead. I can't believe it!"

Amanita's mouth opened and hung there as tears streamed down her face. Connor had seen this type of look only on small children who'd suffered a bad injury or were lost in a supermarket looking for their mother. It was the state of someone lost and angry and afraid.

"Mom, Dad! You left me! Where did you go?"

Amanita's mother hugged her again, babbling her words around her cries of happiness. "We caught a ride into Victorville with a friend."

"What!"

"We knew you were going to the party," Amanita's father said, his hands shaking. "All the parents in this town know about the Drake's parties. We're not stupid, you know. But no one ever gets hurt so we went to have drinks with a friend. He picked us up after you left."

"You went to smoke weed with your stupid friends while I was running around watching people die! Don't you know I came home? I came home and you weren't there, you abandoned me! You hate me and you've never cared!"

"That's not true, Am, we love you. We heard an explosion but we didn't know what it was. By the time we heard a plane crashed and we tried to get back into town the roads were blocked and then there were those people attacking each other and—"

"You were either too drunk or too stoned to know what was going on. You hate me and I hate you!"

Nobody said anything after that, but all three of them continued to hug. Connor couldn't blame them. Even if they were bad parents they clearly still loved their daughter.

He envied her.

Sunday, 11:00pm

Despite the dark sky, the residents of the camp could see the massive towers of black smoke spreading out over Victorville, testament to the fire cleansing an entire small town. Many sat and watched in a daze, others touched the pictures of their loved ones on the bulletin boards and prayed for another story like Amanita's.

But no more came.

Connor found a cot and slept. Amanita slept in the cot next to him. Her parents were not far away. After talking to her for a couple of hours, they relented and let her have her alone time.

At some point in the night, she stretched out her hand. "Connor?"

"Yeah?"

"You awake?"

"No."

"Very funny. Will you hold my hand?"

"Yeah."

Later on their hands fell apart as they both slept.

EPILOGUE:
I DONT LIKE MONDAYS

Monday, 9:23am

They were awakened to shouts and gunfire and men in fatigues rousing everyone from sleep. "Get up, get up! *Move move move!* Make your way to the trucks out front and don't look back. Leave all possessions and get out now!"

Connor and Amanita jumped out of bed, followed the crowd out of the tent and into the courtyard. More men in uniform directed them where to go with their guns. Amanita's parents grabbed her and held her hand as they were all led out of the gates and into convoy trucks.

Out near the white science domes marines were firing into the trees. Others were yelling and screaming. A klaxon suddenly sounded and the crowds gathering into the trucks began to scream as well.

"Connor, hurry," Amanita said, reaching down for him from the back of the truck. Her parents were gripping her shoulders, afraid to let her go.

He turned to look at the fighting across the small field. Hissers were pouring out of the woods. Some of them loping like long distance runners with sprained ankles, others at a full on dash. Bullets ripped into their chest but did not slow them down. One or two caught a bullet in the head and fell, but they jerked so much it was hard to hit their brains.

And then there were the spiders, even bigger and faster than before. No longer just bulbous beasts with a handful of arms and legs, they were now massive monstrosities with hundreds of limbs and too many heads to count. The missiles had no doubt blown the hissers into tiny bits which were picked up by surviving creatures. They scurried forth like tanks and swallowed the young marines under their abdomens, tearing them to bits.

Even as Connor watched, a young man was lifted skyward by one of the hissing spiders. Some ten heads bit chunks out of the boy before dropping him again. And in a second that boy was up, hissing and ravenous for blood.

They bombed the town and still couldn't stop it, Connor thought. *It's too fast and too willing to survive.* If there was any hope, it was possible he carried it in his pocket.

"Connor, get up here!" Amanita struck him in the shoulder, grabbed his shirt and pulled him up.

Finally he obeyed, got his foot on the truck's bumper and jumped up into the back.

The truck started moving, across the flattened, dead corn stalks and out toward a long winding road that would take them through Victorville into whatever future lay ahead.

As they rode, Amanita put her arm around him and hugged him close. He returned the sentiment and held her tight. Together they watched out the back of the truck as the farm fields filled with running undead, tackling and leaping on marines. Bodies stumbled under gunshots, mists of red puffing in the air as the bullets ripped through veins and arteries.

For the briefest moment Connor thought he saw General Ryan firing his pistol as four creatures slammed into him from behind and tore into his flesh.

The trucks turned onto the winding road and made their way out of sight of the farm. Connor watched as massive spider monsters demolished the two white domes. Farther behind the carnage, Castor's smoke signals continued to blacken the sky.

Then the truck was speeding down a country road, nothing but woods on either side. The smoky skies turned blue once again, and a deer leapt gracefully behind some trees.

"What do you think will happen?" Amanita squeezed him harder.

Connor looked into her eyes and saw a grown woman trapped in a teenager's body. He felt the same way. He glanced at her parents and noted the way they also hugged each other. *Yeah, they'll be alright,* he thought.

He didn't know what would happen to the world from here on out. Needless to say it would never be the same. Maybe Ryan's men would stave off the attack and finish off the rest of the monsters. Maybe the military would end up burning Victorville and any of the areas surrounding Castor. Maybe they would never contain this new threat that robbed people of the right to rest, that stole away nature's design.

He had grandparents in Connecticut, but he had not seen them in a few years despite the calls on his birthday and holidays. He had an aunt and uncle in Florida, and two cousins who were both years older than he was. He didn't know them that well. He had second and third cousins as far away as Portugal, but he didn't know how to get in touch with any of them—the phone numbers had been in his house, which was now just cinders.

He rubbed the flash drive in his pocket one last time. It had gotten wet and might not even work, but perhaps even a wet drive could be salvaged. It was worth a shot. No, it was worth everything, and he sure as hell was going to give it his all.

He remembered the name of Nicole's father's biotech company in San Diego: *Aminodyne.*

It was a long way away from Castor, but if he could survive this, he could survive anything.

At some point the truck would have to stop or slow down; wherever they were headed, there had to be red lights, there had to be sharp turns. There would be a window of opportunity.

He would jump out of the back of the truck and run. On his bad leg and with no idea where he was, he would run and find his way to Nicole's father.

The two marines sitting in the back of the truck, keeping a watchful eye on these fine Castor folk, might get up to give chase, but he doubted it. There was too much fear and exhaustion written in their faces. Besides, Am would stop them even if she didn't understand why he was running, he knew she would.

She was still waiting for an answer.

"I think things will get a lot worse before they get better."

The truck continued on. The sun shot pink bands of light through the summer treetops and gave the birds a reason to sing.

Eventually, the truck slowed, and Connor stood up.

About the author

Ryan C. Thomas is the author of the novels *The Summer I Died* and *Ratings Game*, as well as the novellas *Enemy Unseen* and *With a Face of Golden Pleasure*. His short stories have appeared in numerous markets over the years. He lives in San Diego where he spends his nights rocking out in the bars with his band, The Buzzbombs. Visit him online at www.ryancthomas.com

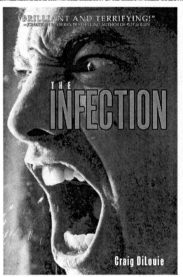
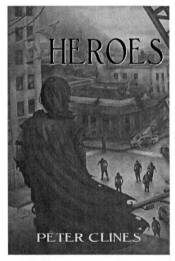

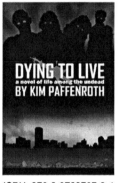
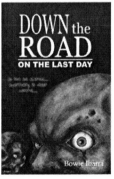

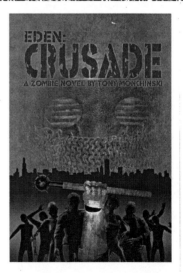

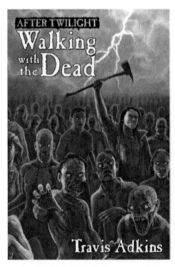

DEAD EARTH: THE GREEN DAWN

Something bad has happened in Nevada. Rumors fly about plagues and secret government experiments. In Serenity, New Mexico, Deputy Sheriff Jubal Slate has his hands full. It seems that half the town, including his mother and his boss, are sick from an unusual malady. Even more worrisome is the oddly-colored dawn sky. Soon, the townspeople start dying. And they won't dead.

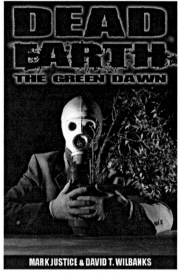

eBook Only

MARK JUSTICE AND DAVID T WILBANKS

DEAD EARTH: THE VENGEANCE ROAD

Invaders from another world have used demonic technology to raise an unholy conquering army of the living dead. These necros destroyed Jubal Slate's home and everyone he loved. Now the only thing left for Slate is payback. No matter how far he has to go or how many undead warriors he must slaughter, Slate and his motley band of followers will stop at nothing to end the reign of the aliens.

ISBN: 978-1934861561

MARK JUSTICE AND DAVID T WILBANKS

MORE DETAILS, EXCERPTS, AND PURCHASE INFORMATION AT
www.permutedpress.com

AUTOBIOGRAPHY OF A WEREWOLF HUNTER

After his mother is butchered by a werewolf, Sylvester James is taken in by a Cheyenne mystic. The boy trains to be a werewolf hunter, learning to block out pain, stalk, fight, and kill. As Sylvester sacrifices himself to the hunt, his hatred has become a monster all its own. As he follows his vendetta into the outlands of the occult, he learns it takes more than silver bullets to kill a werewolf.

BY BRIAN P EASTON

ISBN: 978-1934861295

HEART OF SCARS

The Beast has taken just about everything it can from Sylvester Logan James, and for twenty years he has waged his war with silver bullets and a perfect willingness to die. But fighting monsters poses danger beyond death. He contends with not just the ancient werewolf Peter Stubbe, the cannibalistic demon Windigo, and secret cartels, but with his own newfound fear of damnation.

BY BRIAN P EASTON

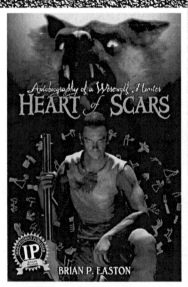

ISBN: 978-1934861639

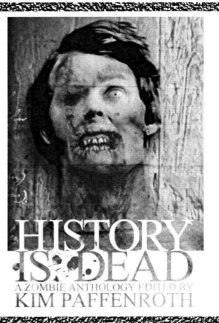

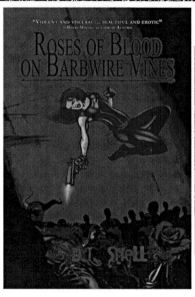

CPSIA information can be obtained at www.ICGtesting.com
Printed in the USA
BVOW021100270212

283903BV00001B/301/P